Journal Entry, June

Terrace, B.C.

Today my son David [...] journey. With us were his wife and my five-week-old granddaughter. We drove in a four-wheel-drive vehicle on a bumpy course where there was no roadway to an isolated spot on the Skeena River.

There I sat on a log in the sunshine cradling the newest member of my family, watching eagles swoop, listening to the roar of nearby rapids. Peace and joy overwhelmed me. I know I have to write a book about fishermen, about families, about this wilderness and the challenges it presents.

A nearsighted black bear waddled out of the forest a few hundred feet from us, and we took refuge in the truck until the wind carried our scent to him. Then he hurried away. So the book will have bears...and romance, as wild and unpredictable as these surroundings.

What if...

∧∧∧∧∧∧∧∧∧∧

~FAMILY~

Bobby HUTCHINSON

Journey's End

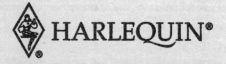

HARLEQUIN®

TORONTO • NEW YORK • LONDON
AMSTERDAM • PARIS • SYDNEY • HAMBURG
STOCKHOLM • ATHENS • TOKYO • MILAN • MADRID
PRAGUE • WARSAW • BUDAPEST • AUCKLAND

HARLEQUIN BOOKS
225 Duncan Mill Road, Don Mills,
Ontario, Canada M3B 3K9

ISBN 0-373-82178-6

JOURNEY'S END

Visit us at www.romance.net

Printed in U.S.A.

Dear Reader,

Journey's End is a story about family, about fathers, daughters and step-parenting. I dedicated it to my father because he was a fisherman, an outdoorsman like the old man in the book. I wanted to illustrate that a family is not a rigid structure, that over time families expand and contract and change, and hopefully grow stronger in the process.

My father died shortly after *Journey's End* was published. I had one grandchild at that time, and now I have four. In so many ways, my life, my family, has undergone immense change.

The single constant element, the ingredient that never diminishes, that can never be destroyed, is the love individuals have for one another. The more love we give, the more we receive.

I wish you and your families great happiness, and I wish you great love.

Happy reading,

Bobby Hutchinson

Journey's End is dedicated to my father,
Robert Rothel.

Thanks to Jim Hinchliffe
for sharing his knowledge of Terrace;
to my son David and his friends,
who took me fishing on the Skeena River;
and to the women of the woods,
Karen, Tammy and Allena,
camp cooks and fishing guides
who educated me about packhorses,
dudes and wranglers.

PROLOGUE

THE DARKNESS WAS DEEP and thick when he awoke, textured, as if he could reach out of the sleeping bag, grasp a handful of blackness and hold it like a ball between his palms.

For a few confused seconds, the old man listened for familiar city sounds, but there was only the muted, urgent rumble of the Skeena River overflowing its banks, swollen with spring runoff, racing on its way to the Pacific Ocean.

The sound reminded him of where he was, and why.

He was a fisherman, and it was May. The salmon were running out there in the darkness, fighting their way upstream, gripped by the urge to spawn in the very creek that gave them birth. Hungry bears waited for them, birds of prey swooped down, fishermen like Doc took their harvest with rods and nets and gaffs, and only a fraction of the salmon that started the journey ever reached their goal. It was a fierce challenge and a final one, and the miracle was that they attempted it at all.

Who could blame Doc for wanting to witness that odyssey one last time?

Once again he heard the soft scuffling that had awakened him—a rodent of some kind scampering across the wooden floor a few feet from his camp cot.

The little animal had probably staked a claim to this

old cabin during the years it had sat empty. Doc was the intruder here, a human in a wild place.

Outside the ramshackle log shelter, the northern wilderness stretched in every direction, miles of virgin forest intersected by rivers and their tributaries, an Indian village here and there, but mostly devoid of human settlement. How long had it been since he'd felt this total aloneness, this sense of being dependent only on his own resources, on his wits, on what was left of his strength?

Many years. Long before his heart attack.

He'd had to scheme and lie to make this trip. They didn't let old men like him go fishing alone. They corralled them instead in places like the lodge and kept them clean and fed and medicated until they died in an accepted manner.

Death. It should be a fierce challenge, a final journey like that made by the salmon in the spring, fighting incalculable odds against distance and time. Instead, all too often, it was a drugged sleep that slipped unconscious into another, final sleep.

Within his warm cocoon, he put one arthritic hand on his chest, feeling the steady heartbeat beneath his palm, wondering how long the old pump would hold up when he started chopping down trees for firewood, lifting logs over his head to make the necessary repairs to the walls of the cabin.

Maybe not long, all things considered, although he felt better right now, here in this drafty, dusty cabin, than he had all winter in that airless excuse for an old folks' home. In fact, he almost felt young again.

He heard his own dry chuckle in the darkness. Maybe he had a dose of spring fever.

meaning is out for three. Come and join us. Leave your message after the beep." ...
Tania shut her eyes and gritted her teeth in utter frustration. She waited for the beep, stopped and her mind went blank, and no words—no words that did nothing to disguise the fact that ... She ... This voice five times I've done this, Mr. Radburn. Don't you ever answer your phone ... I can ... expected you at three. Three ...

CHAPTER ONE

TANIA WALLACE DIALED the eight digits of the long-distance number without once having to glance at the paper where she'd written them down. She'd dialed them five times in the past twenty-four hours; she'd have to be some kind of idiot not to remember them by now.

She waited as the ringing began, tension making her stomach convulse. One long ring. Tania's fingers clenched around the receiver, and she stared out the window, willing someone to answer.

Outside her Vancouver office a gentle May rain cast a misty pallor over the coastal city. The grayness was relieved somewhat by the beds of daffodils and jonquils planted along the sidewalk that led into the brick building that housed the small newspaper where she worked.

The flowers glowed, snow-white and sunshine yellow, determined symbols of spring, oblivious to the cold breeze or the steady stream of passing traffic.

Another ring. Three. *Please let him answer. Please let him be there this time....*

But the answering machine clicked on and the familiar recording began. A deep male voice, sounding a bit self-conscious and abrupt, rumbling, "Hi, this is Matthew Radburn of Northwest Fishing Tours. I'm not in the office just now, but if you leave your name and number, I'll get back to you. If you're wondering how the fishing is up here in Terrace, wild steelhead are spawning, which means we're out for trout. Come and join us. Leave your message after the tone.''

Tania shut her eyes and gritted her teeth in utter frustration. She waited for the beep, snapped out her name and telephone number, and in a voice that did nothing to disguise her feelings, she said rapidly, ''This makes five times I've done this, Mr. Radburn. Don't you ever answer your calls? Again, I'm concerned about my father, Murdoch Wallace.''

She emphasized the name and repeated it, using her father's lifelong nickname. ''Doc Wallace. He was one of that group of seniors you took out fishing eighteen days ago.''

Tania forced herself to talk as fast as she could, to finish her story before the tape ran out, as it had done on two of her other fruitless calls. ''I'm worried about him. He was due back here May 15. It's now May 19 and I haven't heard from him.'' The rest of her speech came out in a frantic babble. ''Please, Mr. Radburn, please call me collect here at work or at my apartment.'' She recited both numbers again, barely finishing before she heard the tape end.

Feeling limp and drained, she set the receiver down in slow motion, aware that the young woman at the reception desk near the door was paying close attention.

The office was small, and with two desks crammed into the minuscule space, no one had many secrets.

''No luck again, huh?'' Jane Kendall screwed her face into a grimace of sympathy. ''Makes you wonder how a business can operate when nobody but a machine ever answers the phone. Must be a lot more laid-back in those little northern backwoods places than it is here in Vancouver. You ever been up to Terrace?''

Tania shook her head, wishing that Jane would attend

to her work and leave her alone. She was getting a head-ache, and she wasn't in the mood to carry on a long conversation with anyone.

Jane was impervious. "My brother's friend Kevin went up there—they were opening a new mine up on top of some mountain. Anyway, Kevin said it's an okay place, lots of fishing and hunting, friendly people. But then, Kevin's not a very particular guy, if you know what I mean. Give him a pint of beer and a pack of cards and he's happy." Jane frowned. "Born with a suppressed libido, Kevin was. I had a thing for him there for a while, so I oughta know. But from what he said, I got the feeling Terrace is crawling with available hunks, if you don't mind the rough-and-ready type. I sure don't, do you, Tania?"

Despite the fact that Tania was thirty-six and Jane only twenty-four, the younger woman talked as if they were united by one common purpose: the determined and over-vigilant search for an available man. Tania had long since given up trying to convince Jane that she wasn't looking for a replacement for the husband she'd divorced more than a year ago.

But Jane had a one-track mind when it came to the male of the species. "I think blue-collar types are sorta cute, long as they wash enough, don't you?" She squinted over the top of her outsize glasses, noticing at last that Tania wasn't exactly involved in the conversa-tion.

"Say, you look kinda drained. How about a coffee? I'll go get us one."

Jane leaped up and swirled out of the room before Tania could answer. She was back in record time with two cups, setting one down on Tania's desk. She stood there for a moment, before she said in a clumsy way.

"Hey, try not to worry too much about your dad. He's probably still fishing up there and that's why this guide doesn't answer his phone. They probably found a good place and forgot everything. You know what men are like about things like that."

Tania slumped back in her chair and picked up her coffee, taking a long sip and giving up on peace and quiet.

"The fact is, I *don't* know what men are like about things like that," she confessed. "You know, I've never been fishing in my life? My former husband never even owned a fishing rod."

But there wasn't much time for fishing, Tania thought with a bitter little grimace, when a university professor spent a great deal of his free time having one affair after another with his students. The time that was left was usually spent dictating erudite papers for his wife to type for him in her own spare moments. John was a brilliant man in many devious ways. He hadn't been a fisherman, though.

"How about your dad—didn't he ever take you with him?" Jane tilted her helmet of sunny hair to the side in her typical birdlike way, giving her glasses another shove.

Tania shook her head. "Nope. Doc believed that boys fished and girls learned to cook."

"Wow, a real textbook chauvinist, huh?"

"Yeah, he was all of that, all right. He and my mother were divorced when I was thirteen, and before that he was off in the bush working most of the time, so I didn't see much of him when I was growing up."

Her brother, Sam, had always gone to stay with Doc in the summer, while Tania remained in the city with her mother. Logging camps were no fit place for teenage girls, anyway, her mother used to declare when Tania cried to go with Sam. No fit place for any female, which was why she'd finally divorced Doc Wallace.

"The coffee tastes good, Jane. Thanks."

"No problem." The younger woman beamed and went back to her own desk to answer her shrilling telephone.

Tania tried to apply herself to the glowing report of the lavish Shaugnessey wedding she was supposed to be covering for Thursday's paper. The attempt was a total failure. Flowers and lace and details of what the mother of the bride wore went right out of her head, and all Tania could think about was why in heaven's name her seventy-year-old father would fail to arrive home on the day his airline ticket stipulated.

She'd checked the ticket herself the night before he'd left, carefully writing down the return arrival time and flight number, noting them in her pocket memo. Then she'd driven to the airport to pick him up at the right time on the right day, feeling like a dutiful, albeit harassed, daughter.

He hadn't been on the plane. Not on that flight or any of the others that had arrived since from Terrace. She was now on first name terms with a friendly clerk from Air B.C. who checked the passenger list each morning so Tania wouldn't have to keep driving out to the airport just to find out that Doc wasn't there.

Where in blazes was he?

If he'd had another heart attack, she'd have heard, wouldn't she? She insisted Doc keep a card in his wallet listing her as the person to phone in an emergency.

The end of the workday arrived at last, and as she cleared her desk and called good-night to Jane, Tania made up her mind to phone the Terrace hospital again as soon as she arrived home. She'd done that once already, and no elderly men had been admitted in the past few days. After that, she decided with grim intent, she'd phone the Vancouver RCMP and report her father missing. It was a step she hesitated to take, because if this was just a big misunderstanding and Doc turned up and found himself the subject of a police investigation, he'd be furious with her. He'd shout and wave his arms and his face would get purple, and then she'd worry about his having another heart attack.

Well, that was just too damn bad, she decided, tucking papers neatly into her leather briefcase. It might teach him to be more considerate in the future.

Tania shrugged into her tan raincoat, her jaw set with resolve.

Doc wasn't exactly famous for his good nature, anyway, so one more raging fit wasn't going to make much difference. She trudged out into the rain, wishing she were a drinking woman. Just this once, it would be comforting to sit in some smoky pub and dull the sharp edges of real life with alcohol. Trouble was, she hated the taste of the stuff.

TWO HOURS LATER, the calls had been made and not one thing had changed.

There had been no admissions to the Terrace hospital that could conceivably be her father, and the RCMP constable at General Investigations Section had suggested the best and fastest route she could follow would be to call the Terrace RCMP and deal with them. To Tania, it sounded like passing the buck.

"You understand, Ms. Wallace, that a seventy-year-old man is considered an adult, fit to care for himself. The RCMP has hundreds of juvenile missing-person complaints we have to regard as more urgent than your concern about your father's return from a fishing trip.'' A cheery little chuckle. "Chances are the trout are biting and he's decided to spend a couple of extra days up there. But here's the number of the Terrace detachment. Ask for Corporal Biggsby."

Once again, Tania put the telephone back in the cradle. She stared down at the number the constable had given her, muttered a couple of obscenities she'd learned from her father and lifted the receiver. But the thought of going through the entire story again and hearing the same answers made her give up before the call was completed.

She'd never felt more frustrated and helpless in her life.

She got up from the worn armchair she kept beside the phone and went into her immaculate kitchen to make a cup of tea and try to figure out what she ought to do next. She was pouring boiling water into the brown teapot when the phone rang.

A man's deep voice asked, "Is this Tania Wallace?"

"Speaking." The voice was familiar, but she couldn't—

"Matt Radburn here, Ms. Wallace. Northwest Fishing Tours."

Tania's heart began to pound with a combination of righteous anger and the wonderful feeling that all her worries had been groundless. Matthew Radburn would know where Doc was. The man had left her hanging all this time, but now, finally, he'd decided to answer her frantic message. She felt an overwhelming urge to be rude to him. Instead, she controlled herself with an effort of will, and as calmly as possible, went straight to the point.

"Where exactly is my father, Mr. Radburn? I've been waiting five days now for him to come home, and—"

"That's why I'm late calling you back, Ms. Wallace," the baritone voice interrupted. "I wanted to do some checking with other guiding companies up here. See, I've never heard of your father. I certainly didn't guide him on any fishing trip. He didn't contact my company at all, and I figured maybe there was some misunderstanding and you had the wrong company."

Tania's knuckles turned white as her grasp tightened on the receiver. Her throat convulsed. This man couldn't be saying this. There had to be some mistake. She opened her mouth to say so, but he was going smoothly on.

"I called as many of the other guides as I could get hold of, and none of them have heard of your father, either." The deep voice paused and then added, as if she were an imbecile, "Are you quite sure he said he was coming up here to Terrace, Ms. Wallace? There are other fishing areas in B.C., and maybe—"

"Stop." Tania's voice was tight and high. "Stop, please. Let me get this straight. Are you telling me you didn't contract to take a group of senior citizens from Vancouver on a two-week fishing trip?"

"Yeah, that's what I'm saying, Ms. Wallace. I was never in touch with any group like that." His voice was earnest and not at all reassuring. "I just came out of the bush with my last party the other day, and I was surprised by your messages on my machine, because I haven't guided any groups of seniors from Vancouver, not this year or any other. I've never heard of your father, this, uh, Doc Wallace. And neither have the other guides I spoke to today. Of course, there are a few guys out in the bush right now—there's always the chance he's with one of them, but quite frankly, I doubt it. We usually know who's guiding whom around here, and nobody knows about this group of old-timers you're talkin' about."

Tania's brain was working in slow motion. Her hands were ice-cold and her face felt as if it were burning.

"But...Doc gave me your card. He expressly said he was going with a group you were guiding. I even got postcards from him from Terrace, saying—"

The baritone voice interrupted with a trace of impatience. "Look, Ms. Wallace, I appreciate how you must feel, but I'm giving you the straight goods here. I tell you, I don't know your father. I have no idea who he's with or where he is. I'm sorry."

The flat denial at last penetrated Tania's numbed senses. The man was obviously telling the truth. He was also paying for this long-distance call, and that wasn't fair. It wasn't his concern at all.

"I—I see. Well, tha-thank you for calling, Mr. Radburn." She could feel blind panic building inside her, and her voice trembled. What was there to do now? What on earth was she going to do?

Her agitation must have been obvious. His voice softened a little. "Look, Ms. Wallace, I'm real sorry about this. I can't hazard a guess as to where your father might be, but I'll tell you what—I'll keep my ears open, and if I hear anything, I'll let you know."

Tania's throat felt as if words couldn't get past the lump there. "Thank you, I appr..." To her horror, she choked up and couldn't go on. She gulped, and still her voice wouldn't work.

The man on the other end of the line waited awkwardly for her to continue. When the silence lengthened, he said with obvious embarrassment, "If there's anything more I can do to help, my home number's 555-9463. Call me there. I'll be around for a few more days, until my next party arrives.''

With shaking fingers, Tania copied the number on the pad by the phone. She managed a garbled thank-you and a formal goodbye before the tears came.

Damn! She hated crying. She'd cried far too much this past year. Oh, hell. Might as well give in and get it over with. She sobbed for several long minutes and then stumbled into the bathroom for tissues. She blew her nose hard. Enough already.

Why was she falling apart over this? The RCMP were right, after all. Her father was an adult, supposedly able to care for himself. Although he'd had a minor heart attack three years before, he was in reasonable health. Sure, he was cantankerous and morose, but he certainly wasn't senile, as many of his contemporaries in Mountain View Lodge were.

So where was he right now?

Tania walked over to the small table in the hall, where she'd put the postcards he'd sent her from Terrace. The strong scrawl on the back was definitely Doc's writing.

"How are you? I am fine…" Doc wasn't an inspired writer. He wasn't a writer at all. Come to think of it, this was probably the first time he'd ever written to her.

She tossed the cards back onto the table, and frustration and a sense of utter aloneness filled her, as well as the familiar, silent scream of outrage that had been building in her during the past months.

Life just wasn't fair. She'd been good, as good a person as she knew how to be, and yet here she was in the middle of yet another crisis. And she was alone. She shouldn't have to deal with all this by herself. Sam should be the one taking responsibility for their father.

After all, Sam had been Doc's favorite, his only son, the apple of his eye.

And Sam had been dead six long years.

No help there.

No help anywhere. Doc was the only living relative Tania had, and if he were in some kind of trouble, she was all the help he could hope for. If he were in some kind of trouble, sick or lost somewhere, there wasn't another living soul who'd look for him. That was the core of it, the reason she felt this way.

Life just kept shoving her into situations she hated and couldn't avoid.

First there'd been Doc's heart attack. Then there was her failed marriage. She'd gotten through her divorce, the sale of the home she loved, the painful dividing up of possessions it had taken ten years of marriage to accumulate. She'd made this apartment into some semblance of a home for herself, and after fourteen months on her own, she felt at times as though she might even have a measure of peace in her life, a calm oasis where the wounds that her marriage to John Felton had opened in her soul might heal.

Now there was this. She thought of herself sometimes as the old comic strip character with the black rain cloud perpetually over his head.

She went into the bathroom and washed her face, removing the smudged mascara and the light traces of makeup she wore during the day. In the mirror, her face was thinner than it had ever been, cheekbones standing out, hollows evident beneath them.

One of the positive side effects of her divorce was this dramatic loss of weight, Tania mused. She'd never been fat, but she had carried around fifteen extra pounds for years. A woman could never be too rich or too thin, she quipped to herself with a sad, lopsided grin.

Well, there was a long way to go on the rich issue, even if the pounds had melted away. She hadn't come out of the divorce a wealthy woman by any means.

The truth was, she didn't look very healthy, either. The pallor of her skin was shocking against the red-gold brilliance of her hair. Well, there wasn't enough sun in Vancouver in the wintertime to color anyone's skin.

She moved slowly to her bedroom and stepped out of her gray skirt, unfastened her beige blouse, slid off the lacy slip and bra. She pulled on a soft blue housecoat, old and worn and comforting, and went into the kitchen to pour a cup of the now-lukewarm tea.

She sat there a long time, thinking about what she should do, what she could do, what she ought to do. What she had to do.

About midnight, she made up her mind, and by one in the morning her suitcase was packed, her few plants grouped in the sink with enough water to keep them alive for a while, the fridge emptied, notes ready for the paperboy and the mailman.

She bathed and lay down, but she didn't sleep much at all.

At eight she called her boss, Dennis Kardom, and asked if she could take her holidays, starting now. He refused, point-blank, as she'd suspected he would. Dennis ran the paper on minimal staff, maximum output and a fair amount of bullying.

Tania announced with calm resolve that if holidays weren't possible, she was taking a leave of absence for personal reasons. Dennis wasn't at all happy about it, but Tania wasn't asking permission.

He grudgingly agreed to three weeks after a long,

threatening lecture about the scarcity of jobs in Vancouver, the number of eager young journalists ready to leap at the chance of a job on his paper, even covering society weddings and funerals. He was right. Tania was taking a chance with her job and she knew it.

The whole thing was Doc's fault.

She called the Air B.C. ticket office and made a reservation on the next flight to Terrace. Checking in at the airport at eleven that morning, she vowed that when she found her father she was going to give him a good piece of her mind.

"GABY, WAKE UP. It's almost noon."

Matthew Radburn stood in the doorway of the narrow little room, peering down at the bed, where his daughter was sleeping. He felt helpless and out of place, and annoyed, as well. He'd been trying for a solid hour to get her up, and he wasn't having much luck.

"Go 'way, can't you see I'm tired?" The muffled, angry groan sounded from the tumbled heap of covers that was Gaby. All that was visible was a wild mass of tousled, tormented hair, bleached a harsh sunflower yellow.

Matt wasn't used to Gabriella as a blonde. He remembered her with hair the same color as his, brown. But then he wasn't used to the rest of Gaby, either—her curvaceous body, her new and blatant sexuality, her easy use of profanity, her rude and angry manner. Matt remembered her as the sweet, plump little girl of fourteen he'd visited for four days a year and a half ago, a girl who'd grown up away from him.

His child was a stranger.

It was an ever-present sadness, having a daughter he didn't know. There hadn't been time on that short visit or the others he'd made through the years to fill in the gaps of Gaby's childhood or to bridge the chasm of time and distance that yawned wider with each passing year.

Now, she was here, living with him, and more of a stranger than ever before.

He tried again, apology and appeal in his voice. "Gabriella, you know we need groceries, there's nothing to eat in the fridge, and I've got a million things I need to do in town. Now either you get up and come with me or you'll be stranded out here in the trailer for five or six hours at least. Make up your mind."

That had some effect.

"Gawd, I can't believe this." Puffy dark brown eyes ringed with unwashed makeup squinted up at him; her downturned mouth was peevish. "Can't you let a person sleep once in a while?"

Matt remembered, as he had so often in the turbulent three days since Gabriella had come to live with him, a tiny, curly haired girl in a crib, holding her arms out to him early in the morning with a smile that spread across her face like sunshine. Something in his chest contracted, and pain filled him for what might have been. Where was that sweet-natured Gaby? Lost forever in this streetwise, smart-mouthed brat his daughter had become?

"Well, are you coming or not?"

A heavy, beleaguered sigh. "All right, yeah, I'm coming. Hold your horses."

Matt bit back the rebuke on the tip of his tongue. "I'll have a cup of coffee, but then I'm leaving, so you'd better get in the shower quick."

Matt made his way down the narrow hallway that separated the bedrooms from the galley kitchen and living room of the ten-foot-wide trailer home. He plugged in the electric kettle, moving a clutter of odds and ends to make room, and scooped a spoonful of instant coffee into a mug he selected from the sinkful of dirty dishes.

The place was a mess. Sometime in the next couple of days he'd have to find time to give it a cleaning. Gaby seemed to have no leanings whatsoever toward home-making, and he had no idea what rules he ought to make about chores.

When the water boiled, he filled the mug and moved to sit on the broken-down couch under the front windows. The springs were shot, and he sank almost to the floor, slopping coffee on the leg of his jeans. With a yelp of pain, he struggled up again, slopping more coffee on the worn rug.

Damn it to hell. He needed fresh air. He needed to think, and he did that best in the open air.

Matt made his way out the front door and down the wooden steps to where he'd built a rough picnic table and a bench under some trees the summer before. There was still an icy nip in the air, and he zipped up the padded green eiderdown vest he wore over his flannel shirt. May, this far north, wasn't exactly sunbathing weather, but spring was in the air.

The sun came filtering down through the tall pines that surrounded the trailer. There were patches of snow in the surrounding woods, but the northern spring was making determined advances on the remnants of winter in the Skeena River valley. Spring salmon would be starting their migration up the river now, making for exciting trout fishing. Matt sipped what was left of his rapidly cooling coffee and thought about fishing.

It was the middle of the month, and there would be more and more dark fish as the river started to pick up glacial silt. Next trip, he'd fish for steelhead the first two or three hours of the morning, then put on flashy lures and try for springs. His next fishing party was arriving in a couple of days, four well-to-do businessmen from Arizona. Five. One of the guys had called to say he was bringing his son with him.

Sons. Daughters.

What the hell was he going to do about Gaby for the fourteen days he'd be in the bush with the fishing party? Could she stay here alone, twenty-three miles out of town, without any close neighbors?

Not possible. So what was he going to do with her?

If only he knew as much about being a father as he knew about fishing. His daughter had been with him less than a week, and with every passing day Matt had the feeling the walls between them were getting higher instead of disappearing.

Inside the trailer, he heard the radio blasting out a rock tune full volume. He gritted his teeth at the racket and sighed. Gaby's preoccupation with the radio might be driving him nuts, but it was fortunate his homestead was as isolated as it was. If he had any neighbors, they'd certainly object to the noise Gaby seemed to consider necessary every moment of the day and half the night, as well.

Well, at least she was up—that was something.

He settled down to worry and wait the inevitable long interval until Gaby considered herself presentable enough to make the half hour trip into town.

TERRACE WAS on the Pacific north coast, only five hundred air miles north of Vancouver, but Tania felt she'd passed through some kind of civilized barrier along the way and landed in a different country.

The village was set in a valley, surrounded by an unlimited expanse of trees, mountains and rivers. The landing strip and small terminal were hewn out of a wild and rugged landscape, and the people in the tiny airport seemed casual and easygoing compared to Vancouver's harried residents.

Tania hired a cab, and the taxi ride through miles of woods into the town of Terrace gave her the feeling she was venturing farther and farther into primitive, foreign territory.

"We're comin' into town now. I always like to use the old bridge instead of the new one—been here since 1926 and got some character, I always figure." Her driver sped with careless abandon across a long, ancient bridge. A traffic light controlled the single stream of vehicles, and it was so narrow Tania felt as if the car were about to crash into the sides at any moment.

She gazed down at the fast-flowing water below. "What's the name of this river?"

He shot an incredulous glance at her over his shoulder. "You're really a stranger, huh? That there's the Skeena. Paddle wheelers used to use it to take supplies up and down, trade with the Indians and such. Terrace is located in what they call the Kitsumkalum watershed. We're only about eighty miles from the coastal port of Prince Rupert."

The lilting Indian names intrigued her, but before she could ask any more questions, they were driving into town.

"Where you stayin', ma'am?" The immensely fat driver peered back at her through the mirror.

"Like you said, I'm a stranger here. Which hotel do you recommend?"

He shrugged, steering with one hand and lighting a cigarette with the other. "Terrace Hotel's always a good bet."

"Take me there, then."

The town had a wide, tree-lined main street, several shopping malls and the usual fast-food restaurants. There were trees everywhere, and a large number of the people on the streets were native Indian.

Tania registered at the hotel and was shown to a small room on the third floor, overlooking the main street. She hung her meager clothing in the closet, found a pen and pad beside the telephone and made a busy list of things to do.

First was a visit to the local RCMP detachment.

A renewed sense of urgency filled her. Her father had mailed postcards from here, walked along the streets outside, maybe stayed in this very hotel, for all she knew. The town wasn't large. It couldn't be that difficult to locate one old man, could it? She sincerely hoped not. She felt alien here, out of her familiar surroundings. She didn't want to stay one moment longer than necessary.

Although being in Terrace did take away the sense of hopelessness she'd experienced in Vancouver, she consoled herself. At least here she felt as if she were taking positive action. Why, down there on the street she might even walk straight into Doc.

She hurriedly washed her face and reapplied her modest makeup, made sure her room key was in her purse and went downstairs. The young clerk at the desk directed her to the RCMP office. His round eyes were curious behind his glasses, but he was too polite to ask questions.

When she walked slowly back toward the hotel two hours later, the afternoon was almost gone. The northern day was already fading to dusk, and she felt heartsick and frightened. She'd accomplished almost nothing, and the conversation she'd had with Corporal Biggsby echoed in her mind.

"Ms. Wallace, I'd like to help you, but looking for your father is like searching for a needle in a haystack," the hard-edged, blunt man had told her. "There're dozens of rivers up here with good fishing where he might have gone. From what you tell me, nobody has the faintest idea where he stayed or when he arrived. If he arrived at all. Nobody knows where he might have headed, if he did in fact go fishing. From what you say, none of the local guides took him out." He spread his hands in a gesture of frustration. "The best I can do is start to check with all the motels and hotels in hopes that someone's seen him, but I'm short on manpower and it's going to take time."

In other words, Tania was back where she'd started, entirely on her own. Alone, lonely and discouraged. Frightened. As evening approached, she was more and more aware of being in a strange place where she didn't want to be at all.

There was a raw frontier feeling to the town, an atmosphere that seemed to intensify as the day faded. A city person since childhood, Tania was increasingly conscious of being surrounded and isolated by formidable wild terrain…and inhabitants to match. The dark-skinned natives and roughly dressed loggers and fishermen she passed on the street were at home here. She was the foreigner.

"Hey, baby. You lookin' fer company?"

"Honey, you wanna beer?"

"Where'd you get that hair, sweet thing?"

Terrace seemed to have a great many rough men like these half dozen grouped around the hotel entrance, rowdy types talking and laughing in doorways and on street corners.

Tania hurried past them, through the quiet lobby. She'd noticed the sign earlier that said Lounge, and she headed toward it. She'd go in, order a drink and swallow the foul stuff like medicine.

She walked into the dark, smoky room, and it took only a second to realize that she was the only unescorted female in sight. Even before she sat down, three different men were eyeing her from the bar. Almost immediately she lost her nerve. She turned and hurried out again, almost running to the elevators.

Upstairs in her small room, she locked the door behind her and tossed her purse onto the bed, disgusted with herself. It was stupid to be intimidated by men in a lounge. She was an intelligent, mature city-smart woman, and she ought to be able to handle situations like that.

She phoned room service, defiantly ordered a gin and tonic and, after a moment's hesitation, dinner, as well.

Silly or not, she felt vulnerable and threatened by her surroundings, and she just didn't feel like braving the dining room downstairs or even one of the cafés she'd noticed along the street.

It wasn't just being in Terrace that bothered her, either. Ten years of marriage, however less than ideal, had handicapped her. She was still far too accustomed to being half of a couple. Well barricading herself in this room wasn't going to help her get over it, was it? Tomorrow, she'd brave the dining room, she promised herself.

How long was she going to have to stay here? Terrace felt like a prison caught in a time warp. She couldn't believe she'd been here only a matter of hours. She wandered over to the window and looked down at the busy, rowdy street below, and panic stirred in her stomach, rising into her throat. She tried to fight it down, but it seemed to have a life of its own, twisting and clawing at her.

What are you going to do now, Tania? It was dumb to rush up here. You should have stayed in Vancouver and simply waited. She'd never felt more alone or lonely in her entire life.

At that moment, Matthew Radburn's voice sounded in her inner ear: "If there's anything more I can do to help, my home number's…"

She picked up her bag and, hands trembling, searched for the torn paper she'd thrust into her wallet just before leaving the apartment early that morning. Where had she…? There it was.

She hurried to the phone and dialed, praying that Radburn would be at home. She had no idea what she expected him to do. She wasn't thinking clearly. She just needed to talk to him.

As the number rang and rang again, she knew only that there had been something in the man's voice that was kind, reassuring. He'd offered to help. Not one other person had offered that.

The ringing was interrupted, and the now-familiar deep male voice came on the line like a blessed reprieve to Tania. The taut muscles in her neck and shoulders seemed to ease a little just at the sound.

"Hello, hello, Mr. Radburn—it's Tania Wallace here," she blurted out. "I'm so glad you're home. You see, I'm in Terrace. I flew up this morning, and…Mr. Radburn, I just don't know what to do.

"You see, I had to come to Terrace, Mr. Radburn, because nobody else seems to be able to do anything, and I thought maybe…"

It took Matt a long, puzzled moment to remember who she was and what the call was about. When the pieces fit together, he shut his eyes and blew out a long, silent breath, cursing himself for ever giving her his home number. The last thing he needed in his life at the moment was Tania Wallace and her father.

CHAPTER TWO

MATT SQUEEZED HIS EYES SHUT and massaged his aching head with his hand. Ms. Wallace's voice went on remorselessly in his ears.

"I thought by being up here, where my father was last heard from, I might be able to trace him."

As her monologue continued, Matt couldn't help but sense the raw panic underlying her words. He felt sorry for her, and at any other time his natural sense of chivalry would have been stirred. He'd have offered some kind of help. But today the well was dry. The afternoon he'd just spent with his daughter had drained him.

At that moment, Gaby was sprawled on the couch in a boneless heap, her denim micromini hiked up so that long, coltish thighs and a triangle of scanty blue panties were in plain sight, and over the top of *Real Woman* magazine, she was sending him looks nasty enough to curdle milk.

"But I'm finding it isn't easy at all.... Are you still there, Mr. Radburn?"

"Yeah, yeah, I'm right here, Ms. Wallace. I'm listening."

Gaby rolled her eyes heavenward as if his polite response were exceptionally stupid.

What was it with this kid of his? He'd wanted more than anything to slap her today, and he'd never laid a hand on a female in his life. She was turning him into a violent person.

He'd come close to starting a brawl that afternoon with a gang of young toughs on the street in Terrace, all because of Gaby and that damned excuse for a skirt she was wearing.

Matt had parked in front of the liquor store and gone inside. He'd been buying a dozen beer when he glanced out the window. His daughter was getting out of the truck. But she hadn't just opened the truck door and stepped out. She'd turned her exit into a production, moving in slow motion and allowing her skirt to hike up to her crotch. Matt hadn't fully realized until that moment just how long and sensually curved his daughter's legs were.

Inside the store, the cashier was watching, too, his hand suspended in midair with Matt's change. He'd pursed his lips in a silent wolf whistle, unaware that Gaby was Matt's daughter.

Matt's face had flamed with embarrassment, and a primitive, protective rage had stirred in his gut. It was then that he'd become aware of four young men lounging outside the door and watching the show Gaby was putting on. Through the open door came their whistles and catcalls.

"Awwright, baby."

"Take it off...."

Instead of hurrying away down the sidewalk, Gaby gave them a provocative smile and said something to them. Matt couldn't hear just what it was, but they all laughed.

The next thing that happened sent him bolting out the door. One of the men sidled over, put one arm around

Gaby and then let his other hand slide down and over her bottom in an erotic, slow caress.

Matt didn't remember going out the door. The next thing he was aware of was nearly tearing the man's shirt off his back as he yanked him away from Gaby. He remembered all too clearly the surge of absolute fury in him that seemed to give him superhuman strength. He'd lifted the younger man off his feet and sent him sprawling against the bike rack a few feet away.

The others seemed frozen into place, at first. After a stunned few moments, however, they'd begun swearing and one of them had lurched toward Matt, fists cocked.

Matt only glared, but after a few choice curses the second man thought better of attacking. The group then subsided into muttered threats, helped their friend to his feet and moved off down the street, hollering insults as they went.

He remembered Gaby standing with her back pressed against the side of the truck, horrified amazement on her face.

"Get the hell in that truck, young lady."

Matt had all but tossed her into the vehicle, slammed the door almost off its hinges and hurled himself around to the driver's side and in. He turned the key and they roared off.

It frightened him how much he had wanted to hit her at that moment. His hands had ached with it. He hadn't dared to turn and really look at her. He'd gritted his words out between his teeth, low and savage.

"Gabriella, how the hell could you do a thing like that, giving those apes the come-on the way you did? Don't...you...understand the consequences of acting that way? You looked like...like some cheap tramp."

No answer. She'd twisted her body toward the window, and all he could see was the back of her tousled head.

Matt's voice rose. "Don't you dare ignore me, young woman. If you're going to live with me, you'll damn well obey some rules, and the first one is that you behave like a lady."

A muffled sound of derision and contempt, a scornful half laugh aimed at her father, and Matt felt hot blood pounding into his head as impotent fury at her attitude filled him.

"If you think I'm going to spend my time protecting you from your own actions, Gaby, you're wrong," he spat through clenched teeth. "If you go on dressing and acting this way, you'll have to—"

"Have to what?" Her sudden shriek sliced through the heavy air in the cab. "Go back to Toronto? Take care of myself?"

Outrage and anger filled the space between them. She gave another harsh bark of laughter, but there was fear in it. "For your information, I can take great care of myself. I've had lots of practice. I've been doing it for a long time, Father dearest." Her voice dripped with sarcasm and tragedy. "You weren't around to protect me when I needed you before, were you? If you don't want me here, I'll go back to Toronto. I know lots of kids there."

Her words drove into him like sharp needles, recalling for him in vivid detail the phone call from her just a short week before, a collect call from a pay phone somewhere in downtown Toronto. He'd accepted the charges and listened, gut churning, to the panicked, terrified voice of his child in serious trouble, reaching out in desperation to the father who should have been there for her all along...and hadn't been.

"Daddy, Mom kicked me out.... Please can I come and live with you...?"

Whatever Gaby had become, it was at least partially his fault. What right did he have to blame her for his own omissions?

He'd phoned her mother, Margaret, to find out what was going on, and had gotten nowhere.

His ex-wife had whined and complained and accused, finally admitting that she couldn't handle Gaby and wasn't going to try anymore. It was Matt's turn, she'd concluded, adding a curt "Good luck."

Guilt and awful grief had compounded to drown his anger. Gaby was only a kid. She deserved better of her parents. Feeling ancient and far less than competent, he'd reached a tentative hand across the cab and laid it on her stiff arm; she'd jerked away.

"Whatever happens, Gaby, you're not going back to Toronto, so get that out of your head," he'd said. "From here on, you're living with me, and that's that."

At the first sign of conciliatory words, she'd pounced like a snarling cat, turning toward him and spitting, "Then get off my case, okay?"

Which had made him want to smack her all over again.

Which was why he didn't have much left for anybody right now, certainly not for this hysterical-sounding Vancouver lady.

"And the RCMP don't seem very concerned, and I just don't know where to turn from here," the low-pitched, husky voice in his ear confided. She made an attempt at a laugh. "You see, I had no idea how rugged the country was up here, Mr. Radburn. There are so many rivers, so much bush. I actually thought it would be easy to just follow some trail or other along a river and locate him. I guess I sort of thought the area was a lot, oh, smaller than it is. It was stupid of me.''

Matt didn't answer in words, although he figured her admission sounded pretty dumb, all right. He made a noncommittal noise so she'd know he was listening, feeling as if the sound were dragging up from his toes. ''Look, maybe you oughta just go back to the city and—'' he started to say, but she interrupted as though she'd read his mind.

A snappish, steely note of resolve came into her voice, surprising Matt. ''Forget that. I'm going to stay here until I find out where he is, so don't bother suggesting that I take the next plane home. I do realize that's probably the logical thing to do, but I've made up my mind.'' The words didn't have the sting they might have, because they were followed by an audible gulp. Matt guessed she was starting to cry.

Female tears made him feel helpless and uneasy. Both times he'd spoken to this woman she'd broken down in tears. She mustn't be very strong emotionally.

Glancing over at his daughter, he realized he hadn't seen her shed a single tear. Gaby caught him looking at her and, with an arrogant twitch of her shoulders, got up and sauntered over to the refrigerator, two feet from where Matt was. She opened the door and made a point of crashing cans and bottles, dropping several of them onto the floor. When that brought no response, she slammed the fridge door and turned on the tap in the sink full force, letting it run on and on.

''Gaby, shut that off. I can't hear,'' he ordered at last, covering the receiver with his hand and meeting her angry glare with a steadfast look of his own.

Matt won the silent duel of wills that ensued. She slammed the taps off so that the pipes shook and flounced off down the hall to her bedroom, banging that door so hard the trailer rocked beneath his feet.

Matt shuddered and wondered what in heaven's name he'd ever done to deserve this. One female was doing her best to wreck his living quarters while another was bawling in his ear.

A loud sniff and the sound of nose blowing came over the lines. "Are you still there, Mr. Radburn?" She sounded as if she had a bad head cold, what with all the crying.

"Yeah, sorry." Talking to her in any sort of intelligent fashion tonight was more than he could manage. He had to go to town in the morning anyway to order the supplies he'd intended to buy today, and he made a reluctant decision.

"Where are you staying, Ms. Wallace? Maybe we could get together for coffee in the morning and talk this whole thing over."

Palpable relief was evident in her quick response. "Oh, could we? I'd appreciate that." She gave him the name of the hotel, and they agreed on ten o'clock.

"And, Mr. Radburn, in case you're wondering how to recognize me," she said just before he hung up, "I have red hair."

He hadn't given the matter much thought. He'd been too preoccupied with his own problems to speculate about what she looked like, but his instinctive reaction was frumpy. He substituted a rusty red for the mousy color he'd imagined. He didn't know how old she was, but she sounded to him like the type of lady who was middle-aged at nineteen. Skinny, kind of neurotic and sexless.

HE HAD TO RESHUFFLE all his preconceived ideas the next morning.

Ms. Wallace looked somewhere in her late twenties or early thirties, Matt guessed when he hurried into the hotel coffee shop half an hour late. She was sitting alone at a small table near the window, and her blazing red-gold hair signaled him like a beacon. Even without it he probably would have picked her out without any problem: she looked different from the other women in the room.

She wore a prim beige shirtwaist, stockings, high heels and tiny pearl earrings, but it wasn't just her formal attire that set her apart, it was her attitude—an air of barely suppressed urgency, her rigid posture as she watched the door. Her fingers toyed impatiently with the unused cutlery beside her coffee mug, becoming still as he walked across the room toward her and stopped beside the table. Her hair was long, and it swirled around her head when she moved. Like her, it seemed to give off waves of nervous energy.

"Ms. Wallace? Sorry I'm late. I'm Matt Radburn."

She began to rise, then sank back as he moved a chair out and sat down across from her.

"Mr. Radburn, how do you do? It's kind of you to meet me."

She was pale, and she didn't seem to be wearing much makeup at all, but even without emphasis, her green eyes and wide, vulnerable mouth dominated her face. She wasn't pretty, exactly, but she definitely had the kind of looks that attracted attention.

"Why not call me Matt?" he said. "Terrace isn't a very formal place."

She was much too thin for Matt's taste. Her wrists as she gripped her coffee cup looked fragile and delicate, but then she wasn't a small woman, either. Tall, maybe five-nine or ten, wide shoulders, small breasts. The dress was too loose to tell about hips, but he'd guess narrow. Long legs, tucked modestly under her chair, feet together. She made an attempt at a smile, and once again his eyes were drawn to her full and sensual lips.

"I'd like that much better than this Mr. and Ms. business," she admitted in the low, husky tones he remembered from the telephone conversations. "Please call me Tania."

A cheerful waitress bustled over to their table. "Morning. How are you this fine day? Can I get you menus? You want coffee to start?" She didn't wait for an answer, turning over the mug in front of Matt and filling it from the pot she held, then topping up Tania's, as well.

Matt had eaten a bowl of cold cereal at six-thirty. He'd had to take care of the horses before he drove in, and there hadn't been time even for instant coffee. Gaby was still sound asleep when he left, and anxious to let sleeping daughters lie, Matt had been as quiet as he could and scribbled a note for her.

Now he was good and hungry. "Bacon, three eggs, a couple of pancakes, toast," he ordered. "You had breakfast yet, uh, Tania?" It felt strange, using her first name.

She shook her head. "I'll have whole wheat toast," she decided.

"That's it?" The waitress had her eyebrows and her pen poised.

Tania nodded, and the woman hurried off.

"Now." Matt wasn't much good at small talk, so he went straight to the reason for the meeting. "This thing with your father. You say he's disappeared, that he sent you postcards and led you to believe he was out on a fishing trip with me. Why do you figure he'd do a thing like that? How old a guy is he, anyhow? Is he in good health?''

He could tell by the way her eyes became remote and by the set of her jaw that she hated being questioned. But there wasn't any other way he knew of to help her, if help was possible.

"The police asked me those same questions yesterday," she said at last with a weary sigh. "My father's seventy and he had a minor heart attack three years ago, but the doctor says he's recovered almost completely. Mentally, he's...well, he's fine. He gets a bit depressed sometimes. As to why he'd do this, I don't know except that he doesn't accept getting older. He's..."

Matt watched her struggle for words, and the unhappy expression on her face told him as much as the information she was giving him.

"He's not an easy man to get along with," she finally admitted. "He used to be a logger. He hates the city, and he despises the minimal-care facility where he's been living since his heart attack. He used to live by himself in a little house in the Fraser Valley, but when he started having blackouts and then that heart attack, I convinced him that he ought to move to Vancouver." She frowned, drawing together thick, winged eyebrows over her long eyelashes. "It was probably the wrong thing to do, because he's never settled down, but at the time I—" she swallowed and cleared her throat "—I was in the middle of a bad marriage, and I just couldn't have him living with me."

She met Matt's eyes with a pleading look that seemed to beg for his understanding. "Not that Doc would have, anyway—he hated my ex-husband. And now he hates my apartment." She ducked her head and stared into her coffee cup. "He's not what you'd call an easygoing, happy old man. He and my mother divorced when I was thir-teen, and I never saw him much after that. We're any-thing but close."

"So you figure maybe he's sort of run away?"

She looked at him for a long moment. "I hate to think so, but yes. Sending those postcards wasn't like him. It makes me suspect he planned this pretty carefully." She lifted her cup and sipped her coffee, and Matt watched her. She was a nervous, uptight lady, but she was also appealing. Vulnerable.

"I can't let him just disappear like this, can I?" The plea burst from her, and her cup clattered in its thick saucer. "I have nightmares about him lying somewhere helpless, sick." She shuddered.

"Why do you think he'd choose this area to disappear in, Tania?"

"He likes it here—he always has. He came up several times, years ago, on fishing trips with my brother."

"Any idea where they fished?"

She shook her head. "None at all. He never..." Her voice came near breaking, but she managed to control it. "He didn't talk to me much, you see. I was—" bitterness and sarcasm were obvious in her tone "—I was just a girl. It was my brother he shared things with."

"Where's your brother now? Maybe he'd have some idea where the old man might be." Matt found himself hoping there was someone in this woman's life who'd share this crisis with her—someone other than him.

"Sam's dead. He died in a car accident six years ago."

"There's no one else who'd be able to help you? A friend of your father's, maybe?"

She shook her head. "Dad's friend at the lodge died a while ago, and he's been pretty antisocial ever since.

He doesn't have any other friends that I know of. And we have no close relatives.''

So she was truly alone. Thoughtful, he smoothed his mustache with his fingers.

The waitress arrived with their orders, and Matt used the interval to digest what Tania had told him, both the spoken and the unspoken messages.

She didn't get along with her father, that was obvious. The old man had clearly made a break for freedom, and Matt felt a rush of sympathy for both father and daughter, because he could appreciate both their situations. He'd already had times with Gaby when he'd considered saddling up Blaze and riding off into the sunset.

He poured syrup over his pancakes, moved the eggs on top of the stack, broke the yolks so they streamed nice and golden over the whole mess and took a huge, mouthwatering first bite.

She watched him and nibbled at her toast as if hunger were something alien to her.

He chewed and swallowed and gulped his coffee, knowing he had to tell her what he'd found out, yet hating to raise her hopes in case it all turned out to be a mistake. He waited until he'd eaten most of his food, wondering how to broach the subject, and at last he just jumped straight in.

''I happened to meet one of the other guides on my way over here this morning; a guy named Danny Macardle. He mentioned that he had a party out last week, and they came across an old-timer all alone in pretty remote country.'' Damn it all, maybe he shouldn't have told her.

''The guy was well dressed and spry, but he didn't volunteer anything about himself or what he was doing up there. It's not an area where casual fishermen usually get to—it's quite a ways north and west of here, designated as wilderness park area on the map. I don't want to raise any false hopes. There could be a dozen different reasons for him to be there. Maybe he's some old professor of anthropology or something doing a study. We get them from time to time.''

But Tania's green eyes seemed filled with light, and her entire expression had changed to one of optimism.

''Look, Tania—'' Matt was feeling worse by the minute ''—it's only a rumor, one chance in a million it might be your dad.'' He hated raising her hopes like this. Danny's story could have any number of explanations besides the one she wanted to believe.

''It's the first encouraging thing I've heard since this whole thing began,'' she said in a soft, quavery voice.

Could it have been her father? Matt pondered. There was a remote possibility, which was why Matt was even telling her about it, but it would take a pretty tough old nut to survive long alone in that country, especially a seventy-year-old codger who'd just come from the city.

Matt knew that the RCMP must suspect, as he did, that her old man had gone off on his own and had a heart attack, that his body would turn up sooner or later, but that it was unlikely he'd be found alive. The upper reaches of the Skeena at Spatsizi were dense, almost impenetrable bush, and the odds were overwhelmingly against Doc Wallace's surviving more than a couple of days up there.

He should have guessed what she'd say next, but he hadn't.

''Will you take me up there, please, Matt?''

He shook his head, caught off guard. ''I'm sorry, but I can't. See, I've got a fishing party arriving tomorrow night.'' Why should he feel a sudden sense of guilt for not telling her that his guiding territory was within a couple of miles of where Danny had said the old guy was, in the Spatsizi park area? There wasn't a reason in the world, beyond common decency, for him to feel responsible for this city woman and her problems.

So why did he?

The last thing he needed in this world was a prim, buttoned-up city woman tagging along with his usual crew of hard-drinking clients. And there were other considerations, as well. Up at base camp, he had old Benny Benson as cook on this trip. Everybody knew about Benny and women. The old coot was one of the best camp cooks around, but if a woman happened to be in the fishing party, Benny had been known to quit on the spot, leaving the guide high and dry. And good food was imperative on these trips.

So what was Benny's reaction going to be when Matt packed in with Gaby in tow?

Sometime in the past night, Matt had admitted that there wasn't a way in the world he could leave that girl at the trailer alone for fourteen days. And he didn't know any females he could ask to baby-sit, either. The females he knew intimately weren't the kind he wanted within ten miles of Gaby.

"I'd expect to pay, of course," Tania was saying.

Matt shook his head again and attacked what was left of his breakfast, but against his better judgment an idea was forming: Gaby needed a full-time chaperon to keep her out of trouble, and Tania was about as respectable as any woman he'd come across in years. She hadn't flirted once with him, hadn't even come close. If he had to drag one reluctant female along on this trip, he might just as well take two, right? Let one sort of take care of the other?

The problems it would create didn't bear thinking about. But there wasn't any way around it. He had the party of men coming; he needed the money the trip would bring; he had to take his daughter with him. He might just as well take Tania, too.

The waitress refilled his coffee cup, and he added cream and looked over at Tania, weighing the pros and cons.

"Look," he finally said, beginning to feel a bit magnanimous and holy about it all. "I might just consider taking you along on this trip, on one condition."

Her eyes were blazing at him again, and now there were patches of bright color in her pale cheeks. She had nice skin, smooth and soft looking.

"What's the condition, Matt?" Her voice was throaty and eager.

He took a deep breath and wondered how the hell he could explain Gaby to her without making it sound as if his daughter were a delinquent. Knowing he was making a bad job of it, he finally blurted out that his daughter had come to live with him a short while ago, and there wasn't anyone he could leave the girl with while he guided his fishing party. So if Tania would agree to keep an eye on her, it would solve both their problems, right?

Wrong. Tania was cautious.

"How old is she?"

"Sixteen."

Tania looked surprised, then frowned. "Oh, I don't think I could do that. I thought you meant a much younger child. She's a teenager—I haven't had any experience with teenagers. I've never really been around kids all that much."

"Well, neither have I," Matt said with morose honesty. "I figure you sort of learn as you go."

Tania looked as if she might be about to ask him how that worked, but she didn't. Instead, she sat thinking for what seemed a long time, and then she shook her head regretfully.

"Matt, I'm sorry. I don't feel I could take on any sort of responsibility right now, especially for a young girl. I'm under a lot of strain with this thing with my father, and I don't think I could give your daughter what she requires."

Remembering yesterday, Matt figured that just might be a good swift kick in the butt, but he didn't say so.

"Perhaps I can find another guide to take me up. Where did you say this old man was, exactly?" Matt had his doubts about her finding anyone, but on a napkin, using Tania's pen, he sketched her a map, anyway, indicating approximately where Danny had been. He told her how to get in touch with a tourist center that listed all the local guides and their phone numbers, knowing as he did so that none of them went that far afield with their parties.

When he was done, he got to his feet and stuck out a hand. She reached out and took it, and for a moment, Matt was aware of her in a disturbing physical way. Her hand was warm, long fingered and smooth, and he found himself wondering if all of her skin was this soft.

"Best of luck then, Tania."

"Thanks, Matt."

He walked to the counter, paid the bill and left the café without one backward glance.

WITH A CONFUSED MIXTURE of emotions, Tania watched him go.

His huge, rangy body, broad shouldered and somehow graceful, disappeared as he went out the door, only to reappear a few moments later, striding down the sidewalk outside the window. As she watched, he turned and crossed the street with his long, loping walk, raising a hand to greet someone and then going into a hardware store.

"You want more coffee?" The waitress was by her side, pot in hand, and although Tania knew she shouldn't have any more, she nodded, anyway. She wanted a few minutes to sit and think over her meeting with Matt Radburn. The story he'd told her about the old man had excited her. Maybe it was silly, but she was convinced that old man was her father. She was determined to travel up the river and find out for herself.

Her thoughts turned to Matt Radburn. For some reason, she'd envisioned him as older than he was, with a beard and a checked shirt, shabby and with an awkward manner—a stereotypical backwoods fishing guide. Stupid of her.

He was wearing a checked flannel shirt, and he had a thick mustache, but that was all she'd been right about. His size was intimidating. He was huge. Six-four or five, maybe? Shoulders and a neck that must make buying clothes difficult. Wide apart, deep blue eyes and a broad face, ruddy from being outdoors. Rumpled brown hair and a handlebar mustache two shades lighter. Crinkles around his eyes and lines from nose to mouth, but she didn't think laughter had put them there.

Matt Radburn's charm ended with his looks, Tania thought. He was grim and a bit intimidating. He hadn't smiled once during the entire meeting, and there was an air of impatience about him, as if he could barely spare the time to talk with her. But after all, he had every right to be impatient. She was imposing on his time. There was no reason for him to be concerned about her problems.

Tania thought over what he'd said about his daughter. Obviously, Matt Radburn had problems of his own to deal with. She thought about his abrupt, awkward proposition, that she take on the chaperoning of his daughter.

She'd sensed it was a move of desperation on his part, and Tania was relieved that, despite her eagerness to travel up the Skeena, she'd had sense enough to refuse him. But now she had to find someone who'd take her there, with no strings attached. It shouldn't be difficult; there must be plenty of guides around.

Leaving a generous tip for the waitress, Tania headed for the tourist center Matt had recommended.

BY LATE AFTERNOON, Tania felt more like throwing herself into the Skeena than traveling up it.

She'd spent hours on the phone in her room, trying to locate a guide. Fishing season was at its peak, and a great many of the names on her list were already out on trips. The few she managed to get hold of gave her an assortment of excuses when she explained what she wanted, and the last call she made left her furious and shaking.

She told her story to the gruff voice on the other end of the line.

"No way."

Exasperated, Tania snapped, "I'm quite willing to pay top rates, you know. I don't understand why it would be a problem for you."

"Look, lady," he said condescendingly, "money's not the issue here. Nobody I know is gonna take one greenhorn city woman on some wild-goose chase to find an old geezer who's no doubt dead somewheres by now, when they could be havin' a good time fishin' with a bunch o' men and earnin' tips besides.''

Bile rose in Tania's throat as the line disconnected.

An old geezer who's no doubt dead somewheres by now....

She changed her heels for flat shoes, grabbed her purse and her room key and stormed out of the hotel.

After half an hour of furious walking, she found herself on a small bench overlooking the town in a quiet subdivision nestled among pine trees. The sun was still shining, although evening was imminent. Dogs had barked at her, pickup trucks had honked, children playing had stared, and she'd hardly noticed.

Deep inside herself, she'd examined her options and come to the only conclusion there was: she had to accept Matthew Radburn's offer. She had to agree to help with his daughter if she wanted to search further for her father.

What would chaperoning his daughter entail? she wondered. What was the girl like?

She tried to remember herself at sixteen, but it was no help at all. She'd been anything but a typical teen, even that long ago. Bookish and shy, she'd never even had a boyfriend. Sweet sixteen and never been kissed. The old, outdated phrase ran through her mind, and she remembered dimly how the truth of it had bothered her.

But wasn't there more to her refusal than just the matter of his daughter? Honesty forced her to admit that being around Matt had left her unsettled, that she was altogether too conscious of him as a virile, attractive man. A rueful smile played across her face. Jane, in fact, would label Matt Radburn a sexy, macho, well-washed, blue-collar hunk. But she wasn't Jane, was she? There was no reason to react like this.

Hurrying back along the streets she'd followed, she

made her way to the now-familiar hotel and climbed the stairs to her room. Inside, she went straight to the phone and dialed Matt's number.

A sullen-sounding young female voice answered before Matt came on the line.

"Hello, Matt, it's Tania," she said to him. "I've decided to take you up on your offer."

As if she'd really had any choice.

"However," she went on without waiting for a response, "I think it's essential that I meet and get to know your daughter before we make the trip."

Silence, for a long, waiting moment—silence that irritated Tania. Gracious, this Matt Radburn could use silence more effectively than anyone she'd ever met. Had he changed his mind? Had he found some other female to supervise his daughter? Anxiety niggled at her gut.

"We're leaving day after tomorrow, so I guess you'd better come out here in the morning. I'll pick you up at ten, all right?"

"That would be fine."

What in heaven's name was she getting herself into?

CHAPTER THREE

MATT ARRIVED at the hotel right on time the next morning, and with a clumsy, old-fashioned courtesy Tania found appealing, he seated her in a battered open-topped red Jeep. Courtesy aside, though, he still didn't smile much.

After making two short stops at a fishing supply store and a bakery, they drove twenty-odd miles over gravel roads out to his homestead.

"You live a long way from town," Tania commented, feeling as if her spine were being jolted into the base of her brain.

"I bought twenty acres of isolated riverside property when I first moved up here," he explained, almost shouting over the racket of the noisy engine and the wind that tore at Tania's hair.

Matt watched the road as he talked, squinting against the dust and the sunshine. "I fancied myself as a country squire in those days. I was going to build a big log house with a deck that overlooked the water. Drew up the plans myself, but setting up in business took all my ready cash, so I bought an old house trailer and set it up to live in—strictly temporary. Still in it after twelve years. Never did get around to building that house."

Tania had a million questions. Where had he moved from? When had his daughter come to live with him? What had he done before he set up his guiding business here? She debated about what to ask first, and by the time she decided, they'd turned off the gravel road onto a narrow, rough dirt trail that followed a rambling path through thick woods into a clearing. She put her questions on hold, fascinated by this first glimpse of Matt's home.

A battered blue-and-white trailer was parked under a stand of towering spruce trees, the wide river a breathtaking backdrop. To the right of the clearing was a large log barn, with a pole corral around it and a horse who trotted over to the barrier and whinnied at them.

The Jeep drew up with a flourish on a gravel area near a blue van and the trailer. As soon as the engine died, Tania became aware first of the ear-splitting racket of hard rock music coming from the direction of the trailer, and second, of the voluptuous and near-naked figure stretched out on a plaid blanket near a makeshift picnic table.

Gaby was lying face-down, fortunately. Her well-rounded bottom was intersected by a minuscule yellow triangle, but the two scraps of fabric making up the top of the bikini lay tossed to one side, and their owner made no effort to retrieve them.

Tania thought she heard Matt groan, but when she turned to look at him, his rugged features were impassive, although his lips were pressed together in a grim line.

He jumped to the ground and came around to her side, taking her arm in a strong grasp and helping her down.

The female on the blanket managed to wave a lazy hand without raising her torso.

"Hi, Pop," she caroled. Beside her was a glass, and now Tania could see the almost empty bottle of red wine lying in the grass within arm's reach.

"Gabriella!" Matt's voice lashed out like a whip.

"Get inside and put some clothes on. It's not hot enough for sunbathing yet. And turn that stereo down."

"Okay, okay, you don't have to get weird about it. I was going in anyhow—the bugs are eating me alive." She managed to cover her breasts with a towel before she got to her feet. She ignored Tania as if the other woman were invisible and sauntered up the wooden steps and into the trailer, swishing her hips and slamming the door behind her.

Tania couldn't help but notice how lovely Gaby's young figure was, rounded at hip and breast, narrow of waist, with long, coltish limbs that gave her an appealing, unfinished air. With her half pound of makeup washed off and her hair color tamed, Gaby would be a beauty.

But Tania couldn't suppress an appalled sense of horror at the thought of spending days and nights around a girl who talked like this one, or of being responsible for her in any way at all.

Matt's face was a mixture of embarrassment and anger when Tania glanced his way. He was standing with his fists planted low on his hips, frowning after his daughter, and it took him a moment to sense Tania's gaze.

"Sorry about that, Tania. I honest to God don't know what to do with her," he said in a quiet, frustrated tone.

That statement alone, sincere and bone honest, prevented Tania from demanding that he take her straight back to town and forget the whole thing. If he'd tried to defend Gaby in any way, Tania would have bolted. Instead, sympathy welled up in her for this big, quiet man. His bald admission hinted that maybe his problems with his daughter were responsible for his silences, his infrequent smiles, his abrupt and often distracted manner. Why, if she had a daughter like that, she'd be at her wit's end, too.

"You never had any kids?" His question was hesitant and rather shy.

"No." But if she had a daughter, the girl wouldn't be at all like Gaby, Tania assured herself, and then felt ashamed of being smug. "I was pregnant twice during my marriage, but I miscarried both times." The admission had always been difficult for her, but telling him seemed easy.

"That's rotten luck. I'm sorry." His voice deepened, and for an instant a warm bond stretched between them, a recognition that each of them had been scarred by living. Her words also seemed to encourage him to talk.

"Gaby was only two when her mother and I divorced," Matt said. "She's grown up on the other side of the country. She only came to live with me about a week ago, and I'm afraid I haven't had much to do with teenagers."

"Me either."

In some obscure fashion, the conversation made Tania feel more confident about the whole thing. Matt didn't sound as if he really knew his daughter, so at least he wouldn't expect instant rapport between Tania and Gaby.

The rock music suddenly died from inside, and Gaby emerged wearing one of Matt's shirts, unbuttoned down the front, tossed casually over the yellow bikini. The top was in place this time, however.

Like a tightwire, tension replaced the easy atmosphere, stretching between father and daughter in a palpable wave.

"Gaby, this is Tania Wallace. Tania will be coming with us on the trip tomorrow."

"Oh yeah? How come?" The response was insolent.

"Haven't you ever heard of 'How do you do?'"

Matt's voice was deceptively even, but it carried a formidable warning.

Tania could see color stain the smooth skin under the artificial blush on Gaby's cheeks, but her brown eyes were hard and defiant.

"How do you do?" she parroted, eyeing Tania from head to heels in a calculated, feminine way. "So why are you coming on the trip, Mrs. Wallace? Do you just like fishing?"

Tania actually felt intimidated by this girl, which was crazy. "No, I've never fished in my life." She paused there, uncertain as to what Matt wanted Gaby to know about the agreement they'd come to.

He rescued her. "Ms. Wallace is searching for her father, Gaby. He's seventy years old, and he's been living in Vancouver, but now he's gone missing somewhere up the Skeena, maybe near my fishing camp. Another guide might have spotted him up there. Tania's coming with us to see if she can find him."

"Oh." Gaby hesitated. Her voice lost some of its brashness when she said, "You don't think anything bad happened to him, do you?" It was an anxious, childish question, and it made Tania think better of the girl. At least there was something inside her that was compassionate.

"I hope not," Tania said with fervent emphasis. "I don't think so. He's a healthy man, so I'm hoping he's just lost track of time, fishing somewhere."

Gaby gave her a long, steady look, as if she couldn't believe the way adults deceived themselves. Then she shrugged and nodded. "That's probably it, all right."

They were still standing outside, and now Matt said with obvious reluctance, "Come on inside for coffee and a doughnut, Tania."

"Hey, you got doughnuts in town? Awwright!" Gaby enthused, leading the way up the wooden stairs and through the trailer door. "There's nothing good to eat in this place."

Tania was just behind her. Matt had gone over to the Jeep to retrieve his parcels.

Tania's first sight of Matt's home caused a sensation akin to nausea in the pit of her stomach. She had always been compulsively neat and tidy, and as she surveyed the chaos of the surprisingly large room, she had to force herself not to roll up her sleeves and find the soap and bleach.

"I'm all sweaty from the sun. I'm gonna grab a quick shower. Sit down. Dad'll be here in a minute." Gaby tripped off down a narrow hallway, leaving Tania standing awkwardly just inside the door, taking horrified stock of the disaster around her.

Dishes littered the counters and overflowed from the sink. Half a loaf of bread sat drying on a cutting board with a messy bowl of butter and an open jar of strawberry jam beside it, not to mention a sticky knife, attracting several flies. A black frying pan with two inches of congealed gray grease sat at a tipsy angle on the stove.

Tania tore her shocked gaze from the kitchen area, but the living room was just as bad. An assortment of crumpled clothing was tossed on the sagging sofa. Tania recognized Matt's checked shirt among the heap, as well as message T-shirts that had to belong to Gaby. Some of the girl's shoes were peeping from under the sofa and chair—one sandal and a mauled-looking sneaker. Dust balls clung to the gray rug. And everywhere she looked there were books: stacked in corners, toppling from chairs, overflowing from a ceiling-high bank of shelves in a corner, filling the ledge below the wide window that fronted the trailer. The books surprised Tania, because they were a messy echo of the neat, orderly shelves of books in every room of her apartment. They were the talisman of the avid reader.

She took a tentative step toward the nearest stack and picked several up, noting two of the latest bestseller paperbacks she hadn't yet had a chance to read, a fat mystery she'd loved, as well as outdoor adventure novels she wasn't familiar with. Matt must devour books, just as she did. She filed away that information as she made her way over to the one armchair in the room that was almost free of clutter. She removed two newspaper sections and the latest issue of *Cosmopolitan* and laid them on the littered coffee table. Then she sat down.

Somewhere in the back of the trailer water was running as Gaby showered, but apart from that, it was quiet. Then the Jeep door slammed, and a moment later Matt came through the door, ducking his head automatically to avoid the doorjamb, arms full of parcels. He sent one sweeping glance around and shook his head.

"No use apologizing for the mess," he said with matter-of-fact candor, shoving a cereal box, a bowl and two cups out of the way so he could dump the bags on the kitchen table. "I'm no housekeeper, and it seems Gaby's like me in that department. It isn't usually this bad, though. I haven't had time or energy to do a proper cleanup since I got back from the last trip. I need a cleaning service, I guess."

Tania thought the place could use something like seven maids with seven mops, a good disinfectant and a garage sale. And both Matt and his daughter were in dire need of a few stiff lessons in maintenance and tidiness. It wasn't something she should say, though, so she kept her mouth shut, watching Matt fill a kettle, put it on the stove and rummage around until he found a clean plate. He took the doughnuts out of the bakery bag, heaping them by twos and threes on the plate with a fine male disregard for arrangement, giving up when two fell off again. He washed the sugar off his hands under the tap, making Tania shudder by using a stained tea towel to wipe dry.

"You take cream, no sugar, right?" He shoveled instant coffee into two mugs he rinsed out under the tap, poured the not-quite-boiling water in and stirred vigorously, frowning with concentration.

Tania studied him as he took a carton of coffee cream from the fridge and carefully poured some into her cup. He tore off several sheets from a roll of paper towels and folded each across the center to double as napkins. Carefully balancing the brimming cup, the plate of doughnuts and the paper towels, he threaded his way across the floor to Tania's side.

"How did you know what I take in my coffee?"

"From the café yesterday morning."

For some obscure reason, the fact that he'd noticed and remembered what she took in her coffee touched Tania's heart. She'd thought he wasn't paying any attention to her on a personal level. She'd lay odds that John, her former husband, for all his glib and empty compliments and charming manners, hadn't bothered to notice what she took in coffee, even after ten years of marriage.

Matt was a curious man, she reflected. He was a strange combination of conflicting traits. He'd responded to her plea for help, obviously against his better judgment. He was a man who didn't reveal his feelings or his emotions with ease, but when he did get around to talking, he was completely honest. He managed to look clean and well-groomed even while living in the midst of this colossal mess. Matt interested her more each time she was with him.

He brought his own coffee over and laid it on the low table, shoving clutter aside with a practiced motion to make room. He lifted a straight-backed kitchen chair and set it down so that he and Tania were facing each other.

She decided to get business matters out of the way first.

"If you'll tell me what you charge for these trips, Matt, I'll write you a check now."

He gulped his coffee down—the entire cup in one long draft—and set it back on the table.

"No charge for you," he said. When she started to protest, he interrupted. "We're doing each other a favor. Far as I'm concerned, we'll come out even."

"But there must be expenses on your part—food, lodging. I'd like to pay my own way."

He cocked an eyebrow at her. With a hint of humor that took her by surprise, he said, "From what I've seen, I don't guess you're gonna break me by eating too much. And you may decide the lodging isn't any hell when you get up there. As for Gaby…well, if you don't charge me, I won't charge you. Deal?"

He was right on target about his daughter. The thought of two weeks in close proximity to Gaby sent a cold shudder rolling down Tania's spine. She met his eyes and gave in. She smiled agreement, and when the glance held a beat too long, she looked away.

"Deal," she said with a catch in her throat. Reaching for her cup, Tania sipped her lukewarm coffee.

Matt folded a paper towel carefully around a doughnut and handed it to her without a word. She accepted it and took a bite, careful not to look into his eyes again. She took another bite, and another. The fresh sweetness was delicious. It was the first thing she'd eaten for a week that actually tasted good. The anxiety that had tied her stomach in a knot was easing now that it felt as though she were taking positive action.

Matt polished off doughnuts with methodical ease, two bites each, and neither spoke.

Moments later Gaby came into the room, soaking hair slicked close to her head, face devoid of makeup. Now she seemed to Tania much younger than her sixteen years, while only a short time before she had looked years older. She was wearing a pair of skintight jeans with a loose red T-shirt over them, knotted in jaunty fashion on one hip. She poured herself a glass of milk from the fridge and took a doughnut from the plate on the coffee table as she made her way past Matt and Tania. She lowered herself to the couch, and Tania understood why Matt had avoided sitting there. The springs were so bad Gaby sank almost to the floor.

The easy rapport that had started to grow between Tania and Matt disappeared. Gaby's entrance seemed to carry tension with it, and that tension filled the room.

To break the heavy silence, Tania said with forced goodwill, "I suppose school is already out for you for the summer, Gaby?"

The girl took a long swig of her milk.

"I quit," she said.

"You quit school?" The announcement shocked Tania. To her mother, and therefore to her, education had been sacrosanct. "So what do you plan to do now?"

Gaby looked at her with a bored expression and chewed half a doughnut with slow relish. Then she shrugged. "Just hang out, for the summer, anyhow. I'll figure out what I want to do in the fall."

Without an education, the choices would have to be

limited, but again Tania didn't say what she was thinking. Instead, she looked over at Matt to see how he was reacting to all this, but his face might have been a stone mask for all it revealed of his feelings.

Tania tried again. "I suppose you miss your friends in Toronto. Moving this far away from familiar surroundings must be difficult for you."

Gaby shrugged again. "Nah, not really. See, we didn't move to Toronto until six months ago. We used to live in Moncton. You know where that is?"

Tania nodded. "New Brunswick," she supplied.

"Yeah. I liked it better there." For a moment Gaby sounded wistful. Then her tone took on its usual breezy, tough note. "But then my mom got divorced when I was thirteen." She shot a look at her father and added in a noncommittal voice, "Again. And then she started living with this guy last year, and he got an offer of a job in Toronto, right? So we moved."

"I see." Tania didn't see at all, but she couldn't think what else to say. Gaby's mother—Matt's ex-wife—sounded as if she might not be too stable. No, she amended, the woman sounded totally self-centered and oblivious to the needs of her daughter. Her assumption was reinforced by the formidable, grim expression on Matt's face, silent witness to what he was feeling about Gaby's story.

"Well, it was probably a very good time to choose to come here and be with your father, then," Tania added brightly, feeling as if she'd ventured into a conversational mine field.

Gaby gave her father an anxious look. "Yeah, I guess so," she said noncommittally. She jumped to her feet. "I'm gonna take Blaze for a ride, Dad."

Matt considered that, then shook his head. "Not until

you do your share of tidying up this place, Gaby. Didn't you read the note I left you this morning about sharing the chores?"

Gaby's bottom lip shot out. "It's not my fault this place is a dump," she whined. "I don't see why I should have to—"

"That's enough. If you've got time to loll around in the sun drinking what's left of my wine, you've got time enough to do some of the work around here. Hop to it. You can start by putting through a couple loads of laundry and hanging them out. It's good and warm out there today."

Tania felt like applauding, but Gaby shot Matt a foul look before she moved with the speed of a tortoise toward the rear of the trailer.

Matt watched her go. The lines around his mouth deepened, and a frown creased his forehead. He pushed his fingers through his hair and sighed. Then, as if remembering Tania was a guest and should be entertained, he said with a determined effort at lightness, "C'mon outside and I'll show you the rest of the place. Not that there's all that much to see, just the barn and the horses."

Tania picked up the coffee cups and the empty plate and deposited them in the sink.

It was a relief to step out into the brilliant sunshine. The air was sweet after the mustiness of the trailer, and in the distance was the muted roar of the river.

"It's beautiful, this place," she commented as they walked across the clearing to where the log barn stood. "I can certainly see why you'd choose to live here."

His face brightened and he surprised her with one of his rare, wide grins. "Yeah? Most women figure this is way too isolated," he said. "They don't mind a night or two, but there's no way…'' His voice trailed off and he cleared his throat.

To Tania's surprise his weather-beaten countenance turned a slow scarlet, and the true meaning of his words hit her like a blow. Why, he'd brought women out here, to… She felt herself blushing, too.

Why should that bother her, for heaven's sake? It was perfectly natural he'd have women chasing after him and even more natural for him to take advantage of it. Matt was a virile, attractive man, and he'd been single a long time. Why should Tania feel, of all things, resentful at the thought of him making love to those women?

He'd stepped ahead of her and was opening the gate to the corral when she caught up. The brown-and-white horse she'd noticed earlier came trotting over, and Tania took several hasty steps back out of the corral. She knew nothing about horses, and she wasn't certain she wanted to meet one this close up.

"Hello, Blazer, old man.'' Matt's voice was a gentle, loving rumble. He rubbed the animal's muzzle and scratched between his ears, and the horse made satisfied noises deep in its throat.

"C'mon inside, Tania.'' Matt turned and held the gate open, and there was nothing for her to do but follow. The horse towered over her, and she gave the animal a wide berth as she bolted over to the barn door and ducked through it.

Please let the animals inside be restrained, she prayed, hovering inside the door and squinting into the gloom.

To her relief, the barn was empty, cool and dim. The smell of hay and animals was clean and pleasant, and everything was neat and tidy. Along one wall, tools were hung in precise, neat rows. Pitchforks and shovels stood in order against another wall, and fresh straw filled the stalls. Obviously, Matt's messy housekeeping didn't extend to his barn. Tania strolled along the wide walkway, aware that he was close behind her.

"You enjoy riding, Tania?" he asked.

She glanced over her shoulder and confessed, "I've never been on a horse in my life. In fact, I've never even been close to one before now."

"I see." The tone was thoughtful. "I wondered, the way you skidded away from old Blazer out there. He made you a little nervous, did he?"

She grinned at him over her shoulder. "Now how did you guess that? Truth is, he scared me silly."

He raised an eyebrow and nodded, seeming to consider his next words carefully.

"I probably shouldn't tell you this right now, but we have to pack in to my fishing territory, Tania."

She turned to face him, hoping she'd misunderstood.

"Pack? As in ride, on horses?"

He nodded, and she could see amusement in his eyes and in the careful way he held his mouth. He was trying not to grin.

"Afraid so."

She swallowed hard. "How...how many miles?"

He shrugged. "Oh, a couple of days' ride. Maybe three. We drive part way and then take horses from there."

"Oh my God!" The exclamation was drawn out and horrified. Three days up on the back of a horse? She shuddered at the thought.

"Don't worry, we go pretty easy. Most of the guys I guide aren't used to horses, either. But they want a real wilderness sort of fishing trip, so that's what I give them."

She was sure, however, that those men weren't actually

scared of the beasts the way she was. The thought of even getting up on one sent bolts of fear down her spine even now. Well, she'd have to get over it—that was all there was to it.

"How many people will be going on this trip, Matt?"

"There'll be nine of us—four businessmen from Arizona, one of their sons, you, Gaby, me and Mario, the kid I've hired as swamper for this trip. My cook, Benny Benson, rode in a few days ago to get things prepared."

"What's a swamper?"

"General all-round gofer, I guess you'd describe it."

"Oh." She was silent, and then she blurted out, "Is it hard to learn, riding a horse?"

His blue eyes twinkled, but he didn't smile.

"Not in the least. You'll catch on fast, wait and see."

Oh, she hoped so. She fervently hoped so.

"Don't give it another thought. You'll probably end up enjoying it so much you'll take up riding as a hobby. Come on outside and I'll show you where I planned to build my house." He reached out and took her hand in a friendly, firm clasp, and at first she considered pulling away. But wouldn't that seem as if she were putting altogether too much importance into a meaningless gesture?

His hand was big and warm and callused.

He led the way out a side door, back into the blinding sunlight. With every passing moment Tania grew more conscious of the feeling of his rough, warm hand surrounding hers, the slight and varied pressures he exerted to emphasize what he was telling her, the bulk of his large body close beside her. How long had it been since a man held her hand, walked beside her, looked down at her and smiled like this?

Far, far too long. She was a woman who'd always

liked being with a man, which was probably why she'd stayed in her marriage so long.

"The other horses are over there in that meadow." He pointed to what seemed a huge number of animals grazing in a distant pasture. "Mario's coming later tonight. We'll load them into a trailer, and he'll drive them up to where we start riding."

Tania was pathetically glad she and Matt weren't heading toward the horses and equally relieved that Blaze was nowhere in sight. Instead, they walked along a well-worn trail in the direction of the river. In the center of a magnificent stand of cedar trees there was the beginnings of a house: a pile of dirt beside an excavation for a basement, an immense pile of logs, the general outline of a spacious building. There was as well an intangible air of desertion. She had a feeling that Matt had started this project with eager anticipation long ago and abandoned it before he was even half-done. His words confirmed it.

"I had big dreams for this place, but they never materialized." He made a disgusted noise in his throat. "Now, I doubt they ever will. See, over here I was going to put solar collectors in, with a glassed-in kitchen-solarium right here, overlooking that view of the river."

"With a deck all around it?"

He grinned and nodded. "For sure. A big wraparound cedar deck, where you could sit and watch the sunset."

"It sounds fantastic. I've never been inside a house built entirely of logs, but I've seen pictures in magazines. They all seem homey and welcoming."

Matt agreed, adding, "Log houses can also be dark inside, so I planned skylights in three different areas." He gestured with one hand without relinquishing his hold on her. He led her around the excavation, pointing here and there to illustrate his words. "The house would be heated mainly with wood, and a tumble-stone fireplace would make up one interior living room wall. That's what those foundations are for over there. The fireplace would have opened into the family room, too. That way it would conserve and use all the warmth it generated without losing half of it up the chimney.''

Tania nodded, watching him out of the corner of her eye. His craggy face was more animated and full of life than she'd seen it before. In the bright sunshine, she noticed a few premature gray hairs at his temples and also in his mustache. She decided she liked his mustache.

''For a long time, I used to work on these blueprints every spare minute I had,'' he confided. ''I almost wore them out making changes, but I haven't even looked at them in a couple of years. Funny how time goes by and you finally realize some things are only dreams.''

Without warning an aching sadness came over her, for Matt, and for herself, as well.

He was showing his faded dream to her, a dream that he'd abandoned somewhere along the way as life grew complicated, just as she'd given up her own fantasies about a happy marriage, a child or two, a successful writing career. Instead, she was one of Vancouver's innumerable divorced women, living in a lonely city apartment, writing tired clichés about weddings and funerals for a paper nobody noticed.

''I wonder if anyone's life goes exactly the way they plan it?'' she mused.

He grunted and shook his head. ''I doubt it. Mine sure as hell took a few unexpected turns along the way.'' He turned and studied her. ''How did you think yours was going to go, Tania?''

They were standing near a pile of lumber, and he sat down, pulling her down beside him. The boards were

warm from the sun, and the warmth, sensuous and relaxing, crept through her tailored pants to her skin. She
could smell wood and the intangible scent of the river.

"My life? Well, I guess I thought it would be different
than it has been, certainly." The surroundings, the song
of the river, the comfortable rapport she felt with him
encouraged her to confide in him. "I married young. I
met John at university—he was my professor. It took a
long time to realize that the person I idolized and married
was incapable of being honest. Or faithful, either." It was
still difficult to confess that John had played around on
her. It had damaged her sense of herself as a desirable
woman.

"It took me even longer to admit he wasn't ever going
to change." She gave a sad little laugh. "By the time it
sifted through my thick head, I'd let years go by, time I
should have been using to further my own career instead
of his. So now, at thirty-six, I'm having to start over, and
I'm not very good at it."

He gave her hand a quick, gentle squeeze. "I know
what you mean. I never figured I'd end up a single parent
at forty, either. And God knows I'm making a mess of
it."

She was going to ask him about Gaby when a sudden,
harsh racket split the silence from what sounded only a
few feet above their heads. Tania shrieked and pressed a
hand over her thundering heart.

"Omigod! What on earth is that?"

Matt laughed and slid a comforting arm around her
shoulders. "It's only a jay, telling us off. He figures
we're trespassing on his territory. Noisy fellow, isn't
he?"

Tania's heart was pounding harder than ever, but it had
nothing to do with the bird. All of a sudden Matt was

holding her tight against his side, and with one strong, easy motion he turned her toward him, his lips only inches from hers.

"Damn it all, I've been wanting to do this all day, Tania," he breathed, and then he was kissing her.

CHAPTER FOUR

HIS MUSTACHE TICKLED. His lips were hard and a little chapped as he brushed them across hers, tentatively at first, exploring, almost polite in his hesitancy, but determined, as well.

Tania began to tremble as her body reacted to his touch. She felt surrounded, engulfed by him. His big, muscular arms were wrapped around her, holding her close, and the world had narrowed to the shape and feel and taste of him. His skin was rough, weather-beaten, and he smelled like hay and fresh air. His kiss stirred responses in her she'd carefully tamped down and filed away a very long time ago.

She'd forgotten what it felt like to be kissed, the delicious, slow swelling deep inside her, the way her lips softened and became pliant at his insistent stroking.

God, it felt good. It felt indescribably good.

She hadn't been kissed by a man for a very long time. Had she ever been kissed in this thorough, slow, attentive way? Matt was intense and clever at it, kissing her deeply and with controlled passion.

Her outer trembling became a deep, inner surge, a desire to have the embrace go on and on, to be held closer and still closer. It felt safe, it felt good in his arms. Her arms lifted and linked around his neck, her fingers tracing the soft, curling hair at the nape, learning the shape of his jaw, tracing the plane of his whisker-rough cheeks, touching the strong cords in his powerful neck.

The jay screamed again, but she was barely conscious of the sound. His tongue asked a question and hers responded. The kiss deepened, and Tania could feel Matt's heart hammering against her body. When they finally drew apart, Tania had trouble getting her breath. Matt was still holding her close, studying her face and frowning. Instead of pleasure, his features registered something closer to anger.

"Damn it all, anyhow. This isn't going to make things a hell of a lot easier," he growled.

His words tore through the illusion of security and joy she'd been experiencing. Tania felt hurt and furious with him for spoiling the moment this way.

She struggled out of his embrace and got to her feet, walking a few steps away and turning her back on him, wrapping her arms around her torso and trying to regain her shattered composure. She felt as if every vulnerable part of her inner being were visible, exposed to him, and she silently cursed herself for allowing her guard to drop this way. Hadn't she been damaged enough by the male species without inviting another wound?

"Don't worry about it. It won't happen again. I'll make certain of that," she managed to choke out, hating the way her voice cracked halfway through the sentence.

"Tania." He was close behind her, and he took her shoulders and turned her toward him. She resisted but she was no match for his strength. He tilted her face up so she had to look at him, ashamed because her vision was blurry with unshed tears. She blinked and they trickled down her cheeks and dripped off her chin.

"Hey, I'm sorry. Don't look like that. Don't cry." His eyes were a deep, soft blue, and they met her gaze with a gentle directness. He used his fingers to rub away her tears, and the rough, clumsy caress touched her in spite of her resolve to be immune to him.

"Kissing you was great—it was wonderful. I didn't mean what I said to hurt you, Tania. Hell, the trouble is I'm no good at all at making pretty speeches. What I said just then was the bald and honest truth. Wanting to kiss you all the time, wanting…" His voice deepened and became a rumble, and his fingers tightened on her shoulders, then loosened as he took her hand and gently guided it to his body, illustrating his words in a fashion that shocked and tantalized her. "Wanting to make love to you the way I do right now, well, it won't make this trip we're taking easier on either of us. That's all I meant. We'll be surrounded by my clients, Gaby will be there, and I'll be busy every minute. We won't have a whole lot of time alone, and right now, that's what I'd like to have. I'd like to be alone with you for the whole fourteen days. Understand?"

She stared up at him, trying to take in what he'd just said, too aware of the hard male anatomy she'd just touched to think rationally.

Wanting to kiss you all the time. Wanting to make love to you. He felt the same way she did. Urgent, wanting, needing.

A wave of relief swept over her, and she felt her body relax, the knot in her stomach unclench.

"I do understand, Matt. I thought you meant…"

The rest of her shaky sentence was lost as he drew her to him, holding her tight against his body. Her head fitted nicely into the hollow of his shoulder, and she let herself rest against him, closing her eyes and reveling in the moment.

"We'll just have to take this slow and easy, but that's

not the way I'd choose, Tania." She felt him sigh, and his arms tightened around her. "That's not the way I'd choose at all, if I had my way."

"Daaa...ad."

Matt's arms dropped away from Tania, and he swore under his breath as he moved back.

His daughter called again.

"Dad, hey Dad! Where are you, anyway? I can't find the lousy clothespins, and that line is too high for me to reach. I hate hanging clothes. Why bother when the dryer's working? It's a big fat waste of time, if you ask me."

They moved still farther apart, feeling like guilty teenagers as Gaby's grumbling voice drew closer. She came around the corner of the barn and stood sullenly leaning against the pole fence, staring at them and waiting for her father to come and help.

"I really should get back to town soon," Tania said as they walked toward the girl. "I need to find a store where I can buy a pair of jeans and some warm shirts, and I have packing to do."

She did have a lot to do, but most of all she felt an overwhelming need to get away from both Matt and his daughter. She needed to be alone again, to think about what had happened here between her and this man and figure out what she should do about it.

"Sure, Tania. I'll just get this kid of mine settled and then I'll drive you back," Matt promised.

Tania felt as if a visible, sensual bond had formed between her and Matt, and she felt herself blushing, of all things, when they reached the spot where Gaby was standing.

She tried to chat with the girl while Matt found the clothespins and fixed a makeshift step so Gaby could reach the long clothesline strung behind the trailer. It wasn't easy. Gaby was sullen and uncommunicative, and Tania found herself resenting Matt's daughter with a passion and intensity that shocked her. It was out of all proportion to Gaby's childish behavior.

The simple truth was that Tania longed to spend the afternoon with Matt here, beside the river, in the place that was home to him. Alone, just the two of them.

All too soon, however, they were bouncing back over the rutted roads in the Jeep, and although Gaby had stayed behind at the trailer, for some reason Tania sensed that the intimacy between her and Matt was gone now. He was quiet and preoccupied during the drive, and when he left her at the hotel, he gave her instructions about the next day instead of saying anything personal.

"My fishing party'll be arriving on tonight's flight. I'll meet them and bunk them here in the hotel overnight, and tomorrow morning I'll pick all of you up good and early. Can you be ready by five-thirty?"

"In the morning?" The incredulous tone of her voice brought a crooked grin at last to Matt's rugged features.

"'Fraid so. We've got a three-hour drive to get to Meziadin Junction, where the horses will be, then a pretty fair pack trip into my fishing territory. It always takes more time than I counted on to get everything organized to leave, too."

"Oh. Well, of course. I'll be ready."

"And don't bring anything that's not essential." He glanced down at the flimsy feminine shoes she was wearing. "I don't suppose you've got a pair of sturdy boots?"

Tania shook her head.

"Well, a pair of good runners will do, I guess. And heavy socks—we'll be doing a fair bit of walking in thick bush. The bugs can get pretty bad—better bring some insect repellent."

Her heart sank. It was sounding worse every moment.

He reached out a hand and took hers, his blue eyes holding her gaze and saying much more than his words. "See you in the morning, then."

He held her hand a moment longer, bent and placed a quick, hard kiss on her lips and then let her go. "Get a good night's sleep. Tomorrow's liable to be a little tiring."

THAT TURNED OUT to be the understatement of the century.

Matt arrived at the hotel promptly at five thirty-five the next morning. Tania, unable to sleep, had been up since four. She'd showered, washed her hair and blown it dry, pinned it up in a bun, decided that wouldn't do, taken it down, then braided it in a pigtail down her back.

She put on a pair of her stiff new jeans—she'd bought two—and the crisp, tailored white shirt she'd decided looked good with them. She had a tweed blazer with her that would serve as a jacket. She was pleased with the high-top black runners the clerk had said would be almost as good as boots, and she'd bought four pairs of white socks as well as some long-sleeved T-shirts with Terrace, B.C., plastered all over them.

Tania surveyed all her things and felt that her wardrobe, at least, would be adequate for any situation. She wasn't so sure about herself. Growing more apprehensive by the instant, she put on a little makeup, washed it off and then redid it, packed and repacked the single suitcase and large bag she was taking, filed and painted her nails with clear polish, locked the other large suitcase the hotel said it would hold for her and then unlocked it to transfer a blouse she thought she might need into her bag. Then she stood at the window, watching the street and getting more nervous with each passing second. By the time Matt knocked at her door, she was half-sick with anticipation.

"'Mornin'." He was wearing a green padded vest over a red flannel shirt. Scuffed Western boots showed under the hem of frayed and faded Levi's. It was obvious he was preoccupied and in a hurry.

"All this stuff isn't going, I hope?" He frowned at the suitcases.

"Only those two, and my shoulder bag, of course." Tania thought he was pretty brusque after the kisses they'd shared the day before. In fact, he made her feel ill at ease. "This big one is staying here at the hotel—they said they'd keep it for me. Do you think it'll be safe here?"

"Might as well bring it along and leave it at the trailer. We have to pick up Gaby, anyhow." He somehow picked up all her bags, heading out the door without another word.

Tania dashed in to check the bathroom one last time in case she'd forgotten something, and by the time she'd caught up with him he was inside the elevator, holding the door and looking impatient. Another man, potbellied, bleary-eyed and yawning, was also in the elevator.

"Tania Wallace, this is Andrew McBain, one of our party."

"Good morning." Tania smiled but Andrew McBain barely nodded.

Because of him, there was no chance to say anything private to Matt even if Tania could think of something. When they reached the lobby, she hurried outside. Matt was stowing her bags in the back of a long van, and he slammed the sliding doors and came around to open the passenger door for her.

The seat beside the driver had obviously been reserved for her, and Tania was filled with gratitude when she climbed in and turned around to smile hesitantly at the other occupants.

The van seemed filled to the roof with suitcases, boxes, crates and a frightening number of laughing, wisecracking men of all shapes and sizes. Matt got in and turned in his seat, rattling off introductions before he started the van.

"Tania, that's Bob Young just behind you, Harry Zalco beside him, Andrew you met already, and in the back are Jim Irwin and his son Scott.

Male faces—some bearded, some clean shaven—peered at her. Two grinned cheerfully, others looked still asleep. She felt as if she'd blundered into a locker room. The air was thick with cigarette smoke, and there was a heavy smell of last night's stale beer from their breath as they called "Hello," "Glad to meet you," and "How'd'ya do?" in loud and boisterous voices. Andrew and Scott merely nodded.

Except for those two, she couldn't remember one of their names an instant after Matt had said them. She managed a polite "Hello," turned frontward and stared at the road as pieces of conversation from the back flew past her like projectiles.

"Hot damn! Did ya hear that good old boy in the bar last night goin' on about the grizzly…"

"…called Susie from the hotel and she…"

"…says he needs those damned projections right away…"

"…so I told him, I said take your goddamn—" interrupted by a hasty, "Hey, Harry, put a cork in it. There's a lady present."

There was a strained silence for long, awful moments, while Tania went on staring out the windshield and feeling like Typhoid Mary. Then she gathered her courage, swallowed hard, turned around in her seat and said, "Look, I work at a newspaper, and my boss could probably outswear anybody in the Western Hemisphere, so don't worry about me fainting at a little bad language, okay?"

She turned frontward again and reminded herself with stern resolve of her reasons for going on this trip.

After talk had resumed behind her, she risked a glance at Matt, and he winked at her and gave her a reassuring grin and a nod of approval, which made her feel a whole lot better. Soon they were bumping down the dirt road to Matt's ranch.

"I'll go get Gaby. The rest of you might like to get out and stretch your legs before we start the drive," he suggested. He retrieved Tania's suitcase from the van and hurried into the trailer. The men struggled out and ambled down to the now-deserted corral, leaving Scott in the van.

Tania hung back, watching them with curiosity. She'd be spending the next two weeks with this group of men, and she couldn't help but wonder what they were like. The first thing she noticed about them was their obviously new, obviously expensive, Western outfits. They had stiff new Stetsons, jeans as new as hers, suede or denim jackets, and they looked as though they might be auditioning for a Western movie.

Tania also noted that two of the men were grossly overweight, Andrew and…was it Harry? They looked as if a sensible diet and an exercise program might do them more good than a fishing trip. The other two, and of course the boy, Scott, were slim enough and fit looking. None of them had Matt's muscles or physique, though, Tania caught herself thinking. They all looked sort of…inconsequential…in comparison. But then, she concluded, so would most of the male population of Vancouver.

Scott was probably about eighteen, and he didn't seem to be enjoying himself much. His jeans had a designer label on the back pocket, and he wore a striped blue rugby shirt under a soft brown leather jacket that emphasized his wide shoulders. His rather long, well-cut blond hair was casually mussed, and he had a small gold ring in one ear. His eyes were dark brown, his features even and classically handsome. He got out and stood leaning on the van with a mutinous look on his face, shoulders slumped.

"Do you like fishing, Scott?" Tania felt uncomfortable, standing right there and not saying anything to him.

He looked at her and then gave his head a vehement shake. "Nope. This is all my dad's idea." His voice was grim.

"Oh. Well, maybe you'll enjoy it, after all."

"Yeah. Maybe." He didn't sound as if he believed it, and Tania gave up on conversation. But a few minutes later, his face took on a more animated expression, and he drew himself erect and squared his shoulders, staring in the direction of the trailer. Tania turned to see what had caught his attention.

Gaby, in formfitting leopard-skin tights and a fluorescent lime-green T-shirt, was sauntering across to the van, swinging a Western hat and her hips with equal gusto. She ignored Tania and homed in on Scott.

"Hi, I'm Gabriella, but you can call me Gaby."

She must have watched old Monroe movies, Tania

thought, caught between amusement and irritation at Gaby's sensual manner with Scott and rudeness to her.

"'Morning, Gaby," she finally said in a cheery tone.

The girl's heavily made-up eyes flicked to her and then disdainfully away.

"Oh, yeah, hi," she said shortly. Then, to Scott, she purred, "My dad didn't tell me there was anybody my age coming along. I figured this was going to be a real drag. Hey, think we could sit inside? It's chilly out here."

Scott almost broke his hand scrambling to open the side door of the van for her. Tania noticed his eyes were on Gaby's well-defined bottom as she climbed up and in.

"My father couldn't get permission from my mom till the last minute. They're divorced, so I almost didn't get to come," Tania heard him say as the van door slid closed.

Well. Gaby certainly knew how to deal with the male of the species, anyway.

Matt was hurrying across the yard now, and the others all hurried over and got in. The first leg of the trip was under way.

IT WAS ALMOST TEN O'CLOCK when they reached Meziadin Junction. They'd driven through several small Indian settlements with lilting names like Kitwancool and Kitwanga, but most of the trip had been through breathtakingly beautiful uninhabited land.

Matt had commented now and then on the colorful history of the area, revealing a deep interest in and wide knowledge of the native people.

"Carbon dating done by archaeologists places the Tsimshian Indian nation and their ancestors in this area for the past forty-eight hundred years. That takes them back to about 2900 B.C., which makes white men

Johnny-come-latelies. The Tsimshian had various tribes living along the Skeena, and before the white men ever settled on Indian land, the Tsimshian sold furs to maritime traders. They called us Ghumshiwa, which means bleached driftwood, and in order to get their kids to behave, they used to say 'Watch out or the Ghumshiwa will get you.''

Tania laughed, delighted with Matt's stories and the way his blue eyes twinkled at her as he told them. In the back, Andrew was snoring in loud snorts, Gaby and Scott were talking in low tones, and Jim, Bob and Harry were leaning forward over the seat, listening to Matt as avidly as she was.

Outside the van, there were rivers everywhere. They followed the Skeena for a time, crossed a bridge, and for the last half of the journey the road trailed along beside a river Matt called the Nass.

"From Meziadin Junction, we'll basically be following the Nass River valley through the Skeena mountain country on horseback," Matt explained in answer to a question from Bob. "My fish camp's situated on the upper Skeena."

Tania shuddered, and nervous tremors began again in her stomach. This part of the trip had been enjoyable. What would the next part bring?

AT MEZIADIN JUNCTION, which was nothing but a crossroads at a small lake, Matt brought out thermoses of coffee, egg and tuna sandwiches and oatmeal cookies for a late and hurried breakfast, and they ate standing up. Some distance away, a large horse trailer sat beside a makeshift corral, and Tania could hear three young men talking to one another and laughing as they worked with the animals.

"That's our swamper, Mario Berzatto, and two friends of his who are going to drive the vehicles back to Terrace for me after we get saddled up," Matt explained.

Tania retrieved her suitcase and bag from the van and tried to stay out of the way. Before she had time to worry about what to do next, Matt called, "Okay, everybody, bring your stuff and come this way," and herded them all in the direction of the horses.

Tania's heart began to hammer. There seemed to be dozens of horses in the corral, milling around, snorting and jumping and rearing up. A rangy young man in dirty jeans was in the middle of them, cowboy hat pulled down around his ears, shouting at them and wrestling saddles and bridles on one animal after the other. The sun was high in the eastern sky, and it shone in golden streaks through the billowing clouds of dust the animals were raising.

"Mario, come over here a minute," Matt called over the noise of the horses and the excited comments the men were making. "I want you to meet our clients." Matt introduced Tania first and then the men.

Gaby had stayed back at the van. Tania saw her, perched in the front seat, using the mirror to apply make-up and fix her hair.

"This is Mario Berzatto, Scott Irwin. Mario's our swamper for the trip. You boys must be about the same age."

The two young men gave each other an unsmiling nod and a measuring look, and Tania compared them.

Mario was tall and well built, although his body was much more wiry than Scott's. Their clothing also set them apart. Mario's blue shirt was ripped at both elbows and none too clean. His green quilted vest was coming apart in places, and when he took his sweat-stained brown hat off, his wavy black hair was in need of a drastic cut. Nevertheless, he whipped a dirty comb out of his pocket and carefully combed the tangles out before he put his hat on again, and there was no question that he was a dramatically good-looking young cowboy.

The riding horses were tied by their reins to the pole fence. They whinnied and moved their massive bodies around restlessly, and Tania could sense that all too soon she would be forced to get up on one of those animals. Her stomach felt sick, and she wished she hadn't eaten that egg sandwich.

Soon the packhorses were loaded and ready to go, as well.

"Okay, everyone, let's saddle up," Matt called. "Tania, over here. I'll give you a hand up." Matt smiled at her, a gentle and reassuring smile. She approached as slowly as she could manage.

"This is your mount, Sultan. Sultan's good-natured and well mannered. You'll get along fine."

Tania's throat felt parched. Her heart was pounding triple time and her palms were soaked. There was nothing to do but climb on.

Matt held the stirrup and she got her foot up in it somehow. Then, as if she were weightless, Matt hoisted her up and into the saddle. The horse stepped several paces to the right, adjusting to her weight.

Tania gulped and fumbled around desperately until she managed to hook her other foot in the opposite stirrup. She gripped the saddle horn with both hands, knuckles white. Mercy. Lordy. She felt a mile off the good solid ground.

"Good girl, that's the ticket. Easy does it now."

It took a moment for Tania to realize Matt was talking to the horse.

"Sul-Sultan isn't a-a boy horse?" Her voice would hardly work.

Matt looked up at her, a wide grin on his face, his blue eyes twinkling with amusement.

"Sultan's a mare. Probably got named by a rabid feminist."

Andrew, standing nearby, gave a huge belly laugh.

Tania wasn't even up to smiling. She concentrated on adjusting her behind to the contours of the hard saddle and hanging on to the saddle horn tight enough to feel marginally secure.

Matt handed her the reins. "Just hold these nice and loose—don't jerk on them. Sultan's tied up, so you can't go anywhere yet."

"Hey, Matt." Harry Zalco was several horses away, and he sounded put out. "Mario here says I'm gonna have to leave my portable computer behind. Now, I can't just walk away from my computer. There's spread sheets I have to work on the next couple of days. Could we talk about it?"

Matt rolled his eyes heavenward and swore under his breath.

"There's no power up at camp, so it's not going to do you much good, Harry." He turned back to Tania. "I'll be right back. Just sit there and get used to things while we get everybody in order. Then I'll come and give you some tips on riding. Where the hell is Gaby?"

He hurried away. Mario was trying to saddle the horse nearest Tania, and the nervous animal was moving sideways in a skittish fashion, threatening to bump into Sultan. Tania sat frozen, afraid to move anything but her head in case Sultan took it the wrong way.

With a fine sense of timing, Gaby chose that moment to make her appearance. She sidled across to the group carrying a duffel bag. Her golden hair was now frizzed out around the brim of a black western hat, and her face was carefully made-up. Her round breasts, obviously bra-less, bounced enticingly inside the green T-shirt, nipples standing out clearly in the cool morning air.

Mario's low, long whistle made Sultan's ears twitch. Tania caught a glimpse of Gaby giving Mario a wide smile, but she couldn't have said for certain what happened next. All she knew was that the horse beside her lunged full force into Sultan. The sudden, unsteady motion beneath Tania made her jerk back hard on the reins just as the other horse slammed into her leg.

Sultan, still tied loosely to the fence, reacted by rearing up until the tied reins jerked her down again. Tania's feet came out of the stirrups and she tumbled to the ground, landing hard on her buttocks and one elbow, almost under the hooves of the other horse. She screamed, dust flew, horses whinnied. Mario swore.

Some of the fishermen weren't on their horses yet, and they came rushing over, trying to help as she struggled up as quickly as she could, her face flaming. She felt humiliated and furious as she stood unsteadily among them, bottom hurting and her elbow sending pain up into her shoulder.

Andrew was the first to reach her. "Nothin' broken, I hope. All we need is a trip in to the hospital before we even get goin'. Hell, how'd ya manage to fall off a horse while it's still tied up, anyway? You ever been on a horse before, lady?"

He sounded disgusted. He was taking swipes at her, trying to brush the dirt off her jacket, and she pulled away from him and glared. She'd never considered kicking a man in a vulnerable spot before, but it was all she could do to stop herself at that moment.

Matt, who'd been reasoning with Harry, came racing over and Andrew moved away, mumbling under his breath about bloody greenhorn women. Matt's hands closed gently around her upper arms, and his voice was concerned and sympathetic, his blue eyes worried.

"You all right, Tania? You sure you didn't crack any bones or anything?"

She nodded, unable to speak. It was all she could do not to burst into tears and throw herself into his arms. She'd never felt as inept and out of place in her life. And to make matters worse, she saw Gaby looking at her with a mixture of contempt and superiority on her lovely young face.

She remembered that Gaby had wanted to go for a ride the day before. Obviously, horses held no terrors for the only other female around, and that made Tania feel even worse. But Gaby's supercilious expression made her determined not to reveal her feelings. She managed to hold her chin high and even to conceal her shock when Matt said, "Okay then, back up on Sultan. We're about ready to pull out, but first, there's a few things I should show you about riding. C'mon, up you go."

She couldn't believe he could be so unfeeling, ordering her back up on that hysterical, skittish horse this fast. Only stiff pride and a deep anger with Andrew got her back up on the horse—anger, outrage and the simple fact that there wasn't any alternative.

For the next fifteen minutes, Matt gave her pointers on riding while the rest of them sat in taciturn silence on their horses and waited to leave without even pretending to be polite about the delay.

BY ONE IN THE AFTERNOON, Tania concluded that Matt had a fine gift for sadism. She hadn't had so much as a drink of water since they'd left Meziadin, and there didn't seem much chance of getting that or anything else to eat or drink in the near future.

She'd been enduring terror, exhaustion, boredom and discomfort in successive waves for hours, and now she added hunger to the list. It didn't look to her as though the day was going to improve, either. In fact, it was moving steadily downhill, right along with the animal beneath her. Sultan was heading down an incline so steep that new bolts of fear went shooting through Tania's overwrought nervous system with each jarring, slipping step her horse took. She was certain she was about to slide right off the animal's neck and probably break her own on one of the massive boulders that were studded all along the trail.

She was more or less alone in her misery. The men were all well ahead of her, already entering the treed meadow Tania could see at the bottom of the hill. The packhorses were strung out quite a ways behind her in a long, winding line; one animal's halter was tied to the next animal's tail, making it possible for Mario to lead the entire string. Gaby had chosen to ride with Mario, and Scott chose to ride with Gaby, so they were all behind, as well.

Matt had turned his mount back half a dozen times during the morning, but there was no intimate exchange whatsoever as he rode distractedly back to Tania, asked brusquely if she was all right, then hurried past her to check on the packhorses. It was silly to feel hurt by his lack of attention; it was obvious he was busy. At the moment, he was up ahead with the others, already hidden by the thick poplars growing in the meadow.

She did feel hurt, however. Tania had never felt as alone, deserted and out of place as she had since they'd gotten on these wretched horses. Worse, she suspected that even the horse viewed her with disdain, she was so uncertain, fearful and clumsy. Fortunately, once they'd started moving, Sultan seemed to know the trail and understand what was required of her, and for that Tania was grateful.

All that was required of Tania was that she somehow stay astride, and that had taken every ounce of her energy and will. She had to remind herself constantly why she was here at all, and with each passing hour it grew more difficult, because as civilization disappeared somewhere behind her, all she could feel for Doc was a deep and bitter resentment for getting her into all this.

Finally, Sultan reached the bottom of the hill, and Tania could relax a tiny bit as the horse's footing became more stable, her back level instead of inclining steeply downward. She wriggled around in the saddle, trying to find a position less uncomfortable. Her bottom had been numb for a long time now, and her back and legs ached from sitting in the same position hour after hour. The thought of being on this animal's back for all of today and tomorrow—and even longer—boggled the imagination.

The scenery was spectacular, though. The scent of wild roses filled the air with delicate perfume. The bushes were growing everywhere, laden with pink buds that contrasted with the new green of the trees. The morning had grown warm, and down here in the little valley there were welcome shadows beneath the thick growth of trees. Tania stretched her shoulders back, relaxing her hold on the reins and tipping her head up to stare into the lacy patterns the leaves made against the blue sky.

Sultan must have got wind of the bear moments before it was visible. The horse let out a terrified snort and gave a lunge that unseated Tania instantly. She fell into the rosebush she'd been admiring seconds before. Sultan reared, screamed and pawed the air. Then she turned around and took off at a gallop back up the hillside toward the pack train just beginning the long descent.

The thorns in the rosebush were tearing at every inch of exposed flesh, but Tania was oblivious to the pain. Terrified, she stared at the black bear not ten feet away from her. Its head was moving rhythmically from side to side as it tested the air.

CHAPTER FIVE

MATT HEARD THE HIGH, terrified scream of a frightened horse and reined Blaze around in one easy motion. The fishermen were all stopping their horses, turning to see what was going on.

"Wait right here. Don't move!" Matt ordered as he trotted past them. He reached down and undid the fastenings on the rifle case beside his leg. He was in time to see Sultan, riderless, galloping back up the side of the mountain toward the pack train.

His heart began to hammer. Where the hell was Tania?

He spotted her a second later. She was sprawled in the center of a large rosebush, a long scratch visible on her cheek. She wasn't making any effort to get to her feet. She was staring with an expression of frozen panic at a small black bear about ten feet away. The bear was standing beside an evergreen, its dish-shaped head moving back and forth as it scented the air. It looked scruffy and still thin after the long winter.

Matt made sure his horse was between Tania and the bear, and he prayed she'd stay quiet until the bear decided what it was going to do next. A scream or sudden movement on her part could spell trouble.

Blaze reared and danced when the wild smell reached his nostrils, and the bear took several menacing steps toward the horse. Matt whipped the gun out of its case and held it ready, hoping he wasn't going to have to use it.

What the bear did next was turn tail and run, but its sense of direction was off. It headed straight up the hill toward the pack train, and a sense of impending disaster settled over Matt even as he called out a warning to Mario.

"You hurt?" he asked Tania next. "Can you move your legs and arms fine?"

Please, God, don't let her be injured, he prayed silently, leaping off Blaze and rushing over to her.

"Matt..." Her green eyes were huge and her freckles stood out in clumps against a face bleached of color. "The...that...it...a...bear. It's...gone?"

"Yeah, it's gone, honey. God, I'm sorry you got such a scare. You sure you're all right? Here, let's get you on your feet."

She seemed dazed, but she got gingerly to her feet with his help, pulling her clothing loose from the thorns that snagged her everywhere. Her hands were covered with scratches and starting to bleed.

"Damn, you would have to fall into a rosebush," Matt swore. He helped her undo the last few thorns and inspected her quickly. She didn't appear to be seriously injured, apart from a few scratches, and he muttered a thank-you under his breath to whatever capricious powers were in charge of this particular fishing trip.

She started to say something to him, but her voice was drowned out by a cacophony of sound coming from the direction of the pack train. Horses screamed, Mario hollered, and Gaby added her voice to the din.

"Son of a gun. That stupid bear's run head-on into the pack train."

Matt had a pretty fair idea what was happening, but he prayed he was wrong.

"C'mon, Tania, up you go."

"I can't. Oh, Matt, I..."

He ignored her protests and grasped her waist, lifting her up on Blaze. He swung into the saddle in front of her, and she gave a startled exclamation and locked her arms around his waist as he urged the horse up the incline as quickly as he could.

The scene was even worse than he'd feared. The lead packhorse, which should have been controlled by Mario, had obviously bolted when the bear appeared. The horse behind him, still tied to the first horse's tail, was forced to follow. The third horse, also tied, decided to take a different route, making for the wrong side of a tree, which effectively stopped the first two in their tracks and tangled the three horses around two solid birches.

The first two had gone down, the third was scrambling to its feet, and the entire pack train was in chaos, blundering around trees, stumbling over each other as they tried to bolt, only to fall and take more horses down with them, making a nightmarish racket. The bear had disappeared.

Mario came galloping up and barreled off his horse to begin the impossible task of untangling the animals.

"Where the hell were you when this was going on? You were supposed to be leading these animals, not lollygagging around a hundred yards back." Matt was furious. He knew exactly where Mario had been, because half a dozen times already that morning he'd ridden back to find Mario dancing attendance on Gaby instead of doing his job.

Gaby rode up now from the back of the pack train,

looking flushed and excited and far too pretty for her own good.

"Wow, would ya look at this! What a mess. Did ya see that bear, Dad? It went charging right past us," she called cheerfully, and Matt rounded on her.

"You get your ass up to the front of this party and stay there where I can keep an eye on you, young lady," Matt ordered between gritted teeth.

"So now it's my fault a stupid bear came along. Why blame me for everything?"

"Just do as you're told."

She gave him a resentful look, but the menace in his voice penetrated. She kicked her mount and headed down the incline. Scott rode up a moment later, took one look at the mess, gave Mario a nasty grin, kicked his mount into a trot and followed Gaby.

By now Mario had tied his horse to a tree and was struggling with the lead packhorse, trying to get it unwound and on its feet. He wasn't having much success.

Matt got down, but first he had to pry Tania's fingers apart to make her let go of her death grip on his waist. When he was on the ground, he reached up and helped her slip off Blaze, conscious even in the middle of chaos how slender her waist was beneath his grasp.

"Better stay well back," he suggested. "These pack-horses can be damned contrary if they want to be. The bear's gone, probably headed for high country, but don't wander too far away, just in case."

Tania looked at him as if he'd taken complete leave of his senses. She had to cling to the saddle for several minutes before she could walk, and then she limped with a rather bowlegged gait over to a spot under a couple of tall pines and sank to the ground, resting her head on her knees and looking as if she might never move again.

Matt surveyed the damage to the pack train and felt sick. Besides the stumbling, neighing horses now struggling to their feet and trying to kick one another senseless, there were sleeping bags, boxes of food, jackets, suitcases and fishing gear scattered on top of, over and through the underbrush, and so far there was no sign of Sultan.

Matt wondered if the horse was already halfway back to the stable. Sultan was no fool, and she probably could sense as well as Matt could how this particular trip was shaping up. If Matt had a choice right about now, that's exactly what he'd do: head for home and let this particular group of happy campers fend for themselves.

Except that this, hotshot, is the way you make your living, remember? Even on days like this, it's got being a stockbroker beat twenty-nine times to Sunday, right? And your darling daughter is at least partly to blame for this, along with that sorry excuse for a wrangler you hired. And the bloody bear.

His anger rose and he tried to find something else to blame and couldn't.

"Matt, is there anything I can do to help?"

Tania had recovered enough to struggle to her feet, and she was close beside him looking around at the mess with a sort of helpless horror.

"Stay out of the way of the horses and pick up as much of that stuff as you can. Just put it in a pile over there under those trees. And if you spot Sultan anywhere, for Pete's sake try and get hold of her bridle." He gave her a reassuring pat on the arm and tried to grin, but it didn't come off.

She nodded, and he felt admiration for her. She wasn't complaining the way he might expect a lady from the city to react after getting bucked off and frightened by a bear. Instead, she gingerly set about doing what he'd suggested. He could tell by the way she was walking that the hours on horseback had already taken their toll on her muscles, but she limped around and gradually moved a little easier.

She was gutsy, he'd give her that.

And she did something disturbing to his innards, something that he just didn't have the time or energy to deal with. She'd surprised him yesterday with her response to his kiss. She was one hell of a passionate woman under that prim exterior, and it lit a fire in him that flared each time he was near her. Why couldn't she have come along at a different time in his life?

He sighed and turned his attention to the monumental task of helping a subdued Mario get the horses untangled and repacked.

It was quite some time before Sultan made her appearance. Matt was cursing Twobits, a particularly obstinate animal who insisted on lying right back down each time they managed to haul her to her feet. He heard Tania call his name, and when he turned toward her, she had Sultan by the very end of the reins, holding them at arm's length and watching the animal as if it were about to bite her.

"She came back on her own. She walked right up to me," Tania said in a nervous tone. "What should I do with her now?"

"Hang on a minute and I'll take her."

Sultan stood quite still until Matt grasped her reins. She gave him a disgusted look, which Matt felt was appropriate under the circumstances. He was relieved and happy to see the horse, because otherwise he'd have had to ride Blaze double with Tania on behind for the rest of the trip, which would slow them down considerably and be hard on old Blaze to boot.

Not that Matt wouldn't enjoy it, but there were practical aspects to consider here.

The rest of the party, curious and tired of waiting, soon arrived to see what was wrong. Matt set them to work helping Mario, noticing that the only two missing were Gaby and Scott. What the hell was his daughter up to now? She already had Mario panting after her. In far too many ways, Matt was beginning to see Gaby as her mother's daughter. His ex-wife had needed the attention of every man in the immediate vicinity.

When Matt asked, Jim said Gaby and his son had chosen to wait at the bottom of the hillside, and Matt began to wonder if he shouldn't tie Gaby's mount to his own for the rest of the trip or think about handcuffing Gaby to Tania for the next two weeks. His daughter was an incorrigible flirt. It made him feel both helpless and enraged.

There wasn't a thing he could do about it at the moment, so he set to work like a man possessed, instead. It seemed to take forever, but at last the pack train was again loaded and neatly linked together, with a chastened Mario sticking close to the lead animal this time.

Matt watched them start down the mountain, fishermen strung out in a single line ahead, the horses in the pack train looking deceptively docile. He sighed with relief and walked over to where Tania was waiting, near the spot where he had Blaze and Sultan tethered.

"Thanks for helping get the gear all collected up, Tania. It would have taken me another hour without help." She'd been much more efficient than the men at arranging things in tidy bundles and organizing what needed to go where.

"I'm glad I could find something to do today besides fall off a horse," she said, her voice trembling.

He stopped short and took a good look at her. She'd taken off the tailored tweed jacket she'd had on when they left that morning. Her cotton shirt, pristine white when they started, was nothing short of a disaster, with a button missing and a dark stain down the front. Her jeans, obviously also new, were no longer clean or crisp looking. Grass had stained them on both knees and bottom. Dust billowed out each time she moved, and her runners were filthy with what looked like horse dung. The scratch on her face was still spurting small droplets of blood, and her hands looked sore and raw where the rose-bushes had gouged them. Her fiery hair was coming loose from the thick braid down her back, and tendrils stuck to her sweaty cheeks. There was dirt streaked across her forehead and over her chin. He noticed she had tiny pearl earrings in the lobes of her ears, and for some reason that incongruous touch of femininity touched him as nothing else had.

Matt felt tenderness and affection well up in him. This was much harder on her than he'd anticipated, and he felt bad.

The sun had turned her pale skin a blotchy pink, and he suspected that by nightfall she'd have a jim-dandy sunburn to add to her other woes.

"I realize I'm not exactly an asset on this trip, Matt. I haven't given Gaby a single thought all morning, because it's all I can do to take care of myself. I'm sorry. I'll try to do better once we reach camp." She looked at him with her chin tilted up and a defiant expression on her face, but he could see that her green eyes were brimming with unshed tears.

He had an irrational urge to gather her into his arms

and hold her tight, protect her from whatever other dis-
asters faced them before the wretched trip was done. But
the others weren't far away, and there was always the
chance someone would come trotting back.

"You look as though you've been through a war," he
said with a husky catch in his voice. "Come over here
and let's put something on those scratches."

He folded her hand into his and led her over to his
horse. He kept a jar of ointment in the saddlebag, but
before he located it he opened his canteen and poured
some water over his hands and then hers.

He fished a clean bandanna out and dried them both
off, wetting and using a corner of the cloth to clean some
of the dirt off her face. Then he opened the ointment and
smeared a gob carefully on his fingers. She'd been standing as patiently as a child being cleaned up by a parent,
but she flinched when his fingers came in contact with
the raw scrape on her cheek.

"Ouch! That stings, Matt."

"Hold still, pretty girl."

She rolled her eyes to heaven at that, and he had to
laugh.

"That's a gross exaggeration at the moment," she said
dryly.

Her skin was hot and velvety smooth to his touch, and
she closed her eyes and obediently tipped her face toward
him. Tenderly, he smoothed the stuff over the deep
scratch, and then, taking each hand in turn, he put more
on each of the gashes on her hands and wrists.

"Rosebush did a number on you, huh?" His breathing
wasn't as even as it could be, standing this close to her,
touching her this way. He could sense the warmth of her
body radiating outward; he had to drag his eyes away
from the small, high breasts that pressed against her shirt

as she breathed. He remembered all too well how she felt in his arms, the yielding, almost fragile feel of her long body beneath his hands, the taste of her lips and mouth when he'd kissed her. Could it have been only yesterday? It felt like a week ago.

"Matt?" Her voice was hesitant.

"Yeah, what?" He had to clear away the hoarseness in his throat.

"Does anybody eat on this pack trip, or do we just fast until we get to your fishing camp?" There was a plaintive note in her voice, and he grinned at her.

"Well, I do feed folks every now and then. We'll be stopping for lunch. You hungry? What time is it, anyhow?" He looked at his watch and swore. He'd expected it to read about noon.

"It's well past two o'clock already." In fact, it was closer to three. "This little caper is gonna keep us on the trail late today. Well, we might as well head down to where the others are and eat before we start out again. Otherwise we'll just be starting and stopping all day."

"Matt?"

"Yeah?"

"Are…would you say there are a lot of bears around here?"

He figured there was no sense lying to her. "There are a few, yeah, but usually they keep their distance and don't bother us. I've only had to shoot two over the years because they were dangerous." He hoped that would reassure her.

"Oh. Yes. I see." She gave a nervous glance all around them, and he was irrationally proud of her when she limped over to Sultan and managed to climb onto the horse's back by herself, with determination if not grace. Of course, the horse was still tied and Matt had to go

over and undo her, but it was a hell of an improvement
over having to be helped on each time. Or was it? Matt
found himself missing the feel of her body in his arms
as he lifted her up to the saddle.

THE REST OF THE DAY disintegrated, just as Matt was
afraid it would. The incident with the bear put them several hours behind schedule, and Matt tried to hurry the
group in order to arrive at the spike camp for the night.
It wasn't an easy task. He had to ride herd on Gaby,
making sure she stayed near him so he could keep an
eye on her.

As if that weren't enough of a headache, he soon realized that two of his fishermen, Harry and Andrew, had
bottles of Scotch stowed in their saddlebags and were
drinking steadily. Neither was adept at riding, and soon
Tania wasn't the only one who'd fallen off her horse.
Andrew toppled straight to the ground like a sack of cement. It was a minor miracle that he didn't break any
bones or crack his skull open, and it took another half
hour to sober him enough to ride again.

And then of course, as the sun beat steadily down,
Harry got sick and had to stop frequently to dash into the
bushes and heave. By late afternoon, everyone was in a
foul mood, hot and sweating, tired and irritable, thirsty
and hungry...including the horses.

Mario had untied Twobits because the ornery packhorse wouldn't stop kicking the horse behind her. They
reached a small creek, and when Twobits felt the cool
water on her flanks, she promptly stopped and lay down
in it.

She was carrying two of the sleeping bags, and Matt
felt like shooting her on the spot. If he did, he figured
he'd save a couple of bullets for Andrew and Harry as

well. Her load was soaked by the time he and Mario prodded the animal onto her feet again, and Matt's pants and boots were also drenched.

The sun was setting and the air had taken on a distinct chill by the time they drew near the open clearing beside the small creek where Matt planned to spend the night.

"Okay, everybody off. We'll camp here." Matt got Mario busy building a camp fire, and then they unsaddled and began unloading the packhorses. They led all the animals two by two down to the creek to drink.

Bob and Jim both offered to help, and Matt was grateful. He was used to the busy routine of making camp, but the problems of the day had drained him and he was tired.

They staked the animals out in the grassy area beside the water so they could graze, and Matt hung the soaked sleeping bags along a rope he strung between two trees. They might dry enough to be usable by bedtime, but he didn't hold out much hope. Then they put up the two large tents Matt had brought along, plus the smaller one he'd added at the last minute for the women.

"Here you go, men, ladies." Matt gave them all bedrolls with dry sleeping bags to arrange in their tents. He and Mario would have to be the ones who suffered the effects of Twobits's midday bath.

"Supper will be along as soon as I get the bacon cooked," he added as cheerfully as he could, turning his attention to the camp fire and the packages of food.

TANIA KNEW she ought to offer to help Matt, but even thinking about moving took more energy than she could muster. She felt a bit nauseous, and every bone in her body was aching. The bones she used for sitting—bones she'd never paid much attention to before—were so sore she felt like weeping.

She took her shoulder bag and her bedroll and crawled painfully into the small orange tent Matt had said was hers and Gaby's, intending to make up some sort of comfortable sleeping place before dark. The only thing in the world she wanted to do right now was sleep. The trouble was, she'd never been inside a tent before, and it was impossible to figure out how she and Gaby would find room to stretch out in such a cramped space. Too exhausted for mental gymnastics, she just abandoned her things and crawled out again.

All day, the problem of where to go to the bathroom had been a major dilemma. At lunchtime, desperation had forced her to walk off a little way into the woods, but she'd been petrified every single moment, certain that another bear would descend on her when she was most vulnerable or that one of the men would walk the same way she had for the same purpose. It was a clumsy, undignified business, and she'd found herself envying and resenting what she'd come to view as the superior design of male plumbing.

It was growing dark, and the woods around the camp were filled with shadows and strange noises. Nevertheless, she was going to have to go again, and it wasn't about to get any lighter before morning.

"Gaby?" The girl was sitting cross-legged beside the camp fire, talking in a quiet voice with Scott.

"Yeah, what?" She sounded surprised and resentful when Tania interrupted, even though she'd been talking to either Mario or Scott all day long.

"Could I speak with you for a minute, please?"

Gaby shrugged. "So speak away." She shot a sideways glance at Scott and giggled.

"Privately."

With obvious reluctance, Gaby slowly got up and sidled over.

"Yeah, what?"

"Would you mind coming with me? I have to find a place to go to the bathroom, and it's getting awfully dark, and after that bear today…" Tania felt like an idiot. It would have made so much more sense to have Gaby asking her to go along.

"Oh. Right." Gaby sounded surprised, but at least she didn't giggle or announce Tania's request to the entire known world. "Sure, all right. I'll just get a flashlight."

Tania was endlessly grateful for Gaby's company, even though the girl didn't say much. They were picking their way through the underbrush on their way back, Gaby shining the flashlight for both of them as well as she could, when Tania said, "You're a good rider, Gaby, and you seem used to all this, this…camping and things. I'm envious. Did your father take you with him when you were younger?"

Gaby avoided a patch of nettles and shone the light back for Tania to see. "Well, like, he taught me to ride once when I was visiting him. I was about six or seven. He never took me along camping, though. I didn't get to see him much, like hardly at all. But I used to go camping with the Girl Guides back in New Brunswick all the time. So, yeah, I guess I'm used to this."

"I wish I'd been a Girl Guide. Or something. Anything."

Gaby didn't answer, and they were soon back at the campground. Tania located the bar of soap she'd thought to bring along and found a roll of paper toweling near the food supplies. She made her way down to the creek and washed her face, arms, neck and hands in the icy stream. The scratches from the rosebushes stung like fury, she had a number of insect bites, and she thought with longing of the hotel room she'd left that morning, of the tub full of steaming water and perfumed bath salts she took for granted, of thick terry towels to wrap herself in when she stepped out.

"Hiya. Bet the water's pretty cold, huh?" Mario grinned at her cheerfully. He was filling several plastic buckets with water, and having him there made Tania feel reasonably safe from bears, although what she figured the boy could do except tell her to run was beyond her. But at the moment, any sort of human company made her feel better. She could see that she was going to have to adjust her thinking and be grateful for minor blessings on this god-awful trip.

She followed close behind Mario when he made his way back to the circle of men now sitting around the camp fire watching Matt cook strips of bacon in a huge, heavy, black iron skillet. The smell was enticing. Her stomach felt better, and Tania thought she'd never felt as hungry as she did right now.

Matt glanced up just then and looked straight at her, and it seemed to her that there was a silent message of encouragement and support—and something more—in that look.

"Supper'll be ready in a jiffy. Soon as I get these spuds fried." He took the bacon out and sliced what seemed like dozens of potatoes into the grease, put a lid on the pan and propped it in the center of the flames, where a blackened coffeepot as big as a soup kettle already simmered. The aroma of fresh coffee mingled with the smell of bacon, and Tania's mouth watered.

"You're gonna make some gal a great housewife," Harry wisecracked.

Matt nodded at him. "I'm not a bad cook, but you ought to see my housekeeping."

Tania had to grin.

Next, Matt tipped half a dozen cans of baked beans into another pot and set them to heat, as well.

"Whoever's sleepin' in that tent with me better go easy on those beans," Andrew growled, and everyone laughed. Harry and Andrew had produced their whiskey bottles and were again drinking steadily. Harry offered Tania a drink, and when she declined he snorted and said something about a stick-in-the-mud. The other men had each had a drink or two and were now slumped around the fire.

Half in a daze, Tania watched Matt's competent movements. The firelight threw his strong features into shadow, emphasizing first his strong jawline, then the shape of his head and wide shoulders. He'd taken his hat and padded vest off and rolled his shirtsleeves up on his forearms, where muscles showed in clear relief. His hair was marked from the brim of his hat, but just like the rest of him, it exuded energy with a life of its own.

Tania felt she might never have the energy to move again, but he showed no sign of fatigue after what had to have been a harrowing day, even for him. He moved from one task to the next like a well-oiled machine, keeping up a lively banter with the men but somehow making them look inept and a little silly by the efficiency and competence of his every action.

"Mario, get the plates out of that box, would you, and the knives and forks, as well. And find some cups. There are packages of buns and a plastic pot of butter somewhere."

"I'll do it." Tania struggled to her feet, wincing at the pain in her thighs, the aching hurt in certain private parts of her body. She was tired enough to fall asleep right where she sat, but she was also voraciously hungry and still fastidious enough to care that Mario's hands were anything but clean. Matt's grateful smile made her feel warmer than the fire had.

Nothing had ever tasted as good as that simple meal. Tania gorged herself along with everyone else, scraping up the last of the beans and sopping up the juice on her plate with extra-large kaiser buns. Dessert was apples and candy bars and leftover oatmeal cookies, and she devoured those, too. By the time she'd had two large cups of coffee, the waistband on her jeans was digging into her flesh, and instead of making her feel more awake, the coffee somehow produced the opposite effect. She could hardly keep her eyes open, but she felt obliged to offer Matt her help in cleaning up.

The fishermen certainly didn't seem to feel any such responsibility. They were paying guests, however, and Tania supposed it was taken for granted they didn't do chores. But it meant the brunt of the work fell to Matt, and that didn't seem fair to her. Matt solved the problem before she had a chance to offer.

"Mario, you put a bucket of water on to heat, and Gaby can give you a hand washing up the dishes," Matt ordered.

"I'll help, too," Scott volunteered, which almost made his father tumble off a log with surprise.

Gaby didn't even complain, which amazed Tania, but when the three young people started gathering up the dishes, she realized that Gaby was neatly playing one young man off against the other and enjoying every minute of it. The girl would say something to Scott as she passed him, giving him a coquettish look from under her lowered eyelashes. A moment later, she'd do the same to

Mario. The boys fawned over Gaby and glowered at each other.

Tania gazed into the fire and with a sinking feeling in her stomach thought about her promise to supervise Gaby and do her best to keep the young girl out of trouble on this trip. How, exactly, was she going to accomplish that? At sixteen, Gaby appeared far more worldly-wise than Tania felt at thirty-six. When in her entire life, she wondered, had she had the womanly skill to keep two males buzzing around her like worker bees while she played the queen? Never. And Gaby also managed to get the men to do most of the actual work. Now that took talent.

"Penny for your thoughts?"

Tania jumped. Jim Irwin had moved over beside her. He was a large man, not tall, but husky. He'd stayed in the background most of the day, and she'd noticed that whenever he tried to talk to his son, the boy either ignored him or grunted rude replies that were all too reminiscent of Gaby.

"I'm afraid I'm too tired to think at all," Tania lied. "In fact, I was about to go to bed."

With considerable difficulty, she got to her feet, giving Jim a wan smile.

"Pretty stiff, huh?" He sounded sympathetic.

"Yeah. Really stiff."

"You'll feel better after a good night's rest. Actually, bed sounds pretty good to me right now, too."

Tania doubted she'd ever feel normal again. The way she felt now, it would take two weeks of bed rest, massage and hydrotherapy before she'd even be comfortable. Instead, she had two whole weeks like today—or even worse—to look forward to. To dread. Not for the first time she felt anger well up in her when she thought of her father and her reasons for being where she was instead of at home in Vancouver in her cozy apartment with a good detective novel.

She shuddered. "Good night, Jim. See you in the morning."

Jim nodded. "Sweet dreams," he said, and there was a wistful look on his face as he watched her walk away.

MATT NOTICED the way Jim had deliberately moved close to Tania. He'd seen the other man watching her today when he thought no one else was looking, and he saw now how she got quickly to her feet and headed toward her tent.

Was this Jim a womanizer, with his eye on Tania? Had he made some clumsy pass at her just now?

Matt felt unreasonable anger toward Jim without even knowing him well or knowing what had passed between him and Tania. For some reason his temper, normally slow to kindle, was all at once as flaming hot as the camp fire in front of him.

First of all, he wished the other man hadn't brought his son along. Matt could already see trouble brewing between Scott and Mario, with Gaby enjoying every minute of it. All he needed was one more thing to worry over on this trip. And for the first time it occurred to him to wonder what four men might get up to with an attractive single woman along. He ought to have thought of it before.

It didn't cross his mind that Tania was certainly old enough to make her own decisions about any man who came on to her and experienced enough to be able to handle men without Matt's interference. Instead, he was already prepared to throttle any one of the paying guests should he make a wrong move in her direction.

Eventually, everyone drifted off to their hard beds.

Matt gave Mario the sleeping bag that had dried enough to be bearable, and after he tended the camp fire and checked on the horses, he wrapped himself in a tarp from the pack train and lay down halfway between the men's tents and the small orange shell where Tania and Gaby were sleeping.

Just in case, he told himself, any of the fishermen got ideas during the night.

He rolled up a jacket to use as a pillow and stared up at the brilliance of the stars, aware for the first time of how tired he was. This was starting out to be one of the most difficult trips of his career. He hoped the next day would be better than this one had been, but he didn't dare even hope. There was still a day and a half's ride before they reached base camp, and judging by today, any damn thing at all could happen.

And probably would.

Harry and Andrew were certain to wake up with hangovers in the morning. And the rest of the crew were sure to be stiff, sore and grumpy after the unaccustomed exercise they'd had today. Gaby was going to drive him out of his head with her antics, and Tania would be lucky if she could even get up on a horse in the morning, never mind stay seated on one for any length of time, judging by the way she'd limped around tonight.

So much for fun and games, outdoor adventure and good healthy living, Radburn. Maybe the stock market has its strong points, after all. He groaned and fell asleep.

A FULL DAY and most of the next afternoon passed before they finally rounded the last corner on the trail, and Matt had never been as grateful to arrive anywhere in his life. The trip had been about half as bad again as he'd expected it might.

Andrew, hung over and sullen, had managed to fall
into the Nass River during their second ford, and Matt
had a few bad moments dragging him out of the rapid,
shallow water. Then Andrew had thrown a fit of temper
because his new suede jacket was ruined.

The second night, a porcupine had decided to try to
chew its way into the women's tent, and Tania had had
hysterics, thinking it was another bear. Matt had come
awake on his feet and running, believing one of the men
was accosting her, and almost fell over the damned porcupine.

But here they were at last.

Ahead was the low, purple sawtooth mountain with a
mile of open green meadow at its base that he'd chosen
years before as the perfect spot for a fish camp. A small
tributary of the nearby Skeena formed a creek through
the middle of the grassy plain, and under a grove of poplars on the bank of the creek was Matt's base camp.

There were two log bunkhouses, a cookshack with a
wall tent stretching out from one side and, down in the
meadow, an open-sided shelter with a rail fence around
it for the animals. Last year he'd added a small cabin off
to one side to use as a storage shed. Smoke wound in a
lazy coil from the chimney of the cookshack. The horses,
sensing an end to the long trip, broke into a trot.

"Heyyya. Hiiiya."

A short, sturdy figure with a long black braid hanging
down his back and a dirty apron tied around his middle
came out of the shack and stood calling to them, one
hand raised in greeting over his head.

Matt felt his gut contract.

For the past few miles he'd been dreading this encounter, the moment when Benny Benson realized that

there were two women in the all-male fishing party he'd agreed to cook for.

Benny Benson wasn't fond of women, and he said so all the time. There was going to be an unpleasant encounter. There might even be a hell of a row.

Matt might or might not have a cook when the explosion was over, and given the odds, Matt figured he'd put his money on not. If he had any money left after outfitting this rig, that is.

And everyone knew that a good cook would make or break an outfitter. Fishermen wanted food, and they wanted lots of it, and for all his bragging, Matt's own cooking was just barely passable on a good day. As for Mario...well, Mario as a cook wasn't even a consideration. Matt was beginning to think that Mario as a swamper was equally suspect.

They needed Benny Benson pretty bad, and somehow he was going to have to calm the old Indian down and convince him to stay on. Feeling like a tired, scarred Ghumshiwa about to engage in a battle with the Tsimshian, Matt gritted his teeth and led his motley crew across the meadow.

CHAPTER SIX

DOC WALLACE MUTTERED foul words under his breath, puffing hard with exertion.

"I'll get ya tied down yet, ya...miserable...sucker."

He was balanced precariously on a chunk of tree stump he'd pushed close to the outside cabin wall. He reached and strained, stretching high over his head to try to grasp the corner rope of the blue tarp he was trying to secure over the peak of the low roof. A breeze had flipped it just out of reach for the tenth time.

A jay swooped from a nearby tree, skimming Doc's head on its way to collect the breakfast scraps tossed amidst the grass of the clearing, and other birds turned the little glen into an amphitheater with their chirping songs.

"Man needs a bloody third arm for a job like this," Doc grumbled to the jay.

It had rained the night before, and Doc had been reminded just how badly the roof leaked. His bedding was damp as well as some of his food supplies. This morning he'd found out that without a ladder and a lot more tools than he had, it was impossible to climb up onto the roof and replace the rough-hewn shingles that were causing the leaks. So, he figured, the next best thing was to cover the whole structure with the large tarp he'd brought along and hope the wind didn't blow the cussed thing to kingdom come, and him along with it.

"Gotcha!" The elusive rope was finally in his grasp. He shoved it beneath the corner post and looped it in a double knot. That made the two opposing corners secure, with two left to go.

Doc was sweating, and he felt a bit light-headed. He leaned against the log wall for a moment, then climbed carefully down from the stump and decided to sit on it for a few minutes before he began the laborious process of rolling it to another corner and fighting with the rope all over again.

"Whew. Hot work." He mopped his head with a hankie he dragged from his pocket.

He'd have liked a cup of the strong coffee left in his pot from breakfast, but somehow he didn't quite have the energy to get up right now and fetch it. He took careful breaths, conscious of the small, tight ache that had been in his chest all morning.

A little bit of rest, that's all he needed. He'd overdone it yesterday, cutting the saplings he'd needed to stuff between the gaping holes in the walls of the cabin. But he'd got it done, hadn't he? And if he needed to sit here and rest a bit, well, it was his own damn business, wasn't it? A man of seventy had to expect little setbacks in his health from time to time. There was nobody here to tell him do this now, either, the way they had back at the lodge.

"Time for your therapy, Mr. Wallace. We want to strengthen those heart muscles, now don't we?"

"Your doctor's appointment is in an hour, Mr. Wallace."

"Aren't you coming bowling, Mr. Wallace? It's great fun."

The staff back there acted as if a day were a pie they could cut in portions and dole out to a man in chunks to suit their fancy. And what irked Doc was that they were doling out his life, his time, not theirs. Surely a man ought to lay claim to the days he had left when those days were numbered, anyhow.

Here, though, days were longer than he ever remembered them being. Not that time hung heavy on his hands, not by a long shot. There was lots to do, no doubt about it. It took more time than he'd have thought to get wood cut and his meals prepared, and each day he tried to do more of the necessary repairs to the cabin. And every afternoon, come hell or high water, he fished to his heart's content, all up and down the riverbank.

He sure had time to think, though. At first, he'd gone over the times he'd spent here with Sam, taking out the memories like gems and polishing them until they shone. But Sam was gone. It was a terrible thing when a man outlived his own son; there ought to be rules about things like that. Then his thoughts would turn to his daughter, and a nagging guilt would start gnawing at him.

He ought to have told Tania the truth about what he was doing. Trouble was, just like her mother before her, the girl had never understood his passion for the wilderness, and she wasn't about to start now. She hadn't inherited anything from his side at all, as far as he could see. Smart as a whip, but not much sense of adventure.

Still, he wished now he'd told her the truth.

The fist inside his chest that had a way of squeezing at his guts tightened somewhat, and he shifted on the rough surface of the log, his heartbeat accelerating as tension grew in him.

Relax, Murdoch. It's just a gas pain. You've been eating too many beans. It's nothing like that pain you had years ago. Now that was a pain for you.

And Tania had been there for him when he needed her.

Anyway, getting his shirt in a knot wasn't about to change anything. A man's time was a man's time, whenever it arrived. But if death was determined to come and find him here, he only hoped it would be fast and clean.

His thoughts returned to his daughter, the way they'd been doing with more and more regularity this past week, and a sense of melancholy overcame him.

Too bad Tania hadn't been a boy. He understood boys; he didn't understand women at all, never had, never would. It was a shame, a man like him having a daughter. He wasn't fit, didn't deserve her.

The teasing pain inside his chest intensified, and he clenched his teeth and prayed.

IF TANIA HADN'T had Doc for a father, she'd have been horrified at the tirade coming from the obnoxious little brown-skinned man Matt called Benny. He'd waved and hallooed at them all across the meadow, friendly and welcoming as could be. Then when they got here and she was able to clamber off her horse at last, the ridiculous man had gone berserk.

"Women? Matthew, you brought women up here?" Benny's low, guttural voice was scathing, and his whole body reflected his outrage the moment he spotted Tania and Gaby among the men getting off their horses. "You didn't say women were coming on this trip, Matthew."

He didn't even bother to keep his comments private. His voice could have been heard a mile away, Tania thought with disgust. Although, of course, there wasn't a living soul to hear him except the birds. And the bears.

"I don't cook for women, you know that. I don't have time for fancy females, and that's that." He was working himself into a frenzy. He stomped up and down in front of Matt, shaking his fist and gesticulating in an insulting way at Tania and Gaby, his braid flying.

Matt quietly gave Mario orders about the horses and the packs, listening to Benny but not reacting in any way. The men were standing around listening, too, and grinning, which added to Tania's rising anger.

"You know I don't need this job. Benny Benson can get a job anywhere. I'm the best camp cook there is, and everybody I work for knows I've got one hard-and-fast rule—no women in my camp. They make me nervous— I burn things, I break out in hives. They want something all the time." His almost toothless mouth screwed itself into a knot. "I'm not working at any camp where there're women, and that's final." His voice reached a booming crescendo, and he tore the stained apron from his waist and threw it onto the ground, breathing hard and glowering at everyone.

Tania wondered if he was going to stomp on it, like a comic figure in a cartoon. And yet, there was a strange dignity to him, as well. He held himself stiff and straight, and his narrow, dark eyes in his wrinkled face flashed outrage.

Gaby had edged over to stand beside Tania, as if just being female was reason enough for the two of them to draw together.

"Has he got an attitude problem or what?" she asked now in an undertone, folding her arms in a defensive gesture across her chest. "I mean, like, what a real C.P. He's never even met us, and listen to him. I hope Dad tells him off good."

Tania felt exactly the same way.

Matt waited until Benny's anger had run down a bit, and when he spoke, his tone was almost too low for the others to hear. It was clear to Tania that Matt certainly wasn't telling Benny off, however. Far from it. It almost sounded as if he were sympathizing with him, placating him.

"Well, Benny, no question at all about you being a great cook—you're the best I ever had, and I'm sorry to lose you. If I could have warned you about Gaby and Tania being with me, I'd have done it. But they only arrived in Terrace a few days ago, see, so I had no chance. Gaby there's my daughter—hadn't seen her in more than a year till she showed up last week. Tania's up from the coast. Her old dad is lost somewhere up here in the bush. She's desperate to find some trace of him. Couldn't really turn her down, not in those circumstances."

Matt reached into the back pocket of his jeans and pulled out a billfold, peeling off a fistful of notes and holding them out to Benny. "The way things stand, I'm paying you up full for the next week, to cover the inconvenience of having to pack out and find another job this late in the season. My apologies, Benny. We're gonna miss you pretty bad, but I'd never ask a man to go against his principles in something like this. If you could wait till morning before you ride out, I could give you an extra packhorse to carry your gear. Not tonight, though. They need a good feed and a rubdown before they start out on the trail again. The whole works of us are pretty weary from the ride, as a matter of fact. Hungry, too."

Benny didn't immediately reach for the money Matt held out to him. Instead, he stood for what seemed a long time with his arms folded across his chest, breathing hard, his mouth compressed into a sour knot. Then he reached down and retrieved his apron from the ground, banging it against his knee to get the dust off and tying it around his middle.

"There's stew on the stove in the cookhouse," he finally growled. "And fresh bread and apple pie." He turned on his heel and stomped into the building without another word.

Matt stood silent for a moment, then drew in a deep breath and blew it out between pursed lips. He put the money back into his wallet, took off his hat and ran a hand through his hair, then clamped the hat back on. He looked over at Tania and Gaby, shook his head, grinned and then gave them a thumbs-up sign, as if the scene with Benny hadn't been that bad, after all.

Tania felt it had been nothing short of disaster.

"I never heard of such an old grouch…" Gaby began in an indignant tone, but Matt put a finger to his lips, shushing her with a frown.

"Benny's a good cook and you aren't, so shut up. Go on in, all of you, and eat," he instructed. "Mario and I'll get these horses unsaddled, and then we'll join you."

Hungry or not, Tania had no desire to be the one to first confront the bad-tempered cook, so she hung back until the fishermen had all gone inside. Gaby stayed behind with her, and by the time the two women hesitantly entered the dusky, low-roofed, long building, the men were already seated at rough wooden tables with immense bowls of steaming stew in front of them. No one was talking; instead, they were all intent on eating.

Tania's stomach rumbled.

Huge loaves of crusty, freshly baked bread stood on the square tables, and the men were sawing off great chunks to dip in the savory stew. Her mouth watered at the smell.

The room was about twelve feet by twenty, with a

narrow doorway at one end leading to what Tania assumed were Benny's sleeping quarters. There were open cupboards nailed to the walls, an old-fashioned wood-burning range at one end and a makeshift sink with a window over it. The walls were of stand-up peeled logs, and the tables and chairs were all hand hewn from rough cedar. Tania was quick to notice a small washstand in one corner with a tin basin and a well-used towel hanging on a nail.

"Let's wash our hands first," Tania suggested, and Gaby groaned.

"I'm about to starve to death. Think he'll even let us have some food?" The girl tilted her head toward Benny.

"All we can do is try. Follow me."

Tania washed quickly, then headed over to the side table where the plates and cutlery were stacked.

Benny was sitting hunched in a big chair against one wall, smoking a pipe and nursing an enamel mug of coffee. He glanced up every now and then to glare at everyone in general and mutter under his breath.

Tania avoided his gaze, took a bowl and filled it with stew from the immense pot on the wood-burning cookstove, expecting at any moment to be attacked either verbally or physically by the obnoxious little man, but he didn't say or do a thing. He ignored Tania and Gaby just as he ignored the rest of the party.

Tania found a space for herself and Gaby at the table farthest from Benny and cut them each a thick slice of bread. Her hands were trembling when she tried to butter it, and she was suddenly aware that she was dangerously close to total exhaustion. The strain and physical exertion of the trip, followed by the nasty scene outside, had drained her physically and emotionally.

"This stuff is just radical! Taste it," Gaby mumbled,

her mouth full. She continued to fork up more as she spoke, dipping her bread into the gravy and making contented humming sounds.

Tania began to eat, and with each spicy mouthful she felt better. Gaby was right. Benny might be a miserable old chauvinist, but his cooking was fantastic.

"Room for one more here?"

Matt's deep, cheerful voice came from beside her, and Tania squeezed over to allow him room between herself and Gaby, pleasure flooding through her at this chance to be near him. He'd brought her a mug of coffee, fixed the way she liked it, and he placed it in front of her, setting a can of diet Coke in front of his daughter.

"Thanks," Tania said gratefully, taking a deep swallow of the hot, strong coffee.

He was a thoughtful man, without being obvious about it. She was aware of his body settling in beside her, of his thigh almost but not quite touching hers beneath the table. He'd washed his hands, rolling his sleeves halfway up his muscular forearms. His wrists and the back of his hands were covered with silky whorls of damp hair.

"Can I go get more stew, Dad?" Gaby was obviously still uncertain of Benny.

"Go ahead. Everybody else seems to have had seconds and even thirds." Matt's voice lowered to a deep whisper. "Besides, it's a compliment to the cook to eat a lot. Remember, there's pie for dessert, so it pays to flatter the old geezer."

Gaby made her way to the stove, and Matt turned his attention to Tania. "You okay? That was a long ride for somebody who'd never been on a horse before. You did real well, too." He kept his voice too low for the others to hear, and he looked at her with affection in his gaze.

His tone was full of concern. "You look pretty done in now, though."

She managed a grateful semblance of a smile. "I'm not bad, a little tired, that's all," she lied valiantly. "Nothing that a good night's sleep won't fix." She remembered the previous night, spent tossing and turning, unable to adjust to the hard ground, the confines of her sleeping bag and the loud snoring that erupted all night long from the men's tents. Then, when she'd just dozed off, the porcupine had come.

"As soon as Mario's eaten, he and I'll empty out the storage shed and set up a couple of extra cots for you and Gaby. Not fancy, but it's private. The men sleep in the bunkhouses over on the other side, so you'll be fine in the shed."

The bunkhouses and storage shed were on opposite sides of the cookshack.

"That sounds like a lot of work for you. I'm sorry to be such a bother, Matt." She'd realized more and more during this endless trip just how much extra work and trouble it caused him to have her along...and how much stronger the attraction grew each time she was near him.

Gaby, after all, was his daughter, his responsibility. Tania wasn't. Besides, the girl had proved far more resilient than Tania on this trip.

He gave her the reassuring wink she was coming to anticipate, but before he could say anything, Gaby plopped down again beside him, bowl full, and Bob hollered from across the room, "What time do we hit the deck in the morning, Matt? We heading out on the river or what?"

"We'll get an early start—breakfast at six—then we'll pack lunches and hike downriver. The chinook are running, so maybe we can land some big ones for dinner."

A general cheer went up at Matt's words, and Tania felt her heart sink. Obviously, she and Gaby were going to be left here at camp alone with Benny Benson for what was sure to be a very long and unpleasant day. Or was Benny leaving in the morning, the way he'd threatened? He didn't seem to be making any move to pack his gear. In fact, he was fixing another pot of coffee.

Tania wasn't sure which was worse, being in camp all day alone with Gaby or having to avoid Benny.

"Dad, can't I come with you? I don't wanna stay here—it's boring." Gaby's voice was a near whine. She was now devouring a huge slab of apple pie, washing it down with another can of Coke.

Tania got up stiffly to get herself a piece of pie. She was going to gain twenty pounds on this trip if her appetite stayed this way, and she didn't care. She cut one for Matt as well and carried it back to him.

"Thanks, Tania. If you can manage to be up and ready by the time we're leaving, Gaby, fine, you can come," Matt said in a stern voice. "But fishing is my business. I won't coax you out of bed and wait for you for hours up here the way I did back at the trailer."

Gaby's lips turned down at the corners. "I don't see why anybody wants to leave at six in the morning, anyhow. That's the middle of the night."

Tania was inclined to agree with Gaby.

"That's when we leave, and that's that."

"Haven't you ever heard that the early bird gets the worm, little lady?" Harry said sarcastically.

Gaby gave him a poisonous glare and concentrated on her pie.

"I suppose that's good advice, if you like eating worms." Tania couldn't resist saying it. She didn't like people spouting clichés, and Harry had disgusted her during the trip in, alternately ingesting and disgorging quantities of Scotch. And in this totally male atmosphere, the women had to stick together.

Gaby shot her a surprised look.

"Mario seems to be done eating, so we'll go and get your cabin ready, ladies." Matt looked amused as he escaped out the door.

It had grown dark in the cookhouse while they ate. Benny lit several lanterns and began heating a large pot of water on the stove. Tania wondered what the rules were about dishes, but she didn't have to wonder long.

"Everybody outa here now. I don't like my kitchen all cluttered up when meals are done," Benny mumbled, and the men hastily filed out the door, with Tania and Gaby right behind them.

Outside, the long northern twilight had succumbed at last to darkness. An owl hooted nearby, and Tania could hear the creek gurgling, the river farther away rushing past. There was no moon, and the thick blackness was disconcerting after the mellow light of the lanterns inside. She could just make out the mountaintops all around, inky shapes against a lighter sky.

Gaby had disappeared, so Tania made her way cautiously along the side of the cookhouse in the direction of the storage shed. She rounded the corner of the building, and now she could see light streaming through the cracks in the small shed where she and Gaby would sleep.

"Hello? Matt, are you in here?" She shoved the rough-hewn door open, but there was no one inside. Matt and Mario had come and gone, leaving a lantern with the wick turned low.

Two narrow cots sat side by side in the small space not occupied by saddles, bridles, sacks of feed, cartons of dried food and empty buckets. Dust was thick on the floor, and cobwebs stretched like lace in every corner. Tania's luggage, purse, tweed jacket, the contents of her saddlebags, her sleeping bag and a large flashlight were plopped on one bed, with Gaby's belongings on the other. There were pillows but no pillowcases.

Tania arranged things as well as she could and pulled a clean T-shirt over the ticking of the pillow to form a makeshift case. She unpacked enough to find the soft peach cotton tracksuit she'd brought along to double as pajamas and laid it on her bed, intending to get undressed. But more than anything in the world, she wanted a bath. Three days on Sultan had left her feeling absolutely filthy. Even a sponge bath would be better than nothing. But to get a basin and warm water, she had to brave Benny Benson, and the thought made her quake.

A tap came at the door, and she opened it. Matt was standing there, balancing a bucket of water, a washbasin and a steaming kettle.

"Matt, you're a mind reader. How'd you know exactly what I needed?"

"Just naturally brilliant, I guess." He smiled at her and handed the things in one by one, then stepped in himself, ducking his head to avoid hitting the roof.

"Sorry this place is still full of junk. There wasn't time enough tonight to do any more than this. Tomorrow, you can make it more comfortable."

"It's fine now that there's a washbasin. I was trying to work up nerve enough to go and ask Benny, but I'm afraid I'm a coward."

He looked weary, and Tania wanted to reach out and put a comforting hand on his shoulder. Instead, she said, "Is he really leaving in the morning because of Gaby and me?"

Matt shrugged and shook his head. "I doubt it. I think he'll moan and groan some, but judging by his actions tonight, he'll stay. At least, I sure hope so." His eyes twinkled. "Unless you've hidden the fact that you're a top-notch camp cook and you'll take over at breakfast? Then we can call his bluff and send the old grouch packing. Teach him a good lesson."

Tania groaned and sank down onto the cot. "I wish I could help. I'm not a bad cook, given a Cuisinart and a blender and an electric range and *Joy of Cooking*. But under these conditions, I hate to think what I'd turn out. Especially for so many hungry men." She looked up at him. "I'm sorry, Matt. I'm strictly a liability on this trip, I'm afraid."

"You'd never be that." His eyes lingered on her face, and he reached out a fist and gently bumped her chin. "Don't take things so seriously. I was only teasing you. Being a camp cook takes years of experience and a nasty streak a mile wide. You're not qualified."

The atmosphere in the crowded room had intensified, the attraction between them flaring at his touch.

"Guess I'd better go make sure things are quiet over in the bunkhouses." His eyes lingered on her, and then he moved reluctantly toward the door. "Any idea where that kid of mine has gotten to?"

"I haven't seen her since we left the cookhouse. I'll go and look for her right now." Tania was suddenly mindful that Gaby was supposed to be her responsibility.

"Don't bother. I'll round her up and send her in to bed. She'll never make it up in the morning in time to go with us. By the way, there's a box of towels and soap and things over in that corner. I'll get out of here now while your water's still warm." He turned and then stopped again at the door. "Tania, take it real easy tomorrow, and as soon as I get these fishermen familiar with the territory, I'll take you out to see if we can scout out any sign of your dad. In a couple of days, okay?''

She nodded. ''After riding up here, seeing how dense the bush is and how wild, I...'' Her voice quavered and a lump stuck in her throat. She couldn't go on.

''What?'' He moved toward her and put both hands on her shoulders, drawing her to him with strong, sure movements, holding her against his chest. ''Don't lose hope till there's good reason.'' He tipped her chin up with a finger and stared down at her, his face somber. ''Honey, you've come all this way, believing. Don't stop now.''

Her eyes were awash with unshed tears, and the tenderness in his tone made them spill over and run down her cheeks.

''Don't cry—don't.'' He angled his mouth down suddenly and kissed her hard, all his pent-up feelings for her contained in the rough embrace. He drew back and groaned, still holding her.

''It's always the wrong time and place for us. I wish...'' He didn't finish what he'd started to say. Instead, he parted her lips with his tongue and boldly invaded her mouth. His hands slid from her shoulders, down her back to her buttocks, holding her against him, showing her with his body how much he wanted her. The evidence of his desire was bold and demanding against her lower body, and a deep wanting grew in Tania's abdomen.

The sound of a soft feminine giggle came from outside, then a boy's voice saying something not quite audible and Gaby's voice answering. Matt jerked away from Tania, paused a moment, then turned in one motion toward the door and stepped outside.

"Gaby? It's time you went to bed. Where the hell have you been, anyway? Scott, you'd better get over to the bunkhouse. Everybody's bedding down over there."

Tania heard the raw anger in his voice and knew it was partly because their own embrace had been interrupted.

"I just went for a walk down to the river with Scott. Jeez, Dad, what are you so steamed about? We weren't gone long."

"I was worried about you. I want to know where you are and where you're going while we're up here, Gabriella. This isn't a place to go wandering off on your own."

"But I wasn't on my own, Dad. I already told you Scott was with me."

Matt snorted. "That isn't exactly reassuring, Gaby. The boy wouldn't know what to do if a bear or a big cat jumped out of the underbrush."

"Well, Mario would. He knows all about the bush. Next time I'll go for a walk with him instead." Gaby's words were insolent and openly challenging.

Tania wished fervently that she didn't have to listen to this exchange between father and daughter, but there was no way to avoid it. They were right outside the door.

"I'm warning you, young lady, I don't want you causing any trouble between those boys. Do you hear me? I watched you all the way up, playing one off against the other, and I want you to quit it right now before you get yourself in a mess of trouble."

Gaby didn't answer, and a moment later she burst through the door of the cabin, knocking into Tania in the small space. It was obvious that Gaby was furious.

She didn't apologize or say a thing to Tania. She dug into her sports bag and extracted a pair of yellow flannel pajamas with Mickey Mouse on them, tore off her clothing and put them on. With jerky movements and a sullen, closed expression, she spread her sleeping bag out on the cot and climbed into it, turning her back to Tania and burrowing down until even her head was covered.

"Good night, Gaby," Tania said at last. There was no response.

Tania didn't know what to do. She felt helpless and horribly out of place, and the very idea of supervising the girl beside her seemed ludicrous. Just having to room with her was bad enough.

When Gaby was finally still, Tania turned the lantern as low as it would go and took off her own clothes, filling the basin with water that was by now barely tepid.

As quietly as she could, she washed herself off, top to bottom, shivering in the cold but grateful for the chance to feel reasonably clean again. Then she tugged on her sweats and turned out the lantern, drawing her own sleeping bag close under her chin, waiting to get warm and wishing she knew what on earth to say to the angry, unhappy young woman in the other bed. And wondering as well where the powerful attraction between her and Matt was leading.

Very soon, she fell asleep.

THE SOUND OF WEEPING wound itself into Tania's dream. She was still married in the dream, and for a few moments the old feelings of desperation and betrayal paralleled the sad sound of a woman crying. Was it her?

She struggled awake, not wanting to be back in those times, but the crying went on, a hopeless, low sobbing.

The darkness was thick, without a trace of light, and apart from the sobbing, everything was silent. The air was chill on her face, and the smells were not familiar:

a mingling of leather and oil and a pungent, musky odor emanating from the sleeping bag wrapped around her.

Bit by bit, Tania realized where she was. It was Gaby who was crying, in choked and muffled gulps, as if she'd been crying for a long time and didn't expect anyone to comfort her.

"Gaby? Gaby, honey, what is it? What's the matter?" Tania's sleep-rough whisper stopped the weeping, but the girl didn't say anything. The wrenching sobs she tried to suppress sounded as if they hurt her chest.

Tania struggled up on one elbow, managed to free herself from the tangle of material twisted around her and swung her legs out of the bag to the floor, wincing at the pain in her thighs, calves and buttocks. She reached out a hand and found Gaby's body, stroking what she imagined must be her back, up and down and up again.

The slender body tensed, but it didn't jerk away.

"You want to talk about it?" Tania asked after a long time had passed in silence.

"Talk. What—what good does ta-talking do, anyhow? It never—never changes anything." The girl's words were punctuated by gulps as she did her best to control herself.

Tania couldn't deny that. She'd never really confided in anyone herself, so how could she encourage Gaby to do so?

"I used to be able to talk to my mother a little, when she was alive," Tania mused, more to herself than to Gaby.

"Well, you're just lucky she's dead," the girl spat into the darkness. "I wish to hell my mother were dead."

The words echoed in the small room, and shivers of

shock and foreboding rippled through Tania's body. It took a great deal of anger, more than Tania could imagine a child having, to wish a parent dead.

CHAPTER SEVEN

THE STARTLING WORDS hung in the silence, and Tania was at a loss as to what to say. Her hand was still rubbing up and down Gaby's back, and she continued automatically for another minute before the girl wrenched herself away.

"Don't touch me—I don't need your pity. It sucks!" Gaby said in a vicious, angry tone. "What do you know, anyway?"

Tania felt wounded, as if Gaby had struck her. She swallowed hard several times, thinking of rejoinders and discarding them. The girl had a talent for making adults angry with her, no doubt about it.

The little cabin felt stuffed full of emotion, smothering feelings that neither female could express. At last, Tania fumbled for the flashlight she'd put beside her bed, stuck her feet into her runners and went outside, drawing in deep lungfuls of the cool, fresh air.

The river sounded far louder than it had earlier, and an owl hooted in a haunting rhythm from one of the pine trees. Tania could hear the horses in their enclosure as they moved around and snuffled at their feed. There was a sliver of a moon, but it was fading.

With the help of the light, she made her way to the outhouse, feeling nervous and wary of every shadow, every new and strange noise that echoed out of the forest nearby. She was hurrying back when a man's voice sounded from somewhere beside her.

"Pretty dark out here, huh?"

Tania jumped and let out a small shriek of alarm, turning her flashlight full on him.

"Sorry, I didn't mean to scare you." The man held an arm up to shade his eyes. "It's me, Bob."

Her heart was in danger of hammering its way through her chest wall. She lowered the flashlight, which was shaking. Her entire body was shaking.

"Oh, hi, Bob." She gulped. She couldn't think of another thing to say.

"What time is it, anyway?" he asked. "I left my watch in the bunkhouse. Weird thing for me to do. I haven't had that watch off my wrist for this long in years, but up here you somehow don't feel it's necessary to know what time it is."

"I'm not wearing mine, either, so I don't have any idea about the time." She had no intention of standing around in the middle of the night talking to him, so she began moving back in the direction of her cabin.

"Can't sleep," he offered next, walking along beside her, puffing a little. She'd seen in the flashlight's gleam that he was fully dressed. "You having trouble that way, too, can't sleep?"

"Not really. I...actually, something woke me up."

"Probably coyotes," he said. "They were howling something fierce a while ago. Or maybe they're wolves—couldn't prove it by me."

He was still keeping pace with her, and Tania wondered if he planned to follow her right back to the cabin. She stopped by the corner of the cookhouse, searching for a way to get rid of him without being out-and-out rude.

He stopped, too, and she could hear him breathing in the stillness.

"Well, good ni—"

"You're from Vancouver, that right?"

Heavens to Betsy. He was planning on chatting the rest of the night.

"Yes, I am," she said shortly. "Now I really have to—"

"Never been beyond Vancouver airport, but they tell me it's a nice city. I'm from Yuma, myself. It's not very big. More of a town than a city, hot as Hades sometimes." And as if it were part of what he'd been saying, he asked, "You married, Tania?"

She was caught off guard, and she was getting irritated with him.

"Divorced," she said shortly. "Bob, I really have to get back to bed. It's the middle of the night."

"Yeah," he said. "Sorry. I'm keeping you up."

"Yes. Well, good night, Bob."

Tania turned to go, and he blurted out, "It's just that nights are hell for me right now. See, my wife died three months back, and the days aren't too bad, but the nights…well, I can't sleep so good. Jim and Harry—I've known them for years—well, they sort of talked me into this trip. Said it would be good to get away from it all, but it's funny, y'know?" He made a sound intended to be a chuckle. "You can't get away from what's inside your head so easy."

"Oh, Bob, I'm so sorry." She felt touched by his loneliness and his loss, and for the second time that night she didn't know what to say to give comfort.

"Yeah, well, Alice was sick for a long time. I knew what was coming, but when it happens, you're still not prepared." He sighed and then forced a lighter tone.

"Anyway, I never intended to keep you out here all night, listening to my life story. I heard Matt say you're up here looking for your father, so you got troubles of your own without hearing about mine. Sorry to bend your ear this way—I don't usually do this. But nighttime…I dunno, it does something to you."

Tania's heart ached for him. Now it was she who detained him. "Did…do you have any kids?"

"Nope. Alice wasn't strong, and I was scared what it would do to her. We just had each other. Eighteen years we were married."

"I'm so sorry," she said again. Why were words ineffective just when you needed them most?

"Yeah, me too, but you know, lots of folks don't have even that much happiness. I keep telling myself I oughta be grateful for those years."

"It still must be hard."

"It is. Damned hard. Look, you go on in now. You're gonna get cold standing out here. And Tania? Thanks for listening."

She reached a hand out and grasped his for a long moment.

"Good night, Bob."

MATT STOOD a short distance away, watching, hearing the soft, intimate intonation of their speech, but he was too far away to hear the exact words they spoke. He could see them well, though, caught as they were in the circle of light from the flash Tania held, and he saw her reach out and take Bob's hand before she walked away. It gave him a sick feeling in his gut.

He'd crawled out of his bedroll to do the usual night check on the horses, half asleep, and he was on his way back when he heard Tania's voice. He hadn't intended to spy on her. He just didn't know a damn thing about these dudes, except that they had plenty of money, and he didn't want her having to fight Bob Young off in the middle of the night.

But it hadn't gone that way at all, had it? He waited in the darkness until Bob ambled off in the direction of the bunkhouse. Matt was sleeping in the other building, and he gave Bob plenty of time to settle in before he made his way back to his own bed.

He couldn't fall back to sleep the way he usually could, however. He tossed and turned and finally faced up to what was bothering him. He was just plain jealous, sick with it in a way he couldn't ever remember being. And he was jealous because a woman he'd known only a few days had talked in a soft voice to another man in the middle of the night and reached out and held his hand for a minute or two.

What the dickens was wrong with him, allowing himself to get this screwed up over her? What had they shared, after all? A few kisses, some soft words, a glance or two? There was no commitment between them. Hadn't he learned his lesson, learned how fickle women's affections could be? Surely his marriage ought to have taught him that.

Evil memories of long-ago hurt swept over him, and for hours he tossed and turned and cursed the snoring men who slept so peacefully all around him, and at last he cursed as well the fiery-headed woman who slept a few hundred yards away.

TANIA WOKE to sunshine streaming through the cracks in the little cabin and reached with bleary eyes for her watch. She couldn't believe what it said. Eleven forty-five.

She'd slept almost till noon. She hadn't heard the fishermen leave or even been aware of the cacophony of bird song outside that filled her ears now with joyous, cheerful racket. She rolled over and squinted at the other cot.

There was a Gaby-size lump curled up on it, with a shock of bleached daffodil hair showing beneath the top of the sleeping bag. So Gaby hadn't made it up to go with the fishing party.

Tania felt a selfish relief. Even a sullen Gaby was preferable to being marooned all day with that Benson man. If he was still here.

As if in answer to her question, a sudden clanging made Tania jump. It was the sound of metal banging on metal, and it was loud. Earsplitting.

"Whaaat?" Gaby's tousled head popped out of the bag, eyes wide open, and both women sat up, jarred by the clamor that went on and on.

"I'll bet he's doing that on purpose just because we slept in," Gaby said with disgust.

"I wouldn't put it past him," Tania agreed. The din finally stopped, and they lay back down in silence for a few minutes.

"Is there anywhere I can shower or wash my hair?" Gaby asked next. "I feel filthy."

"We'd have to ask for hot water."

Gaby snorted. "Good luck. He'll probably take a fit all over again if a female dares to speak to him."

"I think we're going to have to try. I mean, two weeks is a long time not to talk to someone."

"No, it's not. My mother once—" Gaby bit off whatever she'd been about to say. She crawled out of bed instead and rooted in her pack, pulling out a small battery-operated tape player. Loud and, to Tania, foreign music exploded into the room.

Tania had to yell over the noise. "I think we're going to have to rely on basins of water to wash in, Gaby. You could shampoo your hair in one, then I'll pour the rinse water over you." She took the bucket Matt had brought the night before and went bravely out the door. The music spilled from the cabin, but outside it didn't quite feel as if her eardrums were about to burst from it. "I'll see if there's any hot water we can have."

The cookshack was empty when she came timidly through the door, but there was a copper-bottomed washtub half-filled with steaming water set on one end of the crackling wood stove.

"Mr. Benson?"

No answer. The place felt deserted.

Feeling like a thief about to have her hands chopped off with a cleaver should the bad-tempered cook catch her, Tania hastily used a long-handled dipper and filled her bucket with the scalding water. There were three galvanized pails of cold water over by the washstand, and she took one of those, as well, on her way out. At the last moment, she tucked the dipper under her arm, too.

Might as well be hung for a gallon as a pint.

IT WORKED FAIRLY WELL, although Tania had to go back and get a second pail of cold water before they were done, and the tiny cabin was almost awash with what they spilled.

"Could we turn the music down just a little?" Tania thought Gaby would refuse, but the girl must have been used to the request, because all she did was grimace, roll her eyes and tone down the noise to a bearable level.

Gaby wet and shampooed her blond mop, then Tania mixed hot and cold water and trickled it over the girl's head, rinsing away the soap.

"That's cold. It's freezing me," Gaby yelped.

"I'm not exactly an expert at this—sorry," Tania apologized, adding more hot water to the dipper. "I'll never again take a shower for granted, I'll tell you that," she added in a grim tone.

"Me either."

Tania poured too hard, getting water in Gaby's ears.

"I'm drowning! Help me, someone."

They ended up giggling helplessly. The whole procedure was clumsy, messy and ridiculous.

"Would you believe I brought my hair dryer along?" Gaby picked the small appliance out of her pack and held it up by its cord. "Like, where's the plug-in?"

"Don't feel bad, I brought my electric razor."

Next they reversed the process and Tania shampooed while Gaby rinsed for her.

"You sure got long hair."

"I've thought of getting it cut, but the idea of change scares me."

"You'd look good in short," Gaby declared, and Tania felt pleased.

"We might as well use the rest of this water to sponge off," Tania suggested a while later. "You go first. I got the worst of my dirt off last night."

While Gaby bathed, Tania sat on the wooden step outside, soaking in the sunshine and brushing the knots out of her wet hair. The necessary physical contact had created a good feeling between her and Gaby. Tania hoped with all her heart that it would last.

Neither had made any mention of the crying in the night.

DAMP BUT CLEAN AGAIN, they braved the cookhouse to find some food.

This time the cook was in residence, and the truculent look he gave them would have curdled milk. He was standing at a table, peeling potatoes, filthy apron in place, shiny black braid hanging down his back.

"Can we make ourselves some breakfast, Mr. Benson?" Tania felt as if she'd been transported to a scene in a Charles Dickens novel, where the orphanage children begged for food.

"Used my hot water," he snarled at Tania, giving her a lethal glare. "Took my buckets of cold, too."

"We had to wash," she said reasonably. "If you show us where to fill them, we'll be glad to—"

"Carry my own water. Don't need no females packing water for me."

"Well, then, could we make ourselves some breakfast?"

Gaby wasn't saying a word. She stood slightly behind Tania, obviously shielding herself in case the old grump threw something at them.

"This is my cookhouse. You want grub, I cook it. Breakfast was hours ago. That's when the men ate."

He tossed the potato he was peeling into the pot. It landed with a splat. He stomped over to the stove, grabbing a heavy iron skillet on the way. In less time than it would have taken Tania to find the butter, he slammed heaping platefuls of bacon, fried bread, hash browns and gigantic bran muffins on the table farthest away from where he was working. He slopped coffee into two enamel mugs from the pot that seemed to be a fixture on the stove, and before they could even thank him, he went out, slamming the door ferociously behind him.

"What's his problem, I'd like to know?" Gaby didn't say it too loud, though. Both women fell on the delectable food as if they'd been on a thirty-day fast.

They spent the afternoon avoiding Benny Benson as best they could and trying to make their cabin more habitable. Under Tania's direction, they carried out most of the clutter and deposited it in the lean-to beside the cookhouse. Now there was room to separate the cots, one against each wall. It gave them much more room to move around.

Gaby found an old broom, and they swept down the cobwebby walls. They swept and mopped the floor, being careful to use a minimum of Benny's precious water. There'd been a hammer in the mess, and they located nails in a barrel in the lean-to. After smashing their fingers several times, they got the knack, and soon rows of nails along the wooden walls held their clothing. They hung Gaby's makeup mirror in the corner set aside as a washing area. Their basin sat on a wooden crate, with towels and cloths hung on more nails.

"Now if we could only figure out how to build a shower," Tania said, turning a couple of boxes upside down by each cot to serve as bedside tables and then standing back to survey their cozy, clean room.

"Y'know what else we need?" Gaby held up her sleeping bag, still damp from their hair-washing efforts. "A clothesline."

"Let's find that rope I saw in the lean-to. There are enough trees out there to tie it to, goodness knows."

Soon the bag was draped over a perfectly decent clothesline they'd rigged up near the bunkhouses. Tania decided she might as well wash out her soiled underwear, and with Benny sending her looks that should have dropped her in her tracks, she defiantly scooped out yet another bucket of hot water from his precious kettle and scuttled away with it.

She'd been smart enough to pack a small box of detergent, and after some scrubbing, her white blouse and two sets of lacy bras and panties joined the bag on the line.

"Except for the pain in my legs and bottom, I'm beginning to feel human again," Tania said with a sigh. "D'you want the rest of this hot soapy water to wash anything in?"

Gaby screwed up her nose in distaste. "I brought lots of underwear. I'll do mine when I run out." She was draped across her cot, tape player blaring just the way it had been most of the afternoon. At some point Tania had grown used to it.

Gaby jumped to her feet. "I'm dying for a Coke. I'm gonna go see if I can get Chief Grumpy to give me one. Want anything?"

Tania slumped down on the front step, weary after the long afternoon of work. "I'd kill for a cup of tea and one of those muffins we had, but don't endanger your life over it."

She watched Gaby's lithe form disappear through the cookhouse door, and she could hear the girl's voice but nothing more for what seemed a long time. Then Gaby reappeared, looking triumphant and balancing a rusted cookie sheet on which there was a teapot, a mug, two fat muffins and two cans of diet Coke.

"Hope you don't need cream and sugar. I don't figure I'd better go back in there for a while."

Tania poured her tea and broke open the delectable muffin.

"I take it clear," she lied. "Gaby, this is wonderful. Was he difficult?"

"Difficult?" Gaby rolled her eyes. "He's, like, morbid. I say, really polite, 'Could you show me where to find a Coke?' right? And he takes a screaming fit about not being hired to serve ladies afternoon tea, and he wasn't hired to listen to heathen—get that, he figures my music's heathen—noise. So, I say, 'Well, we're not helpless. If you show us where things are, we'll get it ourselves,' right? And y'know what? He goes back to this being his kitchen and he doesn't want us in it.'' She pulled the tab and tipped the can to her mouth. "I ask you. I've got a perfect right to have a Coke if I want. My father paid for all this food, not old Chief Grumpy in there.''

Tania sipped her tea and wondered how to phrase what she had to say so that it wouldn't crack the new and fragile rapport between them. ''We're going to have to come up with a plan here, Gaby,'' she began, feeling nervous and hoping it didn't show. ''See, Mr. Benson was here first, and your father needs him desperately, because there's no one else who could do his job.''

Gaby swallowed and opened her mouth to argue. ''So does that give him the right—''

''No, it shouldn't,'' Tania interrupted. ''But things aren't always the way they should be. So I think we should keep the music turned down some and do our best to make peace with him.''

Gaby's face had taken on the blank, long-suffering look Tania had noticed before.

Tania tried harder. She leaned toward the girl and said urgently, ''Look, Gaby, I'm scared to death that if Mr. Benson leaves, you and I'll get stuck trying to feed those men. And unless you're a lot better cook than I am, we'd be in serious trouble.'' As an afterthought, she added, ''Right?''

To her immense relief, Gaby grinned. ''Right,'' the girl agreed emphatically, and getting to her feet, she turned her tape player down forty decibels.

At that moment, Benny Benson emerged from the cookshack with two empty pails, heading down to the creek to fill them.

"Are you sure we can't help, Mr. Benson?" Tania called to him, trying to put into action what she'd just been preaching.

He didn't even turn his head. Instead, he made a rude sound in his throat and spat hard on the ground. It left no illusions about wanting any help from the women.

"Oh, gross," Gaby whispered. "If you expect me to try and make friends with him, just forget it. He's too mean to even live. He's a mastodon."

Tania didn't answer, but she agreed wholeheartedly all the same. In many ways, this old native was a grossly exaggerated version of her own father, and it seemed ironic to her that she'd come all this way looking for Doc just to be confronted with still another old man who didn't bother to hide his contempt for the female species.

She'd been feeling lighthearted and almost gay, chatting with Gaby and soaking up the late afternoon sunshine, reveling in the chance to relax after the arduous pack trip. Now, her spirits plummeted and she wondered again just what she thought she was doing, coming to this wilderness and this primitive camp on a whim, believing she might really have a chance of finding a seventy-year-old man with a bad heart with whom she'd never shared even an hour's true intimacy.

But then she thought of Matt, and something softened and warmed inside her. There really were men in the world different from Benny Benson and Doc Wallace. And, she thought with a grimace, different from John Felton, the devious man she'd married.

Matt was honest and warm and generous with his affections. In spite of his own bad marriage, he really

seemed to like women. He liked her. She felt the warmth
grow and spread, becoming a sensual tingle as she remembered the few times she'd been held in his arms,
kissed and caressed.

Matt was all the things she'd dreamed of a man being,
back when she still had dreams of happily ever after. She
couldn't wait to see him, to tell him about the day she'd
spent with his daughter, to show him the changes they'd
managed to make in the cabin.

He was making very definite changes in her heart.

BY THE TIME supper was over that night, Tania couldn't
help but notice that Matt could also be remote, cool and
curt with her for no reason she could fathom.

The fishermen had arrived back just at sunset, jubilant
about the four impressive steelhead they'd caught and the
others they'd hooked and released again in accordance
with the conservation practice Matt had explained on the
way up.

"You still get the pleasure of landing the big ones, I'll
be sure to take snapshots of your catch, and by careful
handling, the fish aren't depleted. Released fish live to
spawn again."

It was a practice that Tania had never heard of, and
she thought it made wonderful sense.

"Hey, Tania, come take a look at this baby," Bob
called, holding up a massive dead fish as the bedraggled
group reached the clearing. "Isn't she beautiful?"

"Yuuuck," Gaby said.

The men looked sunburned and dirty, but all of them
were smiling, joking with one another, as eager as little
boys to show off their catch to Tania, Gaby and even
Benny Benson.

Tania's eyes searched for Matt, but all she saw of him

was his broad back, heading down toward the horse corral.

Supper was noisy, and Matt didn't appear until the rest of the group had almost finished. Voices catcalled back and forth and laughter exploded as details of the day's fishing were retold over the potpie and giant-size biscuits Benny served up.

Tania ended up sitting between Jim and Bob, even though she'd tried to arrange it so there was an empty place beside her for Matt. But the other two men made a point of moving over to sit with her, and short of being rude, there was nothing she could do.

"And old Harry, well damned if he didn't fall right in the creek trying to get that hook undone," Dave was saying when Matt came through the door.

Tania was watching for him, and she looked straight at him and smiled, all her feelings in her eyes.

His eyes met hers, then slid away as if he hadn't seen her.

"Hey, Matt, you better hurry. We nearly finished off the food," someone called.

"If I know Benny, he'll have plenty more ready," Matt replied.

He filled a plate with food and went to the farthest table, gracefully straddling a chair between Andrew and Harry and immediately becoming involved in whatever they were saying. He didn't so much as glance in Tania's direction. It took a while, but at last she realized he was deliberately ignoring her.

Tania felt cold and then burning hot. The food she'd been enjoying seemed to lose its flavor. She did her best to smile, to make the right noises in the right places during the animated fishing story Bob was telling her, but her heart wasn't in it.

She waited until the men beside her got up to get some of the chocolate cake and whipped topping Benny had set on a side table for dessert. She slid her chair back and slipped out the door.

The light was fading, the western sky rosy behind the snow-capped mountains. Birds trilled and an owl was hooting somewhere off in the trees at the edge of the meadow.

Tania walked down the slope, struggling through the bushes that grew beside the river, hardly aware of where she was going. She reached the place where Matt had built a makeshift dock. Two float boats and a sleek motor craft were tied there.

She slumped down on a log and put her elbows on her knees, trying to figure out what could have happened in the space of a day to make Matt act this way toward her. Lost in her thoughts, she couldn't have said how much time had passed before she became aware of the crackling and breaking of branches over to her left.

Her heart jolted and then began to race as she remembered Matt's warnings to Gaby about bears and cougars. She got to her feet and frantically tried to figure out which way she should run. A second later, Matt himself stepped into the clearing.

"You scared me, Matt," she heard herself babble. "I thought you were…" Her voice trailed off.

He was standing, hands on his hips, looking at her in a way she couldn't decipher. There wasn't a bit of warmth in his expression or a trace of a smile under the mustache. He looked formidable and angry.

"Regardless of who you were hoping I might be, Tania, it's my job to keep you safe while you're on this trip," he growled. "If you want to meet Bob somewhere private, you'll have to find a better place to do it."

CHAPTER EIGHT

As soon as the words were out of his mouth, Matt could have kicked himself for being obvious, for letting his hurt feelings show in such a blatant way.

"Meet Bob? What the heck are you talking about?" Tania frowned at him. "I don't understand what this is all about, Matt."

"Look, it's none of my business who you choose to—" He bit off the rest of the sentence. "I'm not your keeper. I just want you to remember there are real dangers up here that dudes like Bob aren't aware of."

He'd done it again, harping on Bob like a jealous teenager, and he'd managed to sound like a pompous ass in the bargain. Damn it, didn't age equip a man with any finesse at all? Embarrassment added fuel to his anger, and he turned away from her, starting back up the bank with long, angry strides.

"Matt Radburn, don't you dare make a statement like that and then just walk away from me." He hadn't realized she was right behind him. She grabbed him by the arm and tugged, making him turn around and face her. Her green eyes were blazing at him, and scarlet flags of anger marked her cheekbones.

"You've been plain rude to me tonight, and I haven't done a single thing to deserve it. I spent a lovely day with Gaby, I did my best not to antagonize that impossible cook of yours, and you come back from fishing acting as though I've mortally insulted you somehow. Well, I won't stand for it, Matthew Radburn. You can darned well tell me what you mean by making leading remarks about me and…and Bob, for heaven's sake. I barely know the man.''

"Come off it." Matt's control was slipping fast. "You knew him well enough to meet him alone in the middle of the night. I saw the two of you, holding hands.''

Tania had all but forgotten the early-morning encounter, and she stared at Matt openmouthed until she realized what he was talking about.

"Meet—oh, for mercy's sake, I'd been to the bathroom. Bob nearly scared me to death, popping out of the darkness the way he did. Then he started talking about his wife, and he seemed so lonely… You see, his wife died not long ago, and he's still pretty upset over it—he can't sleep. I felt sorry for him, and I kept trying to get away, but it was difficult.''

It was obvious she was telling the truth. Matt stared down at her open, honest face, into those intensely green eyes. Her nose was peeling and her lips were chapped, and she didn't have any makeup on, but she was lovely all the same.

Desirable. Very desirable. What made him want this particular woman so much?

"Matt, are you…you aren't…are you…jealous? Of Bob? Of me?" Her voice was hesitant, tremulous.

His first reaction was to deny anything of the kind. But then his basic honesty took over. He groaned and pulled her roughly into his arms.

"I'm sorry, Tania. Yes, I'm jealous. I was up checking on the horses last night, and I saw you take his hand. It was all I could do to stop myself from rushing over like a wild bull and tearing him apart." He held her clamped against him, and they were both aware of his desire. He had to fight the urge to lay her down right here on the riverbank, loosen her clothes and his and claim her as his own in the most basic act of possession.

He'd never experienced more primitive emotions or more urgent ones. And when he kissed her, taking her mouth with a desperate need, using his tongue to show her what he intended, what he wanted to do to her, he sensed that her desire was every bit as great as his, and an unholy joy filled him.

"Tania, it's too soon, it's crazy, it doesn't make any sort of logical sense, but damn it all, I don't want anyone else touching you. I thought about you all day when I should've been paying attention to what I was doing. Poor old Harry almost drowned in the river because I was thinking of you. I knew I had no right to be jealous. But I was, anyhow."

He kissed her again, before she could answer, because he was afraid of what she might say or do to dissuade him. He was rushing her—he knew it—but he couldn't seem to stop himself.

But she put her hands on his jaw and drew away for a moment, looking up into his eyes. "I feel the same about you," she whispered, and he shut his eyes tight and just held her.

But having her in his arms made his sexual desire more potent. He kissed her again and again, and his hands explored her body, touching her smooth skin under the thin T-shirt she was wearing, cupping her small, firm breasts and shuddering when the nipples grew hard beneath his fingers. His body was pulsing, and the feel of her against him drove him almost beyond reason. At last he drew away, struggling to get himself under control again.

"One of these days," he promised, holding her at

arm's length, stroking his hand over her silky, flaming hair, studying every line, every curve of her face and throat. They were both breathing as if they'd just swum across the river.

She gave a jerky nod, and he took it as a promise.

"We'd better get back to camp before somebody sends out a search party," he said, and his voice was rough and uneven from wanting her.

"I think so," she replied. "Besides, the mosquitoes are starting to eat me alive."

Neither had even noticed the hordes of insects until that moment.

She stood for a moment, looking up the river to the place where it curved and disappeared in a tangle of trees and undergrowth. Matt knew she was thinking of her father, out there alone somewhere.

"We'll take a couple of horses tomorrow afternoon, if I can get away, and ride upriver to the place where Danny saw the old man," he promised.

"Thanks, Matt." The gratitude in her eyes was mixed with something else, and it warmed his heart.

He took her hand and tugged her up the bank. They emerged from the trees, and Matt was aware of his daughter, watching them from the railing of the horse corral. She was straddling the top rail, with Scott on one side of her and Mario on the other.

"Hi, kids, how ya doin'?"

Gaby was the only one who didn't reply, and she shot Matt a malevolent look. It made him very aware that he was still holding Tania's hand, and he squeezed it and let it go as they neared the camp.

Now why the hell should Gaby be able to make him feel guilty about holding a woman's hand?

BY THE NEXT AFTERNOON, Matt had the fishermen set up in pairs, each a few miles apart on strategic spots along the banks of the Skeena, and it looked as if they'd be set for a few hours, at least. They'd settled in for a long afternoon's fishing, and even Andrew didn't seem to have any booze along today to cause problems.

Matt gave Mario strict instructions about supervising and then headed back to base camp to pick up Tania.

His only reservation about being absent for the afternoon concerned Gaby. She'd surprised him by being up for breakfast before six that morning, insisting she wanted to go fishing with the others.

Matt had found her a rod and some gear, and of course she'd paired off with Scott. But Scott's father, Jim, had stuck close to the two youngsters all morning, and the three of them were still fishing more or less together.

What concerned Matt was the way Mario had managed to find reasons to seek out the trio all morning. Gaby was like a magnet to both Scott and Mario, and they vied with each other to bait her hooks, set her pole for her, carry her gear and even offer her morsels of their packed lunches.

Matt had finally taken Mario aside and explained in no uncertain terms that Gaby was not a paying customer, that Scott and his father were, and therefore Mario's wages might be secured by paying a lot more attention to the rest of the fishing party and a lot less to Gaby.

Tania was sitting on the steps of her cabin, waiting for him, but before he could head over to her, Benny popped out of the cookshack and sidled up to him.

Matt's heart sank. Benny was still put out with him for bringing Tania and Gaby along. Last night, Matt had listened to a string of complaints concerning the way the women had spent their day.

"Sleeping the morning away, then wanting food when I'm busy." And that was only the beginning.

Gaby had played heathen music on that tape thing of hers all day, so loud that Benny figured he was going deaf from it and all the game within twenty miles would have left the territory. Tania had strung a clothesline up with Benny's second-best lariat and then hung her private rigging where Benny could see them, out in plain view.

Matt figured out that the "private rigging" was the lacy underwear he'd noticed on the makeshift clothesline. It certainly hadn't humiliated him, he mused, listening patiently to the rest of the complaints.

Benny had had to make them tea in the middle of getting supper together, and they'd used all his hot water twice, what with their washing and carrying-on. And they'd put all the things from the storage shed into Benny's lean-to without so much as a by your leave.

That was yesterday. Today was obviously a whole new ball game.

"Matthew, can I have a word with you?" Benny always used that opening when he was going to bellyache.

Matt sighed and nodded. "Sure, old-timer. What's up?"

"Your lady friend there. She washed out all my clean dish towels this morning and hung them on that line she made with my rope while I was down at the creek." Benny's voice was quivering with outrage. "Next thing, she'll be taking over my kitchen. It's my kitchen. She stays out and that's final."

Matt bit back the obvious comment: Benny's dish towels looked cleaner than Matt had ever seen them. Benny was a good cook, but he wasn't a particularly hygienic one. A touch of cleanliness wouldn't hurt the old codger one bit, much less his dish towels. Matt didn't say so, however. He fell back on the same placating line he'd used the night before.

"I appreciate that this is tough for you, Benny. I'll certainly have a word with Tania, tell her to stay away from your dish towels. I'm taking her upriver now to see if we can spot any sign of her father. Think you could fix me a thermos of coffee and maybe some of those cookies we had in our lunches?"

Benny grunted and pulled his apron down. "You should tell her she's on a wild-goose chase. No old city man's going to hole up in these parts all by himself and stay alive. An Indian could. Maybe." He stomped back into the cookshack, slamming the door, but in a few minutes he reappeared, thrusting a thermos flask and a fat lunch bag at Matt. "Watch out for cougars in the bush. I heard one out there the other night."

Matt saddled the horses, Blaze for himself and Sultan for Tania, and soon they were out of the clearing, following a barely discernible trail that roughly paralleled the river.

"You've turned into a pretty fair rider," he said approvingly, watching Tania take control of Sultan.

"I was sort of forced into it." She grinned at him.

Tania was wearing a green shirt that intensified the color of her eyes, and Matt couldn't help stealing glances at the way her jeans outlined the long, lean stretch of her legs in the saddle. Her blaze of hair shone in the afternoon sunshine, and her burned complexion was now turning to a golden-brown tan. She looked pretty.

He reminded himself over and over again that this excursion had only one purpose: to find Doc Wallace, if that were humanly possible. That was the reason she was here at all, and Matt had promised to help her in her search.

But he couldn't subdue the awareness that for once they were entirely alone. For the first time, there weren't fishermen and teenagers and a million responsibilities weighing down on him.

More than anything, he wanted to find her father, find the old man safe and healthy and enjoying himself. But, he was ashamed to admit, he just didn't want to find him in the next couple of hours or so. Surely he deserved that much time alone with Tania.

He didn't allow himself to dwell on how he wanted to spend those hours, but flashes of inspiration kept popping into his head regardless of how he tried to subdue them.

TANIA COULDN'T HELP FEELING excited about riding off with Matt, just the two of them.

She'd spent the morning alone, and although she enjoyed the solitude—Benny Benson made a point of avoiding her, just as she did him—there really was nothing for her to do once the cabin was tidied and her complex bathing ritual completed.

She'd scouted around for chores that wouldn't antagonize Benny and ended up hand washing a pile of filthy tea towels she'd found in the cookshack, draping them over her makeshift line to bleach in the hot sun. After that she'd lazed in the sun herself, thinking wistfully of her father perhaps enjoying this same sunny morning not far away. She'd gone for a walk along the creek and found a place sheltered by willows that would be perfect for bathing.

"Were the fish biting this morning?" The horses were ambling along, almost side by side. Matt seemed deep in thought, but when she spoke he smiled at her and nodded.

"Everybody but Andrew was getting good strikes. He's just not very lucky with a fishing pole."

"The fish probably smell the alcohol on him a mile away," she remarked. "Do all your fishing parties have somebody along who drinks as much as he does?"

Matt nodded. "Unfortunately, a lot of guys think having a good time in the bush involves drinking themselves blind every night. I had a fishing party up here last year and one of the dudes got so drunk he fell out of his bunk and broke his leg. We had to arrange for a helicopter to come and lift him out." A thought struck him. "Y'know, we should have checked with the local copter pilots. Maybe one of them would have had some information about your father. Things were so rushed before we left I never thought of it."

"If we don't find him, I'll do that when we get back to Terrace."

"Is your pop a drinking man, Tania?"

"No." It took her a few moments to enlarge on her answer, because Sultan was maneuvering down a steep, rocky incline. Tania didn't imagine she'd become a horsewoman in the past few days; she had, however, learned to give the big mare lots of rein and trust her to navigate. She was developing a definite fondness for the dignified animal beneath her.

"Doc enjoys a drink of Scotch now and then and an occasional beer, but I've never known him to get drunk. How about your father, Matt? Is he a drinking man?"

Matt shook his head. "My parents are far too reserved to do anything to excess. Dad was an accountant in Vancouver. When he retired a few years ago, he and mother moved to a seniors' residence down in Florida, the sort of place where they don't allow kids or dogs or loud noise. I visited them a couple of years back. The place almost drove me berserk in two days, but they're happy, so I guess that's all that matters."

"You're not close to them." It seemed sad to Tania, this eternal division between parents and children. "Were you an only child?"

"I've got one sister, Valerie. She lives down in Florida, too. She was a schoolteacher, never married, never did anything to make the old folks disapprove of her." He gave her a wry look. "Not like me."

It was fascinating for Tania, hearing about his family, his life. "They disapprove of you, Matt? What on earth for?"

Tania was used to her own father thinking she should live her life differently, but for parents to feel the same way about Matt, well, the idea seemed preposterous. Surely a man like Matt, big and strong and handsome, intelligent and ambitious and responsible, would make any parent proud. She told him so, and he laughed, but it had a bitter ring to it.

"They figured I'd lost my mind when I quit my job in the city, sold my house and sports car and moved up here. It was important for them to be able to say their son was a stockbroker. It's quite a comedown to have to say their son's a fisherman."

"You were a stockbroker?" It was an amazing revelation for her, thinking of him in a proper business suit, heading down to the financial district early each morning, spending his time watching printouts on computers and making frantic phone calls.

"I was only moderately successful, because my heart wasn't in it. I always wanted to work outdoors, but my parents really steered me away from this sort of career when I was growing up. Then, a couple of years after my divorce, I developed severe asthma. My life was pretty much a mess, and I took the illness as a sign that something needed changing. I'd hardly been sick a day in my life till then. About that time I heard of this fishing territory up here for sale. Within a month, I converted all my assets to cash, bought the rights to the territory and moved. The asthma disappeared completely, but so did my money and a lot of my big plans, as well." He gave her a crooked smile. "You saw the house I was going to build and how far I got with it."

"You'll still build it, Matt."

He looked over at her, and under the hat brim there was tenderness and gratitude in his blue eyes. "I appreciate the vote of confidence. The problem at the moment isn't money so much as time. I've started a secondary business that keeps me busy all winter—a small factory in Terrace. Three guys work for me. We build those Fiberglas float boats we use on the river. We only work in the winter, when fishing is over."

He constantly surprised her. He hadn't said a word about the factory till now. She questioned him, and he explained how the boats worked.

"They're environmentally sound because they don't use motors or pollute in any way. They're quiet, and I anchor them in the middle of the river and let the guys fish like that. They get good results. The only problem is getting them back upriver after the day's fishing. That's why I have the jet boat. I use it to tow them."

"How did you get the boats up here in the first place?"

"By helicopter. I had a lot of the materials brought in by copter when I was building the camp. It was expensive."

He changed the subject abruptly. "What about you, Tania? Is your job at the newspaper important to you or is there something you'd rather be doing? Do you want to marry again, have a family?" His voice was serious. He really wanted to know.

Something clenched in her stomach, the way it always did when she was forced to assess the vast distances between dreams and what really was.

"I don't know. I want that, sure, but the fact is, I'm not getting any younger. My job is just that—a job that pays me reasonable wages. But I'd quit tomorrow if I thought I could make it as a novelist. As for having children, well, I've already miscarried twice. I'm divorced. Thirty-six isn't the optimum age for starting a whole new life. Besides…" She was about to add that having babies required a partner, but she thought better of it. What if he thought she was hinting, in some coy fashion?

"Besides what?"

He'd reined his horse in, and Tania stopped Sultan beside him. They were in a small clearing, surrounded by spruce trees. The grass was thick and green underfoot, and the horses began to graze. The roar of the river was muted here, pleasant background music underscoring their conversation.

"I have to work all day, and there just never seems time to start planning a novel," she improvised weakly.

"What would you write about if you had the chance?"

That was easy. "Relationships," she said at once. "The way people are with one another, the problems they have. Love between men and women, parents and children. It should be so easy when we love one another. But it never is, is it?"

"Nope." His tone was rueful. "We always manage to complicate it, one way and another."

Matt had swung down from his horse, and he was pulling a thermos and a brown bag out of his saddlebag. "C'mon down, we'll have a coffee break," he suggested.

He held Sultan while she slid off, and then he led both horses over to a tree and tethered them.

Tania sat down on the ground, but Matt insisted she get up again so he could spread his denim jacket under her.

''It's still damp—the earth won't be really dry up here until later in the summer.'' He squatted beside her and took several large cookies out of the bag, giving her one and pouring coffee into the thermos cup, offering it to her before he drank himself.

Tania took it and sipped, although she wasn't thirsty. Her heart was thumping against her ribs. What was there about him that made her body react like this to his nearness? She couldn't remember being affected in this particular way ever before, even by her husband, even in those long-ago days before trust and love and respect for John had disappeared. There were obviously degrees of attraction she'd never experienced till now.

Till Matthew Radburn.

He was lounging beside her, propped on an elbow, munching cookies. She could smell his special scent, a mixture of clean sweat and horses and leather. She could feel body warmth emanating from him, surrounding her like a cloud. He gave off waves of vitality, of good health and something she could only describe as vibrant maleness.

''There's a high plateau up ahead a ways. We can see a lot of the surrounding countryside from up there. We're only about half an hour's ride from it. We'll be able to make it there and back again before evening.'' He took his hat off and ran his fingers through his rumpled brown hair. Then he set the hat down in the grass and took her fingers in his.

''Tania?''

''I need to kiss you.'' He reached up and took the back of her head in his palm, drawing her down toward him.

There was no forcefulness in his touch, only a tender coaxing.

She allowed herself to be drawn.

His kiss was tentative, a light butterfly brush across her lips and cheek, down to the base of her throat and back again in a path that always led back to her lips.

"There's time now, for us, for making love, if you want it to be that way. Do you want that as much as I do?"

Her skin tingled, her body grew hot and heavy at his merest touch. He flicked his tongue across her mouth, wetting it, running the hot tip just between her lips in a tantalizing, teasing promise, waiting for her reply.

Fear and uncertainty mixed with desire. It had been a long time since she'd made love with anyone. It had never been a thing she was particularly good at, or so her husband had led her to believe. Would Matt also find her clumsy, inept?

"Tania?" he breathed again, and now she was lying cradled in his arms, her breasts pressed against his broad, hard chest. His hands were spread wide, supporting her back, moving across her shoulders, caressing even as he cradled.

She was thirty-six years old, for heaven's sake. How many times did love beckon in a lifetime? When she was old, would she be sorry for the things she hadn't done? She met his eyes, but she couldn't speak. She swallowed hard and nodded instead, a jerky little nod that must have revealed her nervousness.

"Tania, I want you bad. Don't be afraid of loving me. I've wanted you from the first time I kissed you, back home."

She could feel his heart slamming hard against his rib cage. His eyes were smoky blue, narrowed, studying every line of her face between kisses, adoring her. Her own heart was thumping madly in her chest, and a liquid heat seemed to fill her abdomen.

"Let me take this off...."

He pulled the bottom of her green shirt out of the waistband of her jeans and tugged it up and over her head. The sun was warm, but goose bumps rose on her flesh as he trailed kisses in a long, slow line from her chin down to where her bra began.

"You, too," she whispered, and with a boldness that surprised even her, she undid the buttons on his shirt, slid it over his shoulders and down his arms. She looked at him and tried for a smile. "If I'm going to be eaten alive by mosquitoes, then so are you."

"Equality all the way. I like that." He grinned, the crooked grin she loved. Golden-brown springy curls covered his chest, and Tania reached out and touched him shyly, running her hands over the broad, muscled expanse, thrilling at the contrast of smooth skin and rough hair.

"That feels good, having you touch me like that." His muscles quivered beneath her caress, and he closed his eyes with delight. At last he groaned and drew her close, deftly undoing the front hook on her bra and sliding it down and off. He devoured her with his eyes and then stroked her breasts, cupping them in his huge palms, touching the tips with his thumbs and making her gasp with pleasure, letting his roughened hands explore her narrow rib cage, the satiny smoothness of her pale skin.

"When I first saw you, I thought you were thin. But you're not at all. You're a lovely woman, Tania. Delicate, and so soft, like silk...." His head dipped, and he drew her breast into his mouth, teasing the nipple at first and then finding the perfect rhythm, a pulsing suction and slow release, a laving with his tongue that made her insides clench and open again, desperate for more of him.

Her head fell back, and her eyes shut. She felt drunk with pleasure, boneless and liquid and needy. He trailed kisses up her chest, nibbled the underside of her chin, made her giggle when his mustache tickled, made her shiver when his mouth claimed her breast again.

"Let's get the rest of these off." He was on his knees now, breathing as hard as she was, gently undoing the snap at her waist, tugging jeans and then panties down. When they caught on her runners, he took one foot and then the other in his hands and undid the laces, slid them and her white socks off, cradling her bare feet in his palms, caressing her instep, tickling the sole a little.

"Matt, it's...well, I've never...never made love outside before," she confessed. Her voice was shaky. "It feels strange to me, being here in the open air like this. Are you sure...no one will come along?"

He smiled at her, a tender, amused smile, and shook his head. "Absolutely no one, I guarantee it. We're miles from civilization. There's only you and me, the horses, the river and miles of wilderness. Till now, there've always been people around, but this time we're really alone." He kissed her forehead, her nose, her closed eyelids. "I've dreamed of making love to you in a place like this, a wild place where there's sunshine and fresh air and the sound of the river. It's almost like being the only man and woman left on earth, isn't it?"

There was something wistful in his voice, and she nodded agreement. He was right; there was a kind of magic in being here, being uninhibited for the first time in her life. The Skeena tumbled along not far away, providing an undertone of sound.

"No bears, either?" She squinted up at him and he laughed, a low, delighted rumbling.

"Bears are shy and sensitive creatures. They'd never intrude on anything like this. Besides, the horses would let us know and I've got this close at hand." He pointed at his rifle scabbard a few yards away. "Just in case we encounter a perverted peeping bear." He bent and kissed her stomach. "You never know—they might just figure out that you taste just like honey."

They laughed together at his teasing. Then Matt sank back on his haunches and simply looked at her, naked as she was in the wash of the late-afternoon sunshine.

Tania had always been a little shy about her body, and having him study her this way should have bothered her, but strangely enough, it didn't. It felt good—and natural—to be here without a scrap of clothing in full daylight. With Matt.

She found she wanted to look at him, too, she wanted to memorize the lines and sculptured planes of his shape, but she also wanted him to hurry, wanted to feel his arms around her, his body against her own.

He wouldn't be hurried, however. He took his time, savoring her, admiring parts of her she'd never thought admirable until now, using lips and hands to excite and tantalize and tease.

"I've spent hours imagining how you'd look, dreaming of this curve—" his fingers traced her waist, the gentle swell of hip "—and these gorgeous long legs." His hand caressed her thigh, trailed back up, slid across her belly, then dipped into the cleft between her legs, sending waves of desire through her.

Her breathing grew uneven, her need for him centering, growing urgent as he stroked her with languid abandon, knowing the place that leaped like fire at his touch.

"Matt, take your clothes off, too. Hold me." Her voice was thick with passion, and he stood up, tugging off his boots and socks, loosening his belt, dropping pants and blue undershorts into a heap on the grass. At last he was naked, fully aroused, powerful and primitive, starkly beautiful against the backdrop of trees and sky. His skin was tawny gold in all the places where the sun hadn't tanned it nut-brown. His form was dusted with silky hair, and his huge, muscular body was lean and hard, his legs well shaped and strong.

"Let's spread my shirt out underneath you and put my jacket here, like this." He eased her down onto his clothing, and his scent, his warmth, seemed to enfold her. "That's the way. Oh, my lovely, lovely Tania."

When at last his body touched hers, he groaned with delight. His skin was hot and moist, burning as if he had a fever. He fumbled in the pocket of his jeans, drew out a prophylactic and pulled away from her for a second.

"Babies shouldn't ever be an accident, my love."

The gentle words, his consideration, touched her soul. Then he was above her again, kissing her, tongue dancing in and out, balancing on elbows and knees as she reached up, pulling him down to her, greedy for the feel of his skin beneath her fingers, his hot body along the entire length of hers.

Hands and tongues and bodies touched, untamed, lustful, and when neither could bear separation a moment longer, he eased into her with a long, slow, tantalizing motion. A ragged sigh expressed her ecstasy.

"Matt…oh, Matt. That feels… Matt, I want—"

"Slowly, dearest. Lots of time.…"

He drew away and thrust again, and her body answered, following his lead until her center became all there was. She abandoned thought, conscious only of sensation, of the aching, burning need he created inside of her. She became frenzied, avid for his stroking, and she moved against him until he shut his eyes tight, holding himself back, quivering, fighting for control. She was lunging with wild abandon against him, drawing him into her.

"Slow down, darlin'. Slow.... I want this to be good for you," he gasped through gritted teeth. "You're making me..."

She wanted to tell him how good it really was, but words were far away. There was only her body joined in ancient harmony with his, moving with single-minded purpose, again and again...and again.

There was a pause, a hovering stillness, and the sound of the Skeena roared in her ears much louder than before. She imagined it surrounding her, carrying her helplessly forward in a rush of warmth and wetness and power she couldn't control, didn't want to control.

There were rapids and she called his name, twisting, falling, at one with earth and sky and water.

When the tumult receded and her body was once again her own, but replenished, renewed, she opened her eyes and gazed up at him, watching him follow the same path she'd taken.

He arched above her, shuddering, and her name was on his lips as his face contorted, the tendons in his throat standing out as spasms shook him. She held him as he trembled, wrapping him with her arms, her legs, her body, exulting in this power she'd never imagined herself having over him.

At last, he sighed and rolled onto his side, holding her close against him. Their bodies were damp and warm, and the light breeze felt wonderful on her heated skin. He opened his eyes and looked at her, and all the feelings she had were mirrored there. He raised a hand and touched her cheek with his fingers, teasing back strands of hair that clung, letting his fingers trail down her jawline.

"I wish I'd met you a long time ago, Tania." There was sadness in his tone. "It feels as if we wasted years looking for each other. Does it feel that way to you, too?"

Her heart seemed to swell until it filled her throat. Her voice was barely a whisper when she began, "Matt, I—"

But he silenced her with his mouth, and when he drew away, he pressed a finger across her lips, frowning at her. "Hush. Don't feel you have to say anything back. I know all the reasons why it's crazy to feel this way. Your father, Gaby, these fishermen of mine—life's complicated enough without me making any claims on you just now."

She reached a hand up and touched his face. She looked into the deep blue of his eyes and read the same uncertainty, the same fears she had. This was an interlude, a few delicious hours stolen from the harsh reality of their lives. There wasn't any use in pretending it might be otherwise.

He caught her in a hug that almost crushed her. It took her breath away, and she clung to his big frame, breathing in the smell and feel of his naked skin, running her fingers through his thick and tangled hair, feeling irrationally happy and perfectly content in the moment, but knowing as well that those feelings couldn't last. Life waited just outside this tiny green glen.

"What are we going to do about this?" he breathed into her ear. "About us?"

"Nothing right now," she said as firmly as she could manage. "As you said before, you're far too busy up here to indulge in much romance, and…and there's my father, and there's Gaby to consider.''

Against her will came the memory of Gaby sobbing in the night. Problems. She ought to tell him, but not now. Not here, in this place they'd made their own. Still…

''You and Gaby don't even really know each other yet. I think it would be difficult to explain to her that something's happening between us, don't you?''

She felt immediate tension in his body at the mention of his daughter, and he made an exasperated sound and drew away from her, reaching for his jeans. The closeness was gone. Tania suddenly felt empty and alone, in spite of the fact that it had been her own practical nature that had precipitated this.

''You're right, I do know that,'' he growled, and she could hear her own disappointment echoed in his tone. ''The only sensible thing to do is keep a low profile for a week or two, until I get a chance to really talk to Gaby.''

Tania reached for her own clothing and began pulling it on. More than anything, she wanted to believe that Matt's relationship with his daughter would smooth out during the next week or so. The trouble was, she couldn't bring herself to believe it would happen.

They dressed in silence, and Matt drew her close for a last, lingering kiss. Then he held Sultan for her while she climbed into the saddle. As they set off upriver, Tania thought again of Gaby. She'd only been around the girl for a couple of days, and what did she know about teenage girls? Enough to know that Gaby was a complex, hidden, troubled young woman with problems that Tania couldn't even begin to guess at. Enough to know that it would take several miracles for the girl to accept Tania into the tentative and very new life Gaby and her father shared.

And what about her own father? Tania looked all around at the heavy underbrush, the denseness and scope of the wilderness surrounding her, and cold icicles of fear trailed up her spine. She was beginning to wonder more and more often whether or not she would ever see her father alive again.

CHAPTER NINE

DOC HUMMED as he rolled the fish fillets in cornmeal and flopped them into the hot grease in the heavy black frying pan. The contrary old wood stove needed another stick of wood, and he stepped out the door and collected an armful from the stack he'd chopped and piled neatly at the front of the cabin. The sun was still a fair distance from the horizon, even though it was past seven in the evening. The northern days were growing longer.

The chipmunk was there again, standing on the chopping block, seemingly watching Doc's every move.

"You like fish? You're welcome to come in and have supper with me."

Doc had caught himself talking out loud this way the past couple of days, sometimes to the chipmunk or to a robin, or sometimes just making comments to the world in general. It was a habit he'd had to guard against back at the lodge, lest he be slotted once and for all into the "pathetic mumbling old man" category. It was hard enough back there to command any respect, or even to maintain any dignity.

He shoved a good-size log on the fire and replaced the heavy iron stove-top lid. The heat inside the cabin was making him sweat, but it was good, healthy sweat, not like that cold, sickly perspiration he'd experienced when he had the attack the other day.

That was over now, he was sure of it. Sure as hell had

given him a scare for a couple days, though. But then he'd awakened this morning feeling ten years younger, and despite the wood chopping and other strenuous jobs he'd accomplished, his old ticker had just been humming along all day. Probably got the muscles in there toughened up finally.

Soon, his fish was perfectly browned, and he dumped some boiling water on a bowlful of dried potato flakes, stirred them vigorously and sat down to his supper.

"Dad, shouldn't you have some salad or vegetables with that?" He could almost hear Tania's voice in his ear, that quiet but disapproving tone she'd always used about his bachelor cooking. She used to bring him big, fresh vegetable salads.

She was right, of course. Meat and potatoes got pretty boring after a while. He used to serve meals like this one mostly when he knew she'd be coming over, just to annoy her. Why the hell did he do that to her, anyway? Do and say things just to get her dander up? Funny how he'd been thinking so much about Tania. About himself and Tania.

When she'd been around, all he'd ever thought about was Sam. She reminded him of what he'd lost instead of making him aware of what he had. Dumb of him. Come to think of it, he'd talked to her about Sam a lot. At least, that's how it seemed now, looking back on his conversations with his daughter. He felt bad about that. He ought to have talked more about her, found out what she was thinking.

He wished he had one of her green salads right now, to go with the fish. If he'd thought of it, he'd have brought some garden seeds up here with him, planted a little lettuce and some carrots and peas. But when he started out on this trip, he still wasn't sure how long he'd be staying up here.

Now, though, he was sure.

BY THE TIME Matt and Tania rode back into camp, it was already evening. The fishermen were back, most of them standing in a group by the corral, talking in loud, boisterous voices interspersed with gusts of laughter. A delicious smell of freshly baked bread and fresh fish cooking floated out the door of the cookshack.

"I'll take care of the horses if you want to go wash up before supper," Matt offered. His eyes went deliberately to her lips, and then he gave a small shrug and added, "Sorry we didn't have a more productive afternoon."

Tania knew he was talking about more than the fact that they hadn't found her father, and she didn't know how to reply. Her body ached and tingled with the aftermath of their loving, and she longed to be able to reach over and at least take his hand, have some sort of reassuring physical contact with him. Instead, they had to appear impersonal and casually friendly.

"Thanks," she said, sliding gratefully down from Sultan's back and walking toward her cabin. She was tired and hungry, and her emotions were in a turmoil.

"Any sign of your father, Tania?" Bob broke away from the other fishermen and hurried over to her. Tania's heart sank. She could feel Matt's eyes on them, and even though she knew he'd accepted her explanations about Bob, she still felt a little uncomfortable with the attention Bob was paying her.

"No sign at all. We rode a long ways upriver, to the place where Matt's friend reported he'd seen an older man, but there was no one there. Not even a trace of anyone ever being there.''

Matt had searched the surrounding bush for signs of a camp, and they'd ridden up to a high bluff and looked down on the immediate area, watching for signs of a cooking fire, but there were none.

"Too bad. Well, tomorrow's another day. You can try again in a different direction. If Matt can't get away to go with you, I'd be happy to." His eyes were admiring and eager.

Tania gave him what she hoped was a grateful smile. "Thanks, Bob. I don't know yet what Matt's plans are, so I'd better just wait and see."

She moved away from him and slipped inside the cabin, closing the door firmly behind her. To her surprise, Gaby was there, slouched on her bed, headphones clamped on her ears. Usually, Gaby was outside at this time of day, tossing a Frisbee with Scott and Mario or balancing on the corral, giggling with them.

"Hi, Gaby," Tania greeted. "You have a good day fishing?"

Gaby waved a laconic greeting to Tania, not bothering to smile or take her headphones off in order to hear what Tania had said. Instead, the girl turned away and stared up at the ceiling, rapping out a rhythm on the mattress with her fingers.

At times like this, she was an irritating roommate. Tania was uncomfortably conscious of having made love with Matt that afternoon but of having no rapport at all with his daughter. She poured a basin of cold water and began sponging herself off, ignoring Gaby as best she could.

"So you finally got back, huh? How come you were

gone all afternoon with my dad? It can't take that long just to ride upriver and back.''

The sarcasm and suspicion in Gaby's voice caught Tania off guard. She was rubbing a washcloth over her face and neck, and she paused and turned to look at the girl. Gaby had taken off her earplugs and was regarding Tania with narrowed eyes and a spiteful expression.

For a moment, Tania felt irrationally guilty and embarrassed, as if Gaby knew exactly what she and Matt had been doing that afternoon. Then she reminded herself that whatever had been between her and Matt was private. Gaby was simply acting like a spoiled child again.

"You know we were looking for my father," Tania began, hoping she sounded more reasonable than she felt.

"Well, it sure took you long enough. You've got no right to monopolize my dad's time that way." Gaby swung to her feet and stomped out the door, slamming it hard behind her.

Pure fury rose in Tania. How dare that…that rude child speak to her like that when she'd done her very best to be friendly? But the anger faded, and in its place was a feeling of helpless frustration. The girl's actions clearly underlined the discussion she and Matt had had about Gaby, and with a sinking heart Tania remembered Matt's optimism about his daughter.

She'd come around in a week or two, Matt had said. But right now, Tania felt a year or two would have been far too optimistic a time period.

SUPPER PROVIDED SOME answers to Gaby's behavior.

Matt and Gaby weren't there yet when Tania entered the cookshack. She filled her plate with fish and chips, took a piece of hot, fresh bread and found a seat next to

Scott. She turned to him and smiled a greeting and then did a double take.

Scott's right eye was grotesquely swollen and turning a vivid shade of purple.

"What on earth happened to you?"

Scott ducked his head and wouldn't answer, but Jim was sitting across the table from them, and he scowled at Tania. "Him and Mario got into one hell of a fistfight this afternoon over that daughter of Matt's," Jim said. He sounded disgusted. "She got to teasing them about which one was toughest, and the young idiots fell for it and ended up fighting. It's just a good thing Scott's nose isn't broken. I'd have a hell of a time explaining that to his mother. I had to practically sign my life away as it was to get her to let him come on this trip with me." He glared at his son, then added in an aside to Tania, "We're divorced. She's paranoid about Scott getting hurt when he's with me."

"Well, I'm sure the bruising will go away in a few days," Tania said in an effort to reassure Jim. She looked around for Mario. He was sitting across the room, and he had a long, ugly gash on one cheek. His face was swollen. Both boys had skinned and bleeding knuckles.

Jim was still lecturing his son. "Fighting over a slip of a girl like that...I'da thought you had more sense, Scottie. Anyhow, she's not your type, a cheap little—"

"I beg your pardon?" Tania's tone was icy, and she was about to give Jim a scathing piece of her mind, but Scott interrupted.

"Just leave me alone, can't you?" Scott got to his feet, overturning his chair with a clatter that drew the rest of the room's attention to their table. The boy was trembling, and his voice was out of control. "What the heck do you know about my type, anyhow? You and Mom don't know the first thing about me. You just spend all your time using me to score points off each other.'' His voice broke and he turned and bolted out the door.

Everyone was quiet. Tania could hear the water bubbling in the kettles on the stove. She felt sorry for Scott, but she was still coldly angry at Jim for his cruel comments about Gaby.

He didn't look up at all. He sat staring down at his plate, and a scarlet flush crept slowly up past his ears.

"There's lemon pie and fresh coffee." Benny's loud voice broke the awkward silence. "Dig in, everybody."

Conversation resumed, and people began eating again, except for Jim. He sat frozen in place, and after a short while, he got up, picked up the chair Scott had knocked over and hurried out.

Matt and Gaby didn't appear until Tania was leaving the cookshack a half hour later. Gaby marched in the door, avoiding Tania's gaze. The girl's eyes were suspiciously red, and her mouth was compressed into a thin line. Matt was right behind her, looking just as grim as his daughter. He caught Tania's eye and gave his head a despondent shake, then stepped back outside with her for a moment, shutting the door so they could talk without being overheard.

"Gaby'll be staying in camp during the day from now on," he said in a quiet voice. "She disrupted the entire fishing party today, and I've grounded her." He rubbed the back of his neck and then added, "Tania, I hate to ask, but do you suppose maybe you could have a word with her for me? I tried to get through to her before about this flirting with Scott and Mario, but damn it all, I can't seem to reach her."

Tania's heart sank. She knew it was a hopeless endeavor, but she couldn't bring herself to tell Matt that.

He looked worried and tired, and she longed to reach out and smooth the lines away from his forehead. But, as usual, there were fishermen around, and Gaby was just inside the cookshack. Would there ever come a time when she could act on her impulses without worrying about who was watching?

"I'll do my best," she promised, and the grateful smile he gave her would have made her try almost anything for him.

TOO TIRED EVEN TO TRY to make sense of the day, Tania went to bed early and slept the night through. She didn't hear Gaby come in, and the girl was still sleeping when Tania got up for an early breakfast with the others. She watched the preparations Matt made for them.

He was using the float boats for the first time, loading fishermen and supplies into the two Fiberglas skiffs for their trip miles downriver to spots where the fishing was good. Mario's job was to saddle and then lead the horses to where the men were positioned, and at the end of the day, bring the fishermen back while Matt used the jet boat to tow the floaters upriver.

Just before they left, Matt came over to the spot under a tree where Tania was sitting with a mug of coffee.

"If you want to come along tomorrow in the boats, I'll have Mario bring the horses down early and we can do some exploring in that direction for your father." His eyes were warm and loving, and she smiled back at him.

"But what about Gaby? She'd be here alone all day."

Matt's features hardened. "She can spend the day with Benny. I'm at my wit's end with her. I don't..." He didn't finish what he'd been about to say because Mario came jogging over at that point with a question for Matt about a trail he wasn't sure of, and Harry hurried over to ask about rods and flies. Bob followed, and Matt was drawn away. There was no chance for any further private conversation.

"Bye, Tania, see you tonight." Bob waved and smiled at her as they took their seats in the boats.

When boats and men were out of sight, Tania made sure Benny was occupied in the cookshack. Mario was swearing and shouting at horses down at the corral, and Gaby was still sleeping soundly when she crept into the cabin and found a towel, shampoo, soap and fresh clothing. Feeling like a pioneer woman, she made her way down to the isolated spot she'd found where the river formed a quiet backwater pool.

Willows and poplars grew high in a protective ring, and she stripped off her clothing and waded in, shuddering when the water touched her thighs and then her breasts. It was decidedly cold, but being able to have a leisurely bath and shampoo more than made up for the momentary discomfort. Her body turned numb after the first few moments, and shock and heady exhilaration made her laugh out loud.

The sun was bright when she scrambled out, slipping a little on the muddy bank before she reached the grass. She dried with brisk roughness, aware of every inch of her body in a way she hadn't been before. It tingled and glowed from the chilly water, reminding her somehow of Matt and his lovemaking. She shuddered with remembered delight.

Funny, she'd never appreciated her body in this special way before. It was as if every separate nerve had awakened, and was singing with joy. She laughed at her own foolishness and tugged on her underwear, then left the rest of her clothing folded on the ground. It was a glorious morning—the sun was already hot, the bugs weren't bad, and she loved the way the heat felt on her skin. She sat down on a log, brushing her hair in long, slow strokes and holding her head back, eyes closed against the glimmering brilliance of sun and sky and water.

Birds were singing in a raucous chorus all around her. The morning air was fresh and clean and sharp. She sat without moving, and an awareness of the world around her that she'd seldom experienced before came creeping over her. She'd remember this moment, this place, all the days of her life.

Sitting there, soaking in the smells and sounds, almost painfully conscious of the wild and pagan beauty of her surroundings, Tania's thoughts drifted to Doc. She felt she understood her father a little more, why he'd left a safe and comfortable home in the city to come up here.

Before this, his actions had been unfathomable to her, just as he was. They'd always been at cross-purposes, her and Doc, and instead of affection, all too often it was a weighty sense of duty that prompted her to visit him, to take what little care of him he allowed. There certainly hadn't been any joy in it, not for Tania, and she was certain not for Doc, either. Why should that be? He was her father, her closest living relative, the reason for her very existence, and yet it seemed impossible to really like him, to get to know him as a friend.

It had been almost a month now since he'd left Vancouver. She tried to avoid the question that haunted her, but it was there, burned indelibly into her brain: was he still alive?

She got up and grabbed her jeans and T-shirt, pulling them on with frantic haste, shoving her feet into her sneakers. She stood on the riverbank, and tears slipped down her face.

"Doc?" she whispered. "Dad?" She hadn't called

him Dad since she was a tiny girl. He'd become Doc, and the nickname served to distance him from her.

"Dad?" Her voice grew stronger, more urgent, and although she felt ridiculous, she couldn't stop herself. "Dad, where are you? Come back to me, let's try again. Let's try again, okay?"

She was shouting now, sobbing, aware that the rush of water muffled her voice, needing release from this new emotion that filled her to overflowing. She cried aloud, holding her arms crossed over her chest. A hesitant touch on her back brought her around with a terrified shriek.

It was Gaby, and she gave a little scream, as well, jumping back, away from Tania.

"Jeez, Tania, what the heck's wrong with you, anyway?" Her tone was accusing. She frowned and stared at Tania as if she expected her to do something crazy.

Tania couldn't speak. She used both palms to wipe away the tears on her face. She felt ridiculous and spied upon. The memory of the girl's rudeness the night before still rankled, and Tania now hurried over to her belongings and scooped them up, giving herself time to recover.

"I was having a bath. This is a good place, but the water's cold," she finally managed.

Gaby was still watching her uneasily.

"Have you had breakfast?" Tania started walking toward the path that led back to camp, and Gaby followed her.

"Nope. That old goat hollered at me when I went in the cookshack, so I told him to go to…"

Gaby's flip rudeness irritated Tania. She turned and confronted the girl, and Gaby's sentence trailed off. She stared back at Tania defiantly, eyes narrowed, mouth set in a rebellious line.

Tania's anger burst out in words. "Gaby, being rude

is no way to get through life. You made comments to me last night that I resented, and even Benny Benson has feelings. We all have to live together for the next ten days. I think it would be a good idea if you gave more thought to what you say and how you say it.''

Damn. That sounded prissy and judgmental, something that Tania's mother would have said. But it was the truth, nevertheless. Tania was breathing hard, and her heart was thumping, partly with anger, partly because she felt she was mismanaging the whole thing.

Gaby's face contorted into an ugly sneer. ''You haven't any right to lecture me, lady. Just because you're hitting on my father, don't think you can tell me how to act, because you can't. You're nothin' to me.'' She all but spit the words at Tania, jutting out her chin defiantly.

''Hitting on…'' The unfamiliar slang took a moment to make sense. ''Oh, Gaby, that's not what—'' Tania stopped at the pure fury and outrage mirrored on the girl's features.

''Oh, yeah? Well, I may be just a sixteen-year-old kid, but I can see how you look at him, how you hang around him all the time.'' Gaby's face was scarlet now, her jealous rage too overwhelming to control or contain. She held out a trembling hand and waved an accusing finger an inch from Tania's nose. ''He blows his stack at me because I play around a little with Scott and Mario, when all the time you and him are getting it on. Some double standard you so-called adults have. You're screwing my father, aren't you? And you've got the nerve to try and tell me how to act.''

Tania was stricken dumb with shock and outrage.

''Bitch, that's what you are…a bitch!'' Gaby spat the words like projectiles.

Before she had time to think about what she was doing,

Tania flung out her hand, and the palm connected with Gaby's cheek, full force.

With the blow, Tania's anger faded and remorse took its place. She thought—too late—of her promise to Matt to try to reason with Gaby. Ashamed and appalled, she watched the girl's cheek stain bloodred.

Gaby's face crumpled like a little girl's, but she refused to cry. Her voice was garbled and nearly hysterical, and she swallowed in between words. "I...I hate you for this. I'll...ne-never forgive you. You...you stay... away...from my dad. Wait till he hears...wh-what you did to me."

"Gaby..." Tania took a step toward the girl, needing to apologize, but Gaby turned and ran out of the thicket.

"Gaby!" Tania called, but the girl didn't stop. Tania hurried after her, watching her sprint across the meadow. Gaby finally slowed when she reached the corral, and Tania saw her climb the fence and start talking with Mario, who was still saddling horses.

Apologizing in front of Mario was more than she could face at the moment. Tania felt ill with shame.

The remainder of the day was wretched. She had no appetite for lunch. She cleaned the cabin with a vengeance, but there was only so much that could be done.

Mario rode out just after noon, leading a string of saddle horses and a pack pony, and Gaby spent another hour down at the corral, slumped on the rail fence. Tania gathered her shattered courage and walked down to talk to her.

"Gaby," she began, "I want to apologize. I'm terribly sorry for—"

"Get lost." The undisguised venom in the girl's tone made Tania flinch. "I've got nothing more to say to you.

Leave me alone. And leave my dad alone, too, if you know what's good for you.''

Defeated, Tania walked away.

Matt was late getting back that evening. The others rode in at dusk, exuberant about their catch and about the day spent on the river, but Matt wasn't with them.

Tania hung back while the others went in for supper, hoping that Matt would arrive and she could talk to him about what had happened with Gaby, apologize to him, try to explain how and why she'd lost her temper so badly. She'd spent the better part of the day agonizing over her actions, feeling like a total failure, full of remorse. She was desperate to talk to Matt, to let him know how seriously she'd failed both him and his daughter.

Would he be furious with her? He had every right to be.

Tania waited under a huge pine while the others ate in the cookshack. She hadn't wanted supper. It was getting dark, and although she watched the river until her eyes ached from squinting into the deepening dusk, there was still no sign of Matt.

The mosquitoes were feasting on her by the time she heard the low growl of a motor and finally saw the dim shape of his jet boat slowly towing the Fiberglas skiffs into their mooring place just below camp. Relief that he was safely back mingled with apprehension as she began walking quickly down toward the makeshift wharf.

A lithe young figure went flying past her, and Tania's heart sank as she heard Gaby call, ''Dad? Dad, I really need to talk to you. I'm glad you got back.''

Tania slowed, stopped. She could see Gaby fling her arms around Matt's neck the moment he stepped onto the dock, and although she couldn't hear the words, she could make out that the girl was sobbing in Matt's arms. There was nothing for Tania to do but retreat.

CHAPTER TEN

MATT STOOD on the dock, supporting his sobbing daughter and wondering what the hell had gone wrong now. He'd never had a trip quite like this one. One problem didn't come right after the other, nothing as neat and tidy as that. Nope, one disaster stacked up on the next, like macabre building blocks.

"Gaby. Sweetheart, what's the matter? What's happened? Are you hurt?"

She was trembling in his arms, and he was more shaken than he cared to admit, because this tough daughter of his seldom cried. Through all the problems, all the harsh words he'd had with her, she'd never shed a tear. But now she was shedding buckets all over his padded vest and sweaty, fishy-smelling shirt.

"It's...it's Tania," she choked out, and a bolt of utter terror shot through him. His hands clamped on Gaby's upper arms, pushing her away just enough to see her face.

"Is...what's happened to Tania? Is she...? For heaven's sake, will you answer me, Gaby? Is Tania hurt?" Awful fear clenched at his innards in the instant it took his daughter to wrench herself out of his arms and peer at him with streaming, resentful eyes, hands planted on her narrow hips.

"Nothing's happened to her. I wish it had. I wish she'd drowned in the river. I hate her. She slapped me right across the face, for nothing. Just because I asked her if you and her…if you were… Jeez, Dad, I needed to know where I was at, y'know, if maybe I should go back to Toronto or something. I don't want to screw up your love life or anything.'' Her voice trembled pathetically. ''I just wanted to know. Anyhow, all I asked was…were you getting it on, and she slapped me, hard.''

Matt was tired and hungry, wet to the skin and sick to death of problems. He'd just spent more than two hours downriver trying to figure out what was the matter with the motor on the jet boat. Then, when he finally got it going, he promptly got stuck on a sandbar and spent another hour getting the floaters free.

Before that, he'd spent most of the afternoon trapped in a boat in the middle of the river with Andrew, who alternately guzzled from his ever-present bottle and regaled the other three with every nasty detail of his most recent divorce in a drunken whine. It was his third, and Matt understood why. He'd only been around the man for a week, but he'd sure as hell divorce him if he could. He'd fantasized about drowning him long before the afternoon was over.

Yesterday, after the fight Gaby had engineered, he'd had all he could do to keep Mario from saddling up his pony and riding out, leaving Matt high and dry for a swamper and part-time fishing guide. Not that Mario was all that great, but there weren't any lineups here to take his place.

Every night Matt spent at least a half hour listening to Benny's string of complaints about having two women in camp. One of those women, Tania, haunted Matt's dreams. The other, Gaby, caused him nightmares that left him sweating and shaking, facing problems he had no idea how to solve.

''What *exactly* did you ask Tania, Gaby?'' Matt narrowed his eyes at her, noting the too-innocent expression, the trembling lips, the woebegone air.

"I just wondered if you guys had any plans, like for when we go back home. I mean, the trailer's pretty small for three of us, and…well, I just wanted to know. I don't wanna be any third wheel."

Somehow, he didn't think the conversation had gone exactly like that. No one knew better than he did that Gaby had a smart mouth, a wicked tongue. He'd had moments when he had to hold back with every ounce of self-control to keep from smacking her for some sarcastic crack or other.

"And you say Tania hit you?"

Gaby nodded, shoulders slumped. She was the epitome of the victimized child.

Oh yes, he'd wanted to hit her, too, but, a small voice reminded him, he'd always held back. He was, after all, the adult. The parent. No matter what this impossible daughter of his did, no matter how little he liked what she did or said or became, he still loved her because she was his child.

She wasn't Tania's child, which made all the rules different. There wasn't any love base there to cushion Tania's anger.

Through it all—meeting Tania, becoming a parent again when he least expected it—Matt had been hoping. He'd been telling himself it would all work out: his love for Tania, his responsibility for his daughter, his desire for a peaceful life that might, someday, include all of them. Now, standing here beside the river, getting bitten to death by mosquitoes and blackflies, sick in his soul over this daughter of his, he wasn't sure anymore.

"I want to talk to Tania about all this," he told Gaby,

putting an arm around her shoulders and walking up the incline toward the camp.

Gaby hung back, grabbing his arms. "How come you need to talk to her? Can't you just take my word for what happened?"

"It's only fair to listen to both sides, Gaby. Yesterday, I made a point of listening to both Scott and Mario as well as you about what occurred."

The light was almost gone, but he could make out the bitterness on her face. "Yeah, and then you believed them instead of me. The same thing'll happen here—I just know it. I wish I'd stayed back east instead of ever coming here to live with you."

Heaven help him, there were plenty of times Matt had wished the same thing lately. He sighed and tried again.

"Gaby, listen to me. You've got to stop being so…" He reached out for her arm, but she wrenched away, out of his grasp, and went running off across the meadow toward the horse shelter.

Matt watched her and let her go. He was far too tired and heartsick to chase after her tonight. With any luck, the bugs would drive her in before long. He forced himself to move, to go to the bunkhouse and find some dry clothes before looking for Benny to see if there was any food left in the cookshack.

He wanted very much to talk to Tania, but by the time he'd changed and wolfed down the leftovers Benny had heated for him while trying not to listen to the old man's complaints about what the females had got up to today, Matt could hardly keep his eyes open.

There was no sign of Tania. The camp was quiet. Everyone had gone to bed, and after a walk around the corral to make sure that Gaby wasn't still out there pouting, he stumbled into the bunkhouse, stripped and crawled into his sleeping bag. Tomorrow. He'd deal with the whole mess tomorrow.

Exhaustion overcame him, and he slept.

THE CABIN WAS HOT when Gaby awoke, and she knew it was late before she read the time on her watch.

Ten after twelve.

Everything was quiet outside. Everybody would have left hours ago, even Mario with the horses, and Gaby was imprisoned for the rest of the long afternoon with grouchy old Benny. Even Tania was gone. She'd heard Scott's father say last night that Tania was going along in the float boats today. It made Gaby mad and sick with jealousy that her father would take Tania along and make her, his only daughter, stay behind to die of boredom.

Gaby crawled out of her sleeping bag. She was sweating and she felt grubby. Her eyes were sore, probably from crying. She didn't always remember crying in the night, but last night she did. She'd awakened with tears running down her cheeks, and as soon as she was aware of it, she'd made sure she didn't make any more noise. The last thing she wanted to do was wake Tania.

Beside her, the other bed was neatly made, all Tania's belongings tidy and in scrupulous order, just as usual. The nutty woman was a neat freak, always washing and cleaning and folding things. She'd even washed some of Gaby's clothing a couple of times, and every day she'd aired the sleeping bags, made the beds, brought fresh water for washing and swept out the cabin.

Gaby figured she could live without that sort of neurosis quite nicely. Her mother hadn't had any hang-ups like that, thank God. Housekeeping wasn't Margaret's strong point, she'd always maintained.

Her mother had other problems, though, that had finally made it impossible for Gaby to stay with her.

Men. Why hadn't it been enough for her mother just to have Gaby? Why did she always have to have some man around? Her mother kept changing men, and they seemed to get worse all the time. Why hadn't she been able to be happy with Gaby's father and stay put? But her mother went from one man to the other.

First there was Derek, her stepfather. Even though she was very young when her mother married him, Gaby had always known Derek wasn't her real father. Oh, he wasn't too bad, except that he acted like a little boy and got jealous when her mother paid Gaby too much attention. Anyhow, he finally dumped her mother for a neighbor lady whose husband left her lots of money.

There were two more, and Gaby always got their names mixed up when she remembered them. They were hopeless, and they didn't last long.

Then came Neil. Gaby thought of Neil, her mother's latest boyfriend, and a shudder rippled through her. Her stomach felt sick and her skin crawled whenever she thought of him, of the way his long hands and hot eyes groped her each time her mother was out.

She'd told her mother Neil touched her, and her mother got mad at her instead of at Neil. Finally, she'd told Gaby to get out if she couldn't get along with him. That hurt so much Gaby didn't want to think about it.

She tugged on shorts and a T-shirt, forcing the ugly memories back into the dark place where they belonged.

She grabbed a towel and her shampoo. Might as well go have an ice-cold bath in Tania's watering hole before she hit Benny up for some food. Maybe the water would take her headache away. Funny how she always got a headache when she thought about Neil.

She arrived at the cookshack forty minutes later, hair still wet but feeling a whole lot better.

"Hi, Benny." She'd decided to try a breezy approach and see what happened. "Can I have some lunch? I missed breakfast, and I'm kinda famished." She fished two cans of diet soda out of the plastic case in the corner and popped the lid on one, taking a long drink.

He was rolling out dough on a table, flour up to his elbows. "I'm busy, any idjit can see that."

"Okay, then I'll make myself a sandwich. Got any peanut butter?"

"I do the cooking."

"But you're busy, Benny," she parroted, imitating his intonation. "Any idjit can see that." She put the cans down on the end of the table where he was working.

The rolling pin paused, and he glared at her. "You need a good crack across the jaw, miss, that's what you need."

For some weird reason, his words hit home. Sudden tears popped into her eyes and rolled down her cheeks, and Gaby was both angry at herself and astonished. She could rustle up tears on command—she had last night with her father—but she didn't need to cry now, for sure. So what was the matter with her, anyhow? She dashed the back of her hand across her cheeks and summoned up her toughest voice.

"Yeah, Benny, well, my dad's girlfriend already did that, so you don't need to bother," she said contemptuously. But there was a catch in her voice, and she turned away so he couldn't see the tears. Damn it all, why couldn't she stop them? She held her breath for several heartbeats, telling herself it was stupid, stupid to cry. Then a racking sob caught her and she nearly choked trying to hold it back.

Benny made a disgusted noise. "Maybe you deserved it if you got hit. When I was your age, my father would have knocked me across the room if I talked back like you do, miss."

His words made her angry, and that at least stopped the tears, but she didn't need a lecture from Benny. If she wasn't so hungry, she'd be out of here. But she was starving.

"Yeah, well, times have changed. There're laws against hitting kids now, y'know? And anyway, my dad would never hit me."

Benny grunted sarcastically. But at least he was slicing some bread, ladling something into a saucepan. Moments later, he slammed a bowl of thick soup and a fat sandwich in front of her.

"There. Don't see why you can't get yourself in here at proper mealtimes. Do you good to get up in the morning, instead of lollygagging around."

She attacked the food, and he watched for a moment and then plopped down two fat muffins in front of her, as well, before he turned back to his pie dough.

She wished she'd brought her tape player over with her, but she was too hungry to get it. Besides, she'd have all afternoon to do nothing but listen to her tapes, and she was getting a little tired of them, anyway. She'd only been able to pack a few. It was boring, boring, boring here in camp. What did her dad expect her to do all day, anyway, alone here with nobody but Benny? Jeez, Benny was worse than nobody.

The edge was off her hunger, and she ate more slowly, watching him because there was nothing else to do.

"How'd you ever learn to cook, anyway?" The question surprised her as much as it did him. He was flipping rounds of pastry into metal pie pans, one after the other. She had to admit he was good at it. She said it out loud.

"You're really a good cook, Benny. Specially your bread—it's radical."

He scowled over at her, obviously expecting a trick, but when she went on eating, he finally growled, "Learned when I was younger than you. Had to feed my brothers. Our father was working all summer in the fish cannery down in Rupert, then he had a trap line in the wintertime."

"So where was your mother? How come she didn't do the cooking?"

The look he gave her was enough to quell further questions, but she was desperate for some entertainment. She waited what seemed a long while, and when he didn't say another thing, she tried again. "How many brothers did you have?"

There was a long, suspicious pause before he answered. "Three. All younger than me."

"I never had any sisters or brothers. My mom got pregnant once when she was still with Derek—he was my stepfather—but she lost the baby. I was kind of sorry. It would have been fun to have a sister or brother." Gaby swallowed a bite of muffin and took a gulp of soda. "Stepsister or brother, I guess," she corrected herself. "But maybe it was a good thing, because Mom and Derek split right after that."

Benny was opening cans of filling and dumping them into the pies, muttering under his breath when the contents stuck in the can, and she was sure he wasn't even listening to her anymore.

"So the kid woulda grown up with a single parent, just my mom to rely on, same as I did. Derek wouldn't have been much of a father, even if he stuck around. Which he didn't.''

Benny wasn't paying any attention to her. He opened the lid of the stove and thrust another log on the fire, then with deft and almost dainty movements, he began putting tops on the pies.

Talking to him was sort of like talking to herself, Gaby decided. "Y'know, there was this girl I knew, her name was Melody? That was her street name—I didn't know her real one. Anyhow, she was fifteen and she'd already had two babies. She couldn't keep them, though. They both got adopted.''

He ignored her, as if she were invisible. It was infuriating. Gaby tried to think of something shocking enough to force him to notice her, trick him into making some sort of response. "She was a hooker, y'know? A prostitute, a street kid. Her mother kicked her out, too. When she was only twelve.''

"Humph.'' Benny could get a lot of mileage out of that one sound. At least she had his attention. He was brushing the pie tops with tinned milk.

"My mom didn't kick me out, though, not really. Oh, she said to leave, but she was just mad. Actually, I left on my own.''

"Humph. Ran away, huh?'' He put three pies in the oven and shut the door. "Seems like that's all you young people today think of is running away. Maybe you should try sticking around. That's what we had to do in my day. Builds character. Kids today, they got too much money, too much opportunity—that's what's wrong. First little thing goes wrong, they run away.''

His words infuriated her and she narrowed her eyes at him and jutted out her chin. "That's just garbage, Benny. You don't know anything about us kids. I got to know some of the street kids besides Melody. None of them had any money at all. That's how they got to be prostitutes, that's why lots of them stole stuff."

"Not enough hard work, too much money."

He was stubborn as well as stupid, Gaby fumed. Her voice was deliberately sarcastic. "Tell me, Benny, who's gonna hire a kid and pay him enough to live on? Tell me that."

"In my day, we didn't get paid for work. Work was there to do, we had to do it. That or get beaten."

"Did that happen to you?" She was suddenly curious. "Did you have to work or else you'd get...get beaten?"

He was scraping the tabletop, getting all the scraps of pastry off of it. He jerked his head up and down again in a matter-of-fact nod. "Many times. My father had a bad temper."

Gaby shivered. "God, that's awful. I'm glad my dad's not mean."

"You have a good father. You don't appreciate him, causing trouble all the time."

"Yeah, well, maybe I'd be different if there was anything to do except just stick around here and be bored all day. This stupid place is so boring I can't believe it."

"Some of us don't have time to be bored, too much work to do. No time to stand around talking with the likes of you, either."

"You might not have as much work if you let somebody else help, y'know, Benny." She wouldn't even mind a few chores. It might make the afternoon go faster.

He gave her a withering look, and she sighed and rolled her eyes. "Don't start with me again about no women in your kitchen. I've got the message loud and clear already."

She flounced out of the cookshack into the sparkling

afternoon, slamming the door as hard as she dared and feeling mean and satisfied when Benny swore at her.

Her watch told her that she'd managed to get through more than an hour and a half. That meant there were maybe five left before another living soul arrived back at camp. Five long hours without a thing to do and no one to talk to. Five hours to block out things she didn't want to think about. And her father had grounded her. Would he stick to it for the rest of the trip?

This was—she counted on her fingers—this was day seven. There were five more days here in camp, then three packing out again. She'd absolutely die of boredom if she had to spend five more long days by herself.

It was enough to make her consider turning around and going back into the cookshack with miserable old Benny and trying to make friends.

WHILE THE MEN FISHED, Tania spent the morning in the middle of the river in a float boat, getting sunburned and being bored to near madness. Matt was in the other boat a short distance away, with the jet boat beached a few hundred yards downstream. Every once in a while she could hear his voice over the noise of the rushing water; they hadn't had a chance to say two words to each other all morning.

"You want to try your hand at this, Tania?" It was Bob who asked, holding out his rod for her to take if she wanted to, but Tania shook her head.

"Fishing just doesn't appeal to me, I'm afraid."

"Not into the better things in life, huh?" he said with a laugh.

Sitting immobile in a boat for hours didn't appeal to her, either, despite the breathtaking beauty of the wilderness all around. It seemed to Tania a sinful waste of usable time, being trapped here as the minutes and hours on her watch crept by in slow motion.

The men in her boat didn't talk much at all except to exclaim now and then when they got a strike or curse mildly when they lost one. The conversation was sparse, limited to the various flies they were using, the merits of one kind of bait over another and the size of the biggest fish they'd ever landed.

Scott was almost as quiet as Tania, not participating in the men's discussions at all, his eye purple and blue from the fight he'd had with Mario, his knuckles bruised and sore looking. It was the expression on his face that made Tania feel sorry for him. He looked lost and sad, and he didn't smile once all morning. Neither did he pay much attention to his fishing line. His father had spoken sharply to him once or twice when the line tangled on a log and Scott didn't bother doing anything about it.

"What will you be doing when the summer's over, Scott?" Tania's question obviously caught the boy off guard, and it was a minute or so before he answered.

"Going back to school, I guess. I've got another year before I'm done."

"Then what?"

He shrugged and she noticed how his gaze slid to his father and then away. "Oh, college, maybe. I'm not sure yet." He didn't sound enthusiastic at all.

Jim had obviously been listening. "No maybe about it, Scott," he boomed in a loud voice. "College is the only thing your mother and I have ever agreed on. This harebrained idea you've got in your head about singing with that half-assed band is just nuts. How many so-called singers ever make any money at it—you tell me that?"

It was obvious that father and son had gone over this

many times, because Jim didn't wait for an answer but went right on. "You have to get an education these days if you want to amount to anything, make any real money. Singers sure as hell can't afford a trip like this one or the kind of fine equipment you're holding there, son. You've got to get an education under your belt if you ever want to live the good life, right, Bob?"

The words were hardly out of Jim's mouth before Scott struggled to his feet and threw the expensive rod, reel and tackle as far as he could into the river. The boat tilted precariously and Tania gave a small shriek as Jim lunged at his son, an instant too late to stop him. The fishing gear disappeared under the rushing water.

"What...what the hell's gotten into you? Are you crazy, boy? D'you have any idea how much I paid for that rod?" Jim roared, red in the face.

Scott was sitting down again, breathing hard, glaring at his father but not saying a word. No one else said anything, either, until a few moments later, when Matt poled the other boat alongside. He must have seen what had happened, but he asked no questions.

"Mario will be along any time now with the horses, so head in for shore and we'll have some lunch. This afternoon, Mario will show you a spot downriver where there's good fishing from a sandbar." His gaze rested on her, and in a cool, impersonal voice he added, "Tania, you and I'll take a ride downriver to see if we can spot any sign of your father. We'll pick up the boats afterward."

THEY WERE ALONE for the first time all day. Matt was slightly ahead of her, letting Blaze find his way through the shoulder-high brush, tramping a path of sorts for Sultan and Tania.

Matt had been unnaturally quiet since they'd left the others, and she had, too. She was worrying over how to tell him about what had happened the day before with Gaby. What she'd done was inexcusable, hitting his daughter across the face that way.

Tania knew Gaby had already given him her version. And, her instincts told her, that version wouldn't have been the absolute truth. The vicious things Gaby had said hardly bore repeating.

The brush became less dense, the trees farther apart, and soon they were able to ride beside each other.

"Matt, I have to—"

"Tania, there's something—"

They looked at each other, and Matt gave a small replica of his usual wide grin.

"Ladies first," he said.

She drew in a deep, shuddering breath, then said, "I slapped your daughter yesterday, and I feel terrible about it."

"Yeah, she said you did." His tone was carefully neutral, and the sigh that accompanied his words was audible. "She's a difficult girl, impossible at times."

"Yes, she is, but...but, oh, Matt, I'm not good with her. I told you in the beginning I've had no experience with teenagers at all. And this trip has confirmed that I have no idea whatsoever how to deal with them. I did try to apologize to Gaby, but she wouldn't respond."

"She's pretty angry, I guess."

"She's also very upset and confused. I've heard her crying in her sleep several times, but when I ask her she won't tell me what's making her cry. Maybe she just misses her mother."

Matt didn't comment on that. Instead, he said, "What caused the blowup yesterday?"

Tania felt at a loss for words. It was impossible to describe the girl's jeering tone, and she just couldn't bring herself to repeat all of the things Gaby had said.

"I guess I lectured her about being rude to Benny, and she lashed out at me about…about chasing after you." Tania kept her eyes downcast. "She accused me of… I think the term she used was 'hitting on' you. And she wanted to know whether…" Tania's throat was dry. She coughed and tried again. "Whether we were…sexually involved."

"That's none of her damned business." Matt's voice was angry.

Tania sighed. That had been her first reaction, as well, but she'd had plenty of time to think the whole thing over.

"Maybe it is her business, Matt. She seems to feel we're competing for your attention, she and I."

He shook his head. "Nonsense. She's my daughter, for heaven's sake, and you're…"

Tania's heart slammed against her ribs, waiting for what he was going to say next. His woman? His lover?

But the path narrowed just then and Blaze took the lead. When they were able to ride abreast again, he changed the subject. "What went on in the boat today between Scott and his father?"

Tania explained, telling Matt as well about the scene at the dinner table the other night, when Scott had stormed out. "The boy seems to think his mother and Jim are using him as a prize in some war of their own, even though they're divorced," she said.

"Maybe they are." Matt squinted off into the distance. "I spent the first year after my divorce fighting with Margaret over one thing and another, mostly about my right to see Gaby. The ties aren't really broken when you still do that. But then she remarried and moved to the other end of Canada, and I came up here, and it was hard to see my kid at all. Besides, I had the mistaken idea that a little girl ought to be with her mother." His face set in bitter lines. "I blame myself for not making more of an effort to have Gaby with me over the years, to get to know her. Now, I feel as if it might be too late to start."

"I feel the same way about my father," Tania blurted out. "But at least you have Gaby with you now. You have a chance to make up for the years you spent apart." She pulled Sultan to a stop, unable to contain the emotions that had been threatening to overcome her all day.

"Matt, this is no use, is it, this searching? We're wasting our time, aren't we? My father's dead, I know he is. Before, I had the feeling he was alive, but when I really saw all this—" she waved a hand at the thick bush that surrounded them, the nearby river that roared like a wild thing over rocks and rapids "—an old man couldn't live up here all alone. Everybody tried to tell me that, but I wouldn't believe them until I saw it with my own eyes." She dropped her head, feeling the tears beginning to form and roll down her cheeks. "I can't believe anymore, Matt. I can't hope." Tears were spilling down her cheeks, and she didn't even bother wiping them away.

"He's dead, and I'm going to have to accept that." A sob escaped, and she added brokenly, "The worst thing about it is that I never really got to know him. He never tried, so neither did I."

"Darlin', don't cry. You can't change the way things are, no matter how you'd like to."

She raised streaming eyes to meet his concerned gaze. "Tell me the truth, Matt. Do you think there's any point in this? Do you think there's the faintest chance Dad is alive up here?"

She saw him struggling, wanting to reassure her, wanting to tell her there was hope. But she saw the truth in his eyes before he reluctantly shook his head.

"No. I'm sorry, honey. I don't think there is."

"Then…then why are we doing this? Why did you go to all this trouble with the horses and everything when you knew…you knew all along…" Her voice rose almost to a shriek, and she felt unreasonably angry with him.

"Tania, don't. Come down, come here, let me hold you."

Matt threw himself off Blaze. "Don't you understand that this is the only way I can think of to be alone with you? This is the only chance I have to talk with you, hold you, make love with you. Goddamn it, Tania, I need this time." He reached up, and his strong hands all but lifted her from Sultan's back.

Tania slid down into his arms, bitterly aware that it wasn't only her hopes for her father she was crying about. She needed this time, too, because there was an end coming between her and Matt. She had to face that. There were only a few days left of this trip, and after that, what?

Gaby's vengeful young face formed before her. Making a life with Matt meant making a life with Gaby, as well, and that was as impossible as finding her father alive.

His arms closed around her, and his lips clamped down on hers. She could taste the salt of her own tears on his lips, but after a while the reasons for them fled, and all she could think of was how much she wanted him to love her.

CHAPTER ELEVEN

GABY SAW THE WAY her father refilled Tania's coffee cup, the way he looked at her when he thought no one was watching.

They'd been in camp nine days now, and Gaby had spent the past three here in camp with Benny. If it weren't for Tania, she knew her dad would have given in by now and let her go with them in the morning. He just wanted her out of the way, that was all.

It tore at her, the way her father looked at Tania. It made Gaby feel as if an icy lump were lodged in her chest. It made her feel panicky and terrified, the way she'd felt during the single endless night she'd spent on the street in Toronto, after she'd left her mother and Neil's apartment. The night she'd phoned her father.

She was sitting beside Scott. He was wolfing down a second piece of chocolate cake. Gaby hadn't finished her first, but she couldn't choke down any more food.

"Want to go for a walk?" She pitched her voice low so that only Scott would hear. He finished the mouthful of cake and gave her an imperceptible nod.

"Meet you by the river, where the boats are. I'll go now. You wait a few minutes."

Andrew left the table at that moment, and Gaby got up and slipped out the door right after him. No one seemed to notice, especially not her father. He was laughing and talking to Harry.

It was nine at night, windy and sort of wild, almost dark. Most nights there was still plenty of light at this time, but this afternoon the sky had clouded over, huge black clouds like bruises forming and rolling overhead. The wind had come up, and there had been thunder, but that was a while ago.

"Smells like rain," Benny had told her that afternoon, standing in the door of the cookshack and sniffing at the air like some kind of hound dog. "My joints are aching. There'll be a storm."

Gaby gave a half smile, thinking of Benny as she ran quickly down the path toward the river.

She'd have gone screaming nuts the past couple of days if it hadn't been for Benny. Funny how your feelings about somebody could change. She'd hated Benny and been more than a little scared of him at first, but she wasn't now. He wasn't her friend, exactly, but at least he didn't scare her anymore. She'd even come to like him in a funny sort of way.

After that first day alone with him, it'd been lots easier to get him talking. She got a kick out of the way Benny talked, in that deep, slow voice without moving his mouth a lot, as if his words were coming from his chest instead of his throat. He used funny words, and he went on and on about the birds and trees and wild game once you got him going. He knew Indian legends, too.

He'd told her just today how the Skeena River got its name. "A giant was tiptoeing from mountaintop to mountaintop, gathering water in a birchbark container. He dipped his fingers in and sprinkled droplets of rain like the sower of seeds. At one point, he bumped his elbow on a cloud and tipped the container. That stream of water gave birth to the Skeena. The name means 'water of the clouds.'"

He'd only gone to school for three years in his whole life. Then his mother had died, leaving his dad with a new baby, two other little boys and Benny. He'd had a rough life. His father had beaten him, but Benny didn't seem to think it was so bad.

"He only ever hit us when he was drinking, and we'd go to my grandmother's place then. He worked hard, took pretty good care of us," he'd told her.

It was weird, but she could talk to Benny. She'd even told him about Neil and why she had to leave her mom's house.

He'd given her that glowering look of his and then said, "Some men aren't men at all. Wild things never act the way these men do. But no good comes from dwelling on such things. They make you sorry for yourself, you lose pride. Better you should start looking inside instead of blaming everybody else. My grandmother used to say a man has to find himself before he can go forward in strength." He'd stared at her somberly. "You have much finding to do. You still blame your father, when it isn't his fault."

Now, waiting for Scott, Gaby thought about what Benny had said. It was her dad's fault, though. Whenever things had gotten bad with her mom, she'd dreamed of him coming and taking her away with him, not letting bad things happen to her ever again.

But he hadn't come on his own. She'd had to phone and beg him to take her, and even though he acted as if it were okay, she knew he really didn't want her around any more than her mother had. All either of them cared about was getting it on with somebody.

Neil.

Tania.

Bitterness and anger made her stomach feel sick again.

She ran down by the wharf and sat on a stump, looking out across the Skeena. The wildness of the wind and water sparked an answering wildness in her, a feeling she had sometimes that she was out of control.

"Hey, isn't it neat out here?" Scott was puffing a bit. "The sky's almost black over there, look." He reached for her hand and pulled her to her feet. "C'mon, let's go for a walk along the river like you said."

Gaby hadn't been alone with Scott much. Despite the boys' fight, Mario was usually with them, and the three of them hung out together in the evenings. She enjoyed it when Mario was there, because she felt safe with both of them, and it was fun to tease and have them scramble for her attention.

This was great, though, kind of romantic, wandering along the riverbank with the wind tearing at her hair. Scott was exciting; he seemed more mature than Mario, more of a man. His arm was around her shoulders now, and he felt big and reassuring, especially when they saw lightning fork across the sky and there was a far-off roll of thunder.

"This is where I take a bath each day. The water's just like ice." They'd reached the place where the willows grew thick and the water formed a backwater pool.

"Oh, yeah?" Scott bent over and stuck his hand in. "Come on, it's not cold at all. What'ya say we take a little dip right now?" He was grinning at her, a challenging grin, and he started unbuttoning his shirt.

"After you," she said with a giggle. Gaby wasn't sure how far he'd go, whether he'd actually take off all his clothes and go skinny-dipping or not. She couldn't tell with Scott, that was the thing about him. She never knew exactly what he was going to do.

The wildness spun inside of her, like a tunnel drawing her in.

His shirt landed on the ground, and his fingers started undoing his belt buckle.

The out-of-control feeling grew, and she laughed a little shrilly.

"C'mon Gaby. I dare you."

She laughed again and pulled off the heavy sweatshirt she had on over her blouse, then bent to untie her shoes. She'd trick him, get him to take most of his clothes off and then shove him in. He'd see how warm the water was, all right.

But his arms reached down and snared her, pulling her up and drawing her close to him. He started to fumble with the buttons on her blouse, his breathing loud and hard, his grin gone.

"Forget your shoes, let's get this off first. C'mon, baby, you're game, aren't you?" He was panting, as if he'd been running, and she laughed again, a little shaky this time, and shoved at him with both hands.

"Hey, Scott, c'mon, cut it out."

But now his mouth came down on hers, open and wet, and he stood with his legs apart and pulled her tight against his body. She'd fantasized about kissing him, but it was way different than this. His tongue was in her mouth, halfway down her throat, and she felt as if she were choking.

His arms were like ropes, trapping her, and his mouth seemed to envelop hers. She was squashed against his bare chest, and she could feel the hard, arrogant swelling of his man's body against her abdomen. It scared her. She tried to pull away and couldn't.

"Scott, let—let me go!"

"C'mon, Gaby." His voice was thick, his lips all over

her face. "You want it as much as I do. You been teasing all the time, giving me the come-on."

"No, I...I haven't...ever done this. I...Scott, let...me...go...please...."

Her hands pummeled his chest, and the raw fear in her voice must have penetrated, because his hold loosened a bit, and he frowned down at her. He was about to say something when a hand landed on his shoulder, pulling him back and away, and Mario's fist connected squarely with his nose. Scott howled and droplets of blood exploded over all three of them.

"You get away from her! I watched you sneak away down here...." Mario was shouting at the top of his lungs and throwing wild punches at Scott.

Scott was holding his nose with one hand, moaning and trying to fend Mario off. Gaby staggered backward, off balance, and Mario hit Scott again, catching him on the shoulder this time. Scott cried out and fell to one knee, but in an instant he was on his feet again, fists doubled, blood pouring from his nose.

"C'mon, you creep. C'mon, tough guy, sneaking up on me...."

In a moment, the boys were tangled in a mass of wildly flying fists, and Gaby moved still farther back, afraid of being hit.

"Stop, both of you, stop! We're all going to get in trouble again if you..." Her panicky voice seemed to blow away with the wind, and the boys paid her no attention.

"What the hell is going on here?"

Gaby whirled around. Her father was leaping down the incline toward them. He grabbed Mario by the back of his shirt and Scott by the hair, holding them apart and shaking them like rag dolls.

"Haven't...you two...learned...better yet? Now what the hell is this all about?"

The boys stopped flailing and stood, heads down, gasping for breath. Scott kept rubbing the back of his hand across his nose, smearing blood over his cheek and down his bare chest. His belt hung loose, the buckle not fastened.

Gaby saw her father's eyes rake over Scott, then flick to her. Her blouse was open all the way down the front. She wasn't wearing a bra.

"Get your clothes on." Disgust was plain on his face.

She fumbled with her blouse, trying to fasten the buttons Scott had undone, but her fingers wouldn't work right. She was shaking. She moved quickly to pick up her sweatshirt from the ground and pulled it over her head, tugging it down.

"Gabriella, I'm ashamed of you. You act like a little tramp. I can't let you out of my sight without you causing trouble." His words were like blows, cold and hard, and she flinched as they fell on her.

"I watched you sneak out of the cookhouse with Scott right behind you. I saw Mario follow you both. I don't blame the boys for this, young lady. I blame you. You've been playing games since the beginning with these two, and much as I'd like to wallop both of them, this is your doing, not theirs."

"But—but, Daddy, Scott was...I didn't..."

Scott shot her a dirty look and she shut up.

"Didn't you expect one of them to call your bluff? You've been playing dangerous games. I tried to tell you that, but you won't listen to a damn thing, will you? What did you expect would happen, teasing these two idiots the way you've been doing?"

She felt utterly humiliated. Both Scott and Mario were

glaring at her now, as if the whole thing really were her fault.

"But, Daddy, I didn't…"

He shook a finger at her. "That's enough. Not another word out of you." He gave each of the boys a solid shove, sending them staggering toward the path.

"You two get up there and clean yourselves up. If there's one more sign of fighting between you, you'll both take me on, one at a time. Understood?"

They hurried away, and he rounded on Gaby again. "I'm at my wit's end with you. I know your mother didn't talk to you about being sexually provocative—she thinks that's the way women should act—but didn't she teach you a damn thing about self-respect? You complained to me about Tania slapping you. Well, I'm telling you, that's exactly what I feel like doing right now."

"Don't you dare say things about my…my mother!" She was shrieking at him, out of control. "I shouldn't ever have come here. I hate it here. I hate you!"

The confusion of feelings inside her exploded into panic. She had to get away from him, from all of them.

"Gabriella…." He reached out to her, but she twisted out of his grasp, turned and started running up the path. She could see Mario and Scott some distance ahead, and she didn't want to be anywhere near them. She veered away, running parallel to the river.

"Gaby!" Her father's voice was full of anger. "Gaby, you come back, do you hear me?"

She had to get away.

There were drops of rain now on her face. Ahead was the dock and the boats. She pelted down the incline, no longer able to think. The agony of feeling filled her to bursting.

She leaped into one of the float boats and heard her

father's running footsteps not far behind. With fumbling fingers she undid the rope that held the boat to the dock, and as she gave it one strong push it rocked precariously and then seemed to develop a mind of its own. It began to move, slowly at first, but it quickly gathered speed as it caught in the current and sailed faster and faster away from the shore.

Panting, her chest heaving, she turned and looked back. Her father was standing on the end of the dock, hands curled into fists, shouting, "Gaby! Gaby!"

In a moment, the noise of the river and the rising wind drowned out the sound of his voice, and she was alone on the water. The boat was swinging dangerously from one side to the other, and she groped for the oars. One was already in the oarlock, but the other lay on the bottom of the boat. It was heavy; she had to use both hands even to lift it, and getting it into the oarlock began to seem an impossible task.

It was getting much darker, and the thunder that had sounded far away before seemed to be coming closer.

She tried to slide the heavy oar into place and failed. She heaved it up and tried again. This time, she dropped the end clumsily into the water. With a wrench that made her feel as if her arms were being torn from their sockets, the current caught the oar and whipped it out of her grasp.

Gaby lunged for it, and the boat tipped crazily. She cried out with fear, aware of how near she'd been to falling overboard. She jerked back, throwing herself to the bottom of the boat, heart thumping.

MATT WATCHED in horrified disbelief as the boat with his daughter in it went hurtling off down the river. Utter panic engulfed him, and he felt paralyzed, as if he couldn't breathe or even move.

His baby, his little girl.

She'd drown, he was sure of it. She'd never managed one of the boats on her own. The river was high and the current strong; it was growing darker every minute. There was a storm coming, maybe a bad one. He fought down the panic, gulping in deep breaths of air, forcing himself to function, to think.

On leaden legs he raced back toward the camp and burst into the cookshack, startling Benny, who was standing at the sink, washing dishes. Except for him, the long room was deserted. The others were probably in the bunkhouses.

A glass tumbled from Benny's hands and shattered on the floor. Both men ignored it.

"Benny, there's bad trouble. Gaby's run off. She's gone downriver in one of the floats. I'm going after her with the jet boat...if I can get the bloody thing started. There's something wrong with the motor again. If I can't, there's nothing for it but to take the other float and hope like hell I can catch her."

Benny was already in action, throwing fruit and muffins and beef jerky into a lunch pack and thrusting it at Matt. "Take this along. How you figure on getting back here if you take the drifter? Might end up miles downstream."

"Walk back, I guess." He turned to bolt out the door. "Tell the others what's going on. And Benny, you're in charge here until I get back."

Benny shoved a flashlight at him. "Don't worry over this crew, they'll be fine," he growled.

Matt was already tearing across the meadow. He heard Benny call after him, "You got matches in the boat?"

Matt waved an arm, not stopping to answer. Both floaters and the jet boat had emergency supplies, waterproof matches and aluminum blankets. He'd never had to use them.

Within seconds, he was in the jet boat. The key was on the ring attached to his jeans. Using the flashlight, he checked the fluid levels and then, muttering a prayer, he shoved the key into the ignition and turned it.

A low grinding noise and then nothing.

He tried again with the same result, and then again and again, cursing under his breath, struggling to keep the rising fear at bay.

A jagged flash of lightning danced across the inky sky, and thunder rolled to the east.

Matt tried one last time. This time there was no response whatsoever. He'd have to take the other drift boat, and without power, he knew his chances of catching Gaby were almost nil. With a feeling that bordered on hopelessness, he grabbed the pack Benny had given him, jumped to the dock and then into the Fiberglas vessel, undoing the rope that held it and guiding it into the current with the oars.

Downriver, where Gaby had gone, there was almost total darkness. The wind was growing wilder, whipping the trees along the shore into a frenzy. As the boat gathered speed, he glanced back along the shoreline to the camp. There was a light in the cabin window, and for a moment Tania's face was clear in his mind.

Then he turned and faced the river, settled the oars in place and urged the lightweight craft onward as fast as he could.

GABY SOON ABANDONED any effort at guiding the boat with the single oar left to her. She crouched in the bottom and her whole body trembled as the boat seemed to go faster and faster, yawing wildly, catching here and there

on a log or a rock and half spinning around before it
dragged itself free again.

"God, please, help me! I'm sorry, help me...." She
repeated the desperate prayer over and over as she sped
and bumped and rocked along, helplessly aware that with
each passing moment she was getting farther and farther
away from the camp, away from her father, away from
any chance of rescue.

If the boat didn't capsize, where would she end up?
Could she keep on flying along like this all night? She'd
never thought to ask much about the river, where it came
out; she'd just totally relied on her father to know those
things and take care of her.

She huddled in the bottom of the boat, clinging to the
seat, hunching even further when lightning flashed, lighting up the sky behind her and sending eerie jagged ar-
rows across the horizon.

Her teeth chattered and her throat was so dry she
couldn't swallow. She was much too frightened even to
cry.

Would the boat hit something and turn over? She heard
her father's voice telling the fishermen how stable and
safe these floaters were. "It's almost impossible to over-
turn them," he'd said. Gaby prayed that he was right.

A light rain had started sometime before, but now there
came a boom of thunder so loud Gaby cried out with
fear. It rumbled on and on, and a few moments later the
next flash of lightning came bluish white and ferocious,
leaping from here to there, seeming to connect at times
with the river.

Gaby's heart pounded in her chest and her breath came
shallow and fast. On the heels of the lightning came a
brief downpour that soaked her to the skin. Wind was
buffeting the boat in gusts, and the current seemed faster

than before. She squinted ahead, trying to see, but it was hopeless.

Her entire body trembled with a combination of utter terror and cold. She scrambled to the front of the vessel, remembering the cubbyhole she'd noticed when she was looking at the boats the other day with Mario and Scott. There'd been a packaged aluminum blanket there, along with matches and a first aid kit.

She found the blanket, tore the package open with her teeth and unfolded the crackling aluminum, holding on tightly in case the wind caught it. With it wrapped around her, she at least felt warmer.

She was probably going to die out here, though, blanket or no blanket, and for the first time, she wasn't entirely certain she had her usual list of people to blame for what was happening to her. She tried for a while, doing her best to convince herself that it was Scott's fault, her father's, Tania's, even her mother's that she was here, hurtling blindly down a river in a stormy northern wilderness.

It *was* their fault, she told herself savagely. If her mother, or her dad, or Tania had…hadn't…would have…

For the first time, it didn't work.

There was a bottom line her basic honesty wouldn't allow her to cross, but still she struggled against admitting that she had only herself to blame. If she accepted responsibility for this, she'd have to take a long hard look at herself, wouldn't she? Like Benny had said she should do.

She didn't want to. It would hurt too much. She concentrated instead on how cold she was, how frightened, how exhausted, how hungry. When that didn't work, she tried to tell herself that nobody really loved her, anyway, that nobody would be sorry if she was never found, but that didn't work, either.

She knew her father loved her. That's why she'd dared act the way she had, because she knew, deep in her soul, that her dad's love would withstand anything. Her mother? She felt the familiar anger flicker. Her mother cared more about men than she did about Gaby.

But what about her? What about Gabriella Radburn? Didn't she enjoy flirting with guys, a little bit like her mother had always done?

What about Scott? her conscience taunted. What about Mario? Was she really just like her mother, after all, as her father had hinted? She didn't want to be. She wouldn't be. She didn't want to have to think anymore.

At last, she simply curled herself into a ball and hugged her legs with both arms, pulling the noisy, crackling blanket over her head to mask the darkness and the terrifying sounds all around her. She was more frightened and miserable than she'd ever been in her entire life, and there was no way to judge how much time had passed. It seemed like an eternity.

In spite of her misery, she must have dozed off with her head propped on the seat, because when the boat collided with the logjam, she couldn't think for a moment where she was or what was happening to her. She was wet and stiff and cold, and she cried out with terror when the grating, grinding sound exploded into her consciousness. She scrambled to her knees and quickly remembered where she was. She unwrapped the aluminum cover, carefully balling it up and shoving it back in the cubbyhole.

The boat was still out in the river. Gaby couldn't see either shore in the darkness, only wild, rushing water on either side of her. The boat was rocking in a terrifying manner, and it was broadside to the current, forced into that position by a tangle of roots and logs and branches that towered high over her head. Just then the vessel gave a sickening sideways lunge and water poured in, covering Gaby's feet. Unless she managed to get around the log-jam and into the current again, she was going to capsize!

The oar. Maybe she could... She lifted it, clinging to it hard, remembering how easily the water had taken the other from her.

She shoved as hard as she could against the twisted mass of roots and wood and nearly overturned the boat in the process. Shaking uncontrollably, she dropped the oar on the floor and crouched in the icy, sloshing water for a long time, trying to curb her panic and think what to do.

The boat bobbed with the force of the current and more water poured in. She had to get loose if she wanted to live.

She lifted the oar again, and this time she shoved more cautiously against the slippery logs. The boat slid along sideways, dangerously tilted to one side, and a sudden lurch almost threw her overboard. Gaby screamed and clung to the oar and shoved again.

Suddenly she was free. The floater shot around the corner of the jam and in another second was once again bobbing along, nose into the current. Gaby put the oar down carefully and sank onto the seat, panting, trembling, feeling her heart hammer as if it were about to burst out of her chest. She'd done it. She turned and looked back.

It was a little lighter than it had been. She could make out the huge, twisted shape of the logjam, and she realized that there was a bend in the river right there, that she'd turned a sort of corner.

The boat was closer to shore than before, but it was the opposite shore from the one she'd started out on. If she could somehow use the single oar to maneuver the boat even closer...

She hefted the oar again, gingerly trying it this way and that in the water, making sure first that it was securely locked in the holder.

After several attempts she found a clumsy and uncertain way to guide the boat closer and still closer to the dark and overgrown shoreline.

There was another slight bend ahead, and she dug the oar deep just before she reached it. The boat shot in a crooked line toward shore, catching suddenly on a sandbar and grating to a stop with a suddenness that sent her jolting forward. Her head hit the seat, and for several seconds she stayed where she was, head throbbing.

When the pain eased, Gaby climbed stiffly out, finding herself up to her knees in icy water. Her first impulse was to make for dry land and abandon the boat, but the past few hours had bred caution.

She might need the boat to get...where? Not back upriver, that was impossible. But what if there were bears or cougars in the dark bush? She shuddered, trying to make out the sinister shapes not far away.

The boat would at least allow her a means of escape.

She grabbed the lead line and tugged as hard as she could, slipping and falling to one knee, pulling the vessel higher on the sand, grateful that it was light and relatively easy to move. There wasn't a tree close enough to tie it to, but she rolled a large rock onto the coiled rope, hoping it would hold. Then she climbed back in and retrieved her blanket and hesitantly made her way farther up the sandbar, farther away from the river.

The bush along the shoreline was dark and menacing.

It was like a black wall in front of her. She didn't want to get any closer than she already was.

There was a huge log just at the edge of the sand, and she collapsed beside it. She struggled with her sodden shoes and finally got them off. She took off her soaked sweatshirt, as well, spreading it on the log. Then she wrapped the folds of aluminum around and around herself, and after a long time she stopped shivering.

She listened to every creak, every strange and scary sound from the woods close behind her, trying to figure out what they were over the noise of the river. But at last weariness overcame fear, and she slid into an uneasy sleep, waking over and over again at some change in the wind, some new frightening sound from the forest.

When the darkness slowly grew less dense and she could begin to see across the river and along the shore, she relaxed. It was almost daylight, and she'd lived through the night. She curled herself flat on the sand and fell deeply asleep.

The warm sun shining on her face and the sound of countless birds singing woke her. She sat up and rubbed her bleary eyes. Her jeans had dried on her, and she felt stiff and sore. Her sweatshirt was almost dry, and she tugged it on.

She'd been having a dream. It was almost as if her father was close by.

"Come and get me, Dad, please...."

But it wasn't that easy. This time it wasn't the same as reversing the charges on a telephone, picking up the money and plane tickets he'd wired to her. If she wanted him to find her now, she had to make much more of an effort.

She'd build a fire. He'd notice the smoke.

There were matches in the boat, part of the emergency supplies. She struggled to her feet and started collecting twigs.

been there huddled together in a corner, deep in conversation.

The four men were in the bunk house now, and Tania assumed they were asleep. They'd been up all the early hours of the night—as had she—waiting for Matt to return with news about Gaby. At length, just about 4:00 a.m., Benny had ordered them all off to bed.

"You'll have to grab the horses and ride them into the...

CHAPTER TWELVE

THROUGH THE WINDOW of the cookshack Tania watched the dawn break. Benny had brewed a pot of fresh coffee half an hour before, and the two of them sat face-to-face across one of the wooden tables, holding the mugs between their palms. The hot, yeasty smell of baking bread filled the room, but it didn't help the sickness in the pit of Tania's stomach.

Mario was down at the corral, saddling his horse. He'd insisted that as soon as it was light enough, he'd ride downstream, looking for Matt and Gaby. Scott had said he was going with him, and Mario, to everyone's surprise, had simply looked at the other boy and nodded agreement.

"You gotta saddle your own horse. I'm not doing it for you," Mario had warned in a surly tone, and it was Scott's turn to nod.

There was blood on the front of Scott's shirt, and his nose was swollen all over again. When his father had asked him about it, he mumbled something about walking into a tree.

Jim took one look at the expression on his son's face and didn't pursue the matter.

Tania was positive the boys had been fighting again, but at least this time they seemed to have resolved their differences. Several times during the long night she'd seen them huddled together in a corner, deep in conversation.

The four men were in the bunkhouse now, and Tania assumed they were asleep. They'd been up until the early hours of the morning just as she had, waiting for Matt to return with Gaby. It was a fruitless vigil, and about 3:00 a.m., Benny had ordered them all off to bed.

"Might have to saddle the horses and ride back into Terrace, get some help up here, so get to bed while you have the chance," he'd told them.

Tania had started back reluctantly with the others, dreading the isolation of her small cabin, the empty bed next to her a reminder that Gaby was somewhere out on that wild river in a small boat. But there'd been nowhere else to go once she left the cookshack. It was still storming outside; she couldn't walk around in that. And there was no possibility of sleep. Since Benny had banged the dinner gong late last evening, bringing them all running, she'd felt as if she were moving in slow motion through a nightmare.

"You figure you can rest, missus?" Benny's question amazed her. It was probably the first time he'd ever addressed her directly.

She recovered quickly and shook her head. "No, I'm sure I can't."

"Humph." He turned away from her, rattling the lids on the stove, shoving in more wood, not looking at her. "Times like this, I cook. Takes my mind off things. I guess if you want to, you can stay here and wash up dishes." His voice was gruff, the words belligerent, but Tania could have hugged him for it.

"Thanks, Benny." She gathered up the coffee cups and plates and poured hot water and soap into the dish basin. It was comforting to wash and rinse and dry, mindless busy work that kept her from going mad with worry over Matt and Gaby.

The storm raged on outside, but in the cookhouse Benny hauled out flour and yeast and mixing pans and set to making bread. It was while he was viciously punching the floury dough that he suddenly said in a disgusted tone, "That girl of Matt's, she's got a chip on her shoulder."

Tania only nodded, not trusting herself to discuss Gaby without saying something harsh about her. Gaby had been foremost in her thoughts all night, and Tania found herself alternately raging internally at the foolish young woman and praying that Matt had found her and that she was unhurt. That they were both unhurt. Tania could hardly bear to think of anyone out in the storm that had been raging for hours, least of all Matt.

At first, after Benny had told them what happened, the men had all been hearty and reassuring, outwardly certain that even without the jet boat, Matt would easily overtake Gaby and that they'd both be holed up in some protected place by now, waiting out the weather and the darkness.

Matt knew the river like the back of his hand, they told each other, he was expert at controlling the floater.

But it had grown later, and they could all hear the roaring madness of the Skeena as the storm grew ever more ferocious. In every mind was a mental picture of two flimsy shells trying to stay afloat in its raging torrent.

After a while, they avoided one another's eyes and stopped making predictions. Benny hauled out a battered mouth organ and played old tunes none of them had ever heard before, and the haunting melodies blended with the wild music of the river. But after the first few hours, Benny put the mouth organ away, and no one could think of anything to say.

That was when Benny had ordered everyone to bed.

Now, in the first grayness of dawn, the only sign of the storm was water dripping from the eaves of the cook-shack. The world was drenched.

Tania and Benny had worked through the small morning hours in a companionable silence, he mixing and baking dozens of muffins, a slab of coffee cake and six loaves of bread while she dutifully washed the pots and pans and bowls he used, scrubbing the wooden counters and wiping down cupboards as she went. Now the kitchen was tidy and spanking clean, and Tania sipped her coffee, knowing it was only adding to the acid sickness in her stomach but needing the warmth it provided.

Benny got up to check the bread baking in the oven, rearranged the loaves and shut the oven door again. "Not done yet." He poured more coffee for them both and then blurted out, "I told that girl I'd show her how to make bread today."

Tania was flabbergasted. She'd been touched at Benny's clumsy efforts at helping her survive the night, but she'd never in her wildest dreams imagined there might have been any friendly contact between Benny and Gaby. She remembered in vivid detail trying to convince Gaby to be even marginally polite to the crotchety old cook and Gaby's scornful reaction. Yet here was Benny, telling her that he and Gaby had formed some sort of relationship during the days they'd spent in each other's company, while Tania's best and most sincere efforts at befriending Matt's daughter had failed dismally.

She felt a sudden surge of rage and resentment, and she set the blue enameled mug down on the table with a bang that sloshed coffee over the rim. Benny scowled at her, but she ignored him.

"I don't even want to think about her," she choked

out. "Gaby is one of the most selfish, thoughtless people I've ever come across." The angry, judgmental words boiled out of her. She'd been holding them back for days, and now she couldn't stop them. "I don't know exactly what happened last night, but I know Gaby well enough to guess that it's something she engineered to get attention. She's spoiled and totally self-centered, and now through her thoughtlessness, Matt might be—" Her voice broke on the last sentence, and she gulped in air.

"Bull. Matt knows the bush, and he can take care of himself. He'll be back. But that girl, she knows nothing about the bush or the river, either." Benny leveled a harsh look at her. "People say don't judge unless you walk a mile in another's moccasins. Gaby has had tough times. That mother of hers, well..." He screwed up his face in disgust. "What kind of woman won't listen when her own daughter tells her some boyfriend is getting funny with her?"

Tania was speechless as the meaning behind Benny's words sunk into her brain. Obviously, Gaby had revealed far more of herself to Benny than she had even to her father. Tania was sure Matt didn't know anything about this.

"Are you saying... Do you mean that some man might have assaulted Gaby?"

Benny nodded. "That's what I'm saying. She told me so."

Was Gaby telling the truth? The girl was devious, Tania knew that. Still, Tania remembered her sobbing in the night and Gaby telling her she wished her mother was dead....

It was the truth.

It hit Tania like a blow to the chest, and she sank back in her chair. She'd told herself that Gaby needed discipline, guidance, a firm hand. The truth was, Matt's daughter had serious psychological problems, and what had Tania done to help?

She cringed at the memory.

She'd slapped Gaby across the face. She'd lectured her without making any effort to understand why Gaby was acting the way she was. She'd defended her own actions by saying she knew nothing about teenagers. But Gaby wasn't just a teenager, she was a human being, a young woman.

Surely Tania could have approached the girl differently, could have tried harder to remember how much it hurt having your father's interests center around someone else when you needed him to love only you.

Tania knew how that felt. Hadn't she been sick with jealousy over her brother's close relationship with their father when she was about Gaby's age? In fact, she could remember vividly how she'd cried herself to sleep each time Doc took Sam for the summer and she had to stay behind. She'd even told herself she hated Sam. She'd turned her anger on her brother instead of on her father, just as Gaby was doing with Tania.

Why hadn't she remembered that, even told Gaby about it?

God, Matt, I've failed you. You asked me to try with your daughter, and I didn't.

The door of the cookshack opened, and Scott stuck his head in. "Mario and I are going to ride along the path down the river now, if that's okay with you, Benny."

Benny sprang into action. "Hold on there. You gotta take lunch packs along with you. I'll put in plenty just in case you find them. Here, fill these." He thrust thermoses at Tania, and she filled them with coffee while Benny made lunches.

When Scott took the lunch packs and left, she followed him outside, shivering in the cool morning air. He looked battered and much older than his years this morning, and Tania hurried after him, gently taking hold of his arm, stopping him halfway across the meadow.

"Scott, could you tell me what really happened last night? Why did Gaby run away?" It was important for her to know. She'd been judging Gaby all along without really knowing the facts, and she didn't want to do that anymore. But it was unlikely this boy would tell her.

"Scott, whatever happened? I promise not to tell anyone else. Not your father, not Matt. It's just...well, it's between Gaby and me, I guess."

He looked at her for several long moments and his mouth trembled, then he said. "It wasn't Gaby's fault. It was all my fault, if that's what you want to know."

"Your fault?"

He nodded and his mouth twisted in pain. "Her dad blamed her, but it was really me. I...I came on to her, I acted like a real schmuck, and I feel bad about it. I'll tell Gaby that. If I get a chance. And I'll tell her dad, too."

Mario whistled from the corral.

"I gotta go." Scott hurried away.

"Good luck." Tania watched the boys ride out, thinking of what Scott had told her.

The early-morning sky was silver, streaked with patches of crimson cloud newly tipped by the rising sun. There was nothing more to do in the cookshack, so she headed slowly to her cabin. She needed to think, to go over the events of the past week and try to make sense of them.

She had plenty of time for thinking. In fact, there was nothing else to do, because although she lay down for a while, sleep was a million miles away. Instead, her brain went over and over the situation between herself and Gaby and Matt, and now that it was too late, she could see that there had been choices, other, better ways of dealing with Gaby, that she hadn't chosen to take.

And by alienating the girl, she'd destroyed any chance of a future with Matt.

She could have tried harder, for Matt, for Gaby, for herself. Just as now, when it was also too late, she could see things she ought to have done differently with Doc. She'd made a total mess of the relationships in her life.

She was convinced she'd never see her father again, but Matt and Gaby just had to be safe.

They had to be.

MILES DOWNRIVER, Matt watched the first faint blush of dawn gradually creep up the eastern horizon. He'd always loved early mornings, but this one brought only anguish.

He'd spent the night battling the river, peering fruitlessly into the darkness and calling Gaby's name until his throat was sore and he was hoarse. By the time the worst of the storm was over, he knew there wasn't any further chance of finding her. He'd reached a place where the Skeena broadened, becoming a small lake, wide and calm.

If she'd made it this far, he'd see her.

He'd steered his boat toward the bank, pulled it high out of the water and slumped down with his back against a huge fir tree, waiting for daylight, trying to figure out what to do next. Exhausted, he had tried not to give in to the utter misery in his soul.

Now the placid water shimmered deep pewter as the early dawn light grew stronger, and Matt could see no floater, no wet and bedraggled Gaby. There was only magnificent wilderness, the steady dripping of last night's deluge from the trees in the forest around him, and the morning song of the birds.

He must have passed her somehow in the dark and the storm. Maybe she'd made it to shore. That must be what had happened. The other awful alternative, the strong possibility that her boat had overturned and she'd drowned, kept creeping insidiously into his mind. Common sense told him that was the most logical answer, but his heart kept screaming no.

It was all he could do not to give in to despair.

He hadn't been able to make friends with his daughter, and that tore at his very soul. Looking back over the few weeks she'd been with him, it seemed that all he'd done was bawl her out for one thing and another.

Not that she hadn't deserved it; he couldn't pretend even now that she hadn't driven him half nuts. But there must have been more that he could have done, should have done, to try to understand her better.

He knew it was senseless, but he found himself bargaining with fate. *Let Gaby survive, and I'll learn to be not only her father but her friend. Just give her back to me, give me a second chance.*

I've spent years putting work ahead of everything else, building up my business, putting my personal life on hold. Now, I'm going to put love at the head of my list of priorities in life.

Not only Gaby was on that list. Tania was there, as well. So far, he'd avoided making any sort of commitment to Tania. Partly, it was because of Gaby. But other single parents fell in love, formed new relationships. Why should he be different? Gaby would adjust; he was positive she would.

There was more to it than just Gaby, though. He was

painfully aware of what he had to offer: a beat-up trailer home in an isolated part of northern B.C., a job that kept him off in the bush for weeks at a time from early May to late October; an uncertain and at times decidedly tight budget.

But surely it was up to Tania to decide whether or not she could put up with his life-style? He intended to give her the opportunity the moment he saw her again.

But what if… He battled with despair, forcing himself to remember a bookmark he'd seen the last time he was browsing in the bookstore. It had read You Can't Afford the Luxury of a Negative Thought. *So get on with it, Radburn, and stop crying into your bloody beer.*

He concentrated on his present predicament.

He was much too far downriver to consider hiking back. Benny would be sending searchers out at daybreak, so if Gaby was between Matt and the fish camp, chances were good that they'd find her long before Matt was able to walk back upriver. The most sensible thing for him to do was get back in the boat and ride the river until he reached a setttlement. Then he'd hitch a ride into Terrace and hire a helicopter.

He wasn't hungry, but he forced himself to eat some of Benny's lunch, and then he dragged the floater down to the water and jumped in, propelling it savagely across the small lake and back into the faster-flowing water.

Doc thought for a time that the wind was going to blow away his tarp and what was left of the damaged cabin roof, as well. He lay in his sleeping bag and worried over it, then finally got up, pulled his pants and mackinaw on and went outside to watch the storm.

It was spectacular, with bolts of lightning and huge rolling cracks of thunder. The wind made the trees creak, sweeping down the Skeena like a mad thing. There was also drenching rain, but Doc told himself he wasn't made of sugar. He wouldn't melt.

When it finally calmed, he dried off and went back to bed and slept.

The birds woke him, as they always did, just before dawn.

It was while he was getting an armload of wood to light the fire that he saw the smoke. It curled above the trees half a mile away along the riverbank. Whoever lit it was having a struggle with wet wood; he could tell by the color and thickness of the smoke. Fishermen, probably.

It had been weeks now since he'd seen a living soul. He decided he might as well go and have a look at whoever it was. He could easily keep hidden in the bush if he decided he didn't want to say hello. Or he could ask them back here for a cup of java.

It didn't take long to get there. During the past weeks, he'd worked out trails for himself all up and down the river. To his surprise, they led him to a bedraggled young girl who appeared to be alone. She was feverishly piling wet sticks on a smoky fire when he stepped out of the woods and walked over to her. She'd had a rough night, by the looks of her. He saw the aluminum blanket folded by the log, the float boat pulled up on the sandbar, the panic on her pale face.

He figured she was in trouble, all right. He just didn't expect her to scream bloody blue murder when she looked up and saw him staring at her. It was enough to give an old man another heart attack...except that his heart was probably as strong as it was ever going to get by now.

When she finished screaming, she started to cry, the way females did when they were scared and angry.

Doc had no handkerchief. He waited patiently until she calmed down a little and then he patted her shoulder in clumsy reassurance.

"What's your name?"

"Ga-Gabriella. Gaby. Radburn."

"Well, now Gaby, no need to be scared of an old codger like me. I'm just a fisherman. My name's Doc Wallace. I've got a little cabin back over there." He gestured with a hand. "We'll head up there if you feel like it, get some hot coffee and breakfast. Got some mush. No milk left, but there's honey. You want to tell me where you're from and how you got here all by yourself? That your boat down there?"

She had control of herself by now, and her big dark eyes were almost popping out of her head, staring at him.

"Doc Wallace? You're…you're Tania's father, aren't you? Tania's been looking for you everywhere. She…we all thought you were—" She bit off what she'd been about to say. "Anyway, she's up at the fishing camp." Her eyes grew even darker and her face got stiff looking. She looked away, back over her shoulder at the river. "My dad's fishing camp. Way back there somewhere, way up the river. I don't know how far, exactly."

He was able to hide the mixture of shock and elation caused by her words. Tania, his city slicker of a daughter, had actually come all the way up here looking for him. It sent a stab of pure pleasure shooting through him, followed quickly by anxiety.

She was gonna pressure him to go back to civilization with her, that was certain. Well, no law said he had to go. The weeks alone had given him confidence.

There'd be sparks flying, though, because he was staying where he was, at least for the time being. Come winter, he'd see. But that was a long time off, and he was having fun. Besides, he was stronger now; he was his own man again. He'd never again give his power away. No one should *ever* give their power away.

He realized the girl was staring at him again, waiting for him to do something, to take charge.

"So you know my daughter, do ya? Well, ain't that something. You want to tell me more about this fish camp of your daddy's while we head over to the cabin? We can have something to eat—ain't nothin' fancy—and after a while maybe we can figure out how to get you back up there—they'll likely be worrying about you. We'll just put this fire out first, and you can give me a hand dragging that boat farther up on shore. We'll have to ford the river. Maybe we can do it dry, thanks to this."

IT WAS ALMOST NINE that evening before Doc and Gaby finally reached the camp. The long northern day was fading as they broke from the trees into the meadow and started wearily across it, heading for the lantern shining in a window of the cookshack. It had been the longest walk of Gaby's life.

"Gaby?" It was Scott's voice. "Gaby, it *is* you, isn't it? Hey, you're back! Wow, everybody, Gaby's back! She's back, she's right here. Awwright!" Scott's excited whoop carried in the quiet evening, and people poured out of doorways.

Tania came hurrying out of her cabin, and when she saw the two figures, she stopped, one foot still on the step, unable to move, unable to breathe. One of them was Gaby, looking weary, dirty and sunburned. The other... the other was a tall, square-shouldered old man.

It was a dream, it had to be. But the lean figure was

coming straight toward her, and she knew that stride, the way he swung his arms....

"Dad...?" Her voice was barely louder than a whisper. "Dad, is it really you?"

He was only yards away now.

"Hello, there, Tania. How the hell are you, girl?"

She threw herself at him, laughing and crying all at once. He laughed, too, an embarrassed rumble she could feel against her body, and it took a few seconds before his arms came up and around her in a ferocious hug. She could count on one hand the number of times she'd ever hugged her father, and it felt good. It felt wonderful.

After a few minutes, she drew away with reluctance, aware of the others gathered around Gaby and her and Doc, everyone talking at once, asking questions and not waiting for answers.

"This is my father, Doc Wallace, everybody." She made introductions, and the fishermen all shook Doc's hand.

Gaby looked straight at Tania, her expression unreadable. "I found him, y'know. I found Doc," she said with a challenge in her tone. "He was on the other side of the river, miles and miles away. You and my dad would never have gone that far."

Tania's father laughed again, more of a chuckle this time. "T'was the other way around, wasn't it, young lady?" His voice was filled with humor. "Nearly broke my eardrums screaming away when you first saw me. Thought I was a ghost, I reckon."

Tania couldn't stop looking at him, amazed at how relaxed, how good-natured he was. How...different.

He smiled a lot. It astonished her. Had he smiled at all the last few years in Vancouver? He was tanned a deep walnut, which made his white hair dramatic. He'd lost weight, but it was a good loss. He looked lean and fit and ten years younger than the last time she'd seen him.

Benny had been standing in the doorway of the cook-shack, watching the scene from a distance. Now he marched over to them, dusting his palms up and down his dirty apron, obviously deciding that someone ought to take charge. He held out a hand to Doc.

"Benny Benson, how do you do? I'm the cook."

"Doc Wallace, how d'ya do?"

They shook hands with solemn dignity, taking each other's measure.

But at that moment, Gaby flung her arms around Benny's waist and hung on. "Oh Benny, hiya! It's so good to see you. Oh, Benny, I was scared. I thought the boat was going to dump over. I thought I'd never see any of you again."

The old cook looked as if he might be about to have a stroke. He held his arms out from his shoulders, obviously not daring to touch the girl hanging on to him like a limpet. His dark skin turned brick red, and his mouth worked but no words came out. He stood like a wooden statue until Gaby unwrapped her arms and stepped back.

"Where's my dad, Benny? I need to talk to him. Where is he? Is he down at the corral?"

The group became quiet and tense all of a sudden.

Benny wiped his hands down his apron again and cleared his throat. "Well, miss, Matt took the other float boat and went off right after you. We haven't seen hide nor hair of him since." His tone was gentle, for Benny, but Gaby flinched as if he'd struck her.

"He came after me? But I...I didn't see him. How come I didn't see him on the river? And Doc and I didn't see him today, either, and we crossed the river and then walked all the way back here. We would have seen the boat, wouldn't we? We should have seen him.''

No one answered her, because no one knew what to say.

''Well, where—where do you think he is, Benny?'' There was desperation in the plea, and Benny's face drew into a formidable frown.

Tania grew tense, thinking the brusque old man was about to blast Gaby, but when he spoke, his voice was almost gentle.

''Don't know, miss. Maybe he passed you in the dark, went on downriver. He's likely hiking back right this minute.''

''But he's…he's been gone all night, hasn't he, and all day, too? Like me? He's had time to get back by now, for sure.'' Gaby's voice quavered, and tears began trickling down her sunburned cheeks. ''Do—do you think my dad's…drown—'' She couldn't finish the sentence. Her face crumpled, her mouth opened wide, and like a much younger child, she began to wail out loud.

CHAPTER THIRTEEN

TANIA STEPPED TOWARD GABY and hesitantly put a hand on the girl's shoulder.

"Gaby, don't cry. I'm sure he's all right. You know—we all do—that your dad's one of the best guides around. Look, it's getting dark, and the bugs are out in force. Come on in. I'll bet you're hungry. Benny's got enough food cooked to feed an army. He made spaghetti and meatballs and garlic bread."

Gaby stiffened at Tania's touch, but she didn't pull away. She allowed herself to be led into the cookshack. The others straggled in behind the women, and Benny bustled into command, relieved to be on familiar ground again. He busily issued orders, setting out food, filling coffee cups.

Doc sat on one side of a table, Gaby and Tania on the other. Gaby's tears were under control, but she was subdued, playing with her food instead of eating. She looked as if she was about to start crying again at any moment, and Tania knew the girl was thinking of her father.

"Gaby, tell me how you and Doc managed to find each other," Tania asked, hoping to distract her.

But Gaby shook her head. "Doc can tell you. I need to go lie down for a while. Excuse me, please." She got to her feet, but when Tania offered to go with her, Gaby refused. "I'd rather be by myself. I don't feel so good."

"Why not let me…" Tania began, but Doc caught her eye and shook his head.

When Gaby was gone, he said, "Leave the girl be, Tania. Best thing for her is sleep. She had a bad night of it from what she tells me, tearing down the Skeena in a little Fiberglas boat, and today we must have walked over twenty miles. Never complained once, either. She's a real plucky little gal, that one. Now she's in a dither over her father. Best let her work it out on her own."

Doc related the story Gaby had told him about her wild ride down the river, about losing the oar and getting stuck in the logjam. "Took a lot of guts for her to do what she did."

For an instant, Tania felt jealous of Gaby, of the praise Doc was lavishing on her. If only once, just once, he'd spoken about her, his own daughter, in those admiring terms. It would have meant so much to her. And then she caught herself up short, ashamed, realizing the harm jealousy had already caused between her and Doc, between her and Gaby.

She had to try to forge a new bond with her father instead of strengthening the old, bad habits. But Matt was foremost in her thoughts, and try as she might, she couldn't help but feel angry and resentful toward Gaby for the trouble she'd caused him.

Was Matt really safe? All day she'd tried her best to believe he was, but the longer he was gone, the harder it became to believe. She decided the best thing to do was talk about something other than Gaby.

"Tell me about this place where you were camping, Doc."

Why did his face and voice become guarded when she was only trying to have a conversation? Her heart sank. Why was it always so hard with him?

"Well, it's a nice spot, close by the river but not too close, sort of in a glen. There's a fair decent cabin and an outhouse. Porcupines chewed away some of it, but it's usable.'' His expression changed, becoming melancholy. "I used to bring Sam up there once in a while, y'know. We had some fine times on the Skeena, him and I. The cabin was in better repair back then, though. I've done some fixing up on it. Main thing it needs is a new roof.''

"Well, maybe you could come up again next year and—''

His steady gaze stopped her, and he shook his head. "You figuring on me coming back with you to Vancouver, Tania? 'Cause I'm sorry, but I don't reckon that's what I'm doing. I'm gonna stay put a while. The fish are bitin' good.''

She swallowed hard, caught off guard. Of course she'd thought that he'd come back with her. It hadn't crossed her mind that he'd do anything else.

"But, Doc, all your things are at the lodge. It was hard to get you into a place like that—it's one of the best around. There's a waiting list—'' She bit off the rest of the sentence, because there was something implacable in his expression that showed her he'd made up his mind. The sick, cranky old father who needed looking after was gone, and in his place was this cheerful, resilient person she didn't know.

Before, she'd have been on the attack, forming arguments, telling him why he had to do what she suggested, why it was necessary, why it was best for him. Now, she wanted it to be different. She returned his level stare, and in the best voice she could manage, she asked, "What exactly are you planning on doing, then, Doc?''

She could tell all his defenses were up, but instead of raging at her, he kept his voice quiet—quiet and very determined. And cool. It hurt her, that coolness. It was as if she'd become a stranger to him.

"I'm staying where I am, at least for the time being. I have to get down to Terrace, have my bank account transferred, get more supplies—I'm running short of grub. I want to find out who owns the cabin I'm using, too. Figure I might buy it if I can. And I'm going to get a boat. I sure like the design of these floaters Gaby's father makes."

Tania's good intentions dissolved. Her voice rose, and she could feel herself losing control. "But Doc, this is so far away from everything, you can't really consider living way up here all by yourself. It's foolhardy, it's…it's just plain crazy at your age."

Something in his face closed against her, like a door shutting. He didn't say anything else, but she could tell his mind was made up. They sat there in strained silence, avoiding each other's eyes.

Tania felt she'd been transported back in time. Wasn't this exactly the pattern her conversations with Doc always followed? Why did they end up in a head-to-head fight every time they were together?

It was a relief when Bob moved over to their table and began asking Doc questions about his camp, about the giant chinook he'd caught and released again. Soon the other men joined them, and Benny came and sat on a bench, too, adding a comment here and there.

Tania excused herself, gathered up the dishes and stood at the sink washing them. She'd been riding an emotional roller coaster for too many hours, and exhaustion was beginning to numb her emotions. The anxiety she felt about Matt never left her, but now a deep depression threatened to overwhelm her. The window over the sink revealed the inky-black night, without a moon or stars, and it seemed to mirror the darkness inside her. Her body felt heavy, and every movement was an effort.

She poured boiling water from the kettle over the clean dishes and left them to drain, slipping quietly out the door. The men were now involved in a discussion about logging, and she didn't interrupt them to say good-night.

The cabin was in darkness. Tania found her flashlight and switched it on. Gaby was curled into a tight ball on her cot, facing away from her. She was wearing her Mickey Mouse pajamas, and she hadn't even crawled inside her sleeping bag. It was crumpled on the floor beside her bed.

Tania drew the sleeping bag gently up over Gaby's recumbent form. The girl was deeply asleep, but her face showed the ravages of tears, and now and then she drew in a long, sobbing breath.

Tania undressed, certain she wouldn't be able to sleep, wishing she had a book, wishing she had something—anything—to distract her from her own despair.

The merry-go-round she was riding with Gaby, Matt and her father hadn't been resolved at all. It had simply rearranged itself and was running in the opposite direction. Now Doc was safe and Matt was missing. And she was still as much at odds as ever with both her father and Gaby. A sense of failure weighed her down.

She crawled into her sleeping bag, turned off the flashlight and closed her eyes in weary resignation. She must have fallen asleep instantly, because the next thing she knew light was peeping through the cracks of the cabin as a loud and angry buzzing brought her bolt upright, heart banging.

It took her a moment to identify the sound of a helicopter. It seemed to be about to land on the roof.

"That's my dad! I'll bet anything that's my dad."

Gaby was scrambling out from under her sleeping bag, oblivious to her pajamas and wild hair. She dashed out the door before Tania could get her own legs untangled from her bag.

Outside, Matt climbed down, ducking under the still-whirling blades, and the first person he saw was Gaby, racing toward him in yellow flannelette pajamas, her feet bare.

Relief actually made his knees feel weak. His head spun, and for a moment he was dizzy, disoriented. *Get hold of yourself, Radburn. Grown men don't pass out just from relief.*

She was safe. God, she was safe, she was here, alive, flinging herself into his arms so hard he had to brace against falling backward, wrapping her arms around his neck tight enough to choke him.

"Daddy, Daddy, you're okay! You're not drowned in the river!"

"I could say the same about you, monkey face." He hadn't called her that since she was a little girl. His voice was hoarse and he had to swallow back the rush of glad emotion that brought dampness to his eyes. His whole body was trembling and his arms held her close. "How'd you get back here, honey? We spotted the floater from the copter—it was upside down on the bank of the river, miles away."

He didn't add that he'd been certain, seeing the boat there, that he'd lost her to the Skeena. He'd told Ed, the copter pilot, to fly here just to pick up some of the men to help him in the search for her body.

"We walked back. We got here last night. Daddy, you'll never guess what happened—it's just bizarre. I found Tania's father, Doc Wallace. Well, actually he found me, but he's over in the bunkhouse right now. Can you believe it?''

Matt couldn't. He was still getting used to her being alive, unhurt. He drank in the sight of her, wild yellow hair, swollen eyes, face devoid of makeup.

His baby girl. She'd be his baby girl no matter how old she grew. Thank God she'd have the chance to grow older. He'd bargained for a second chance, and it had been granted.

Her words finally began to penetrate.

''Doc Wallace? Here?'' He felt thickheaded, unable to deal with anything except his overwhelming relief and gratitude that Gaby was alive.

''Yeah, here he comes now. Hey Doc, my father came back.''

A tall, white-haired old man was striding across the meadow with the others, a wide smile on his face. His eyes were hazel, not the green of Tania's, but they were the same shape as hers, and Matt could see where Tania's long, lean body had come from.

''Doc, this is my dad, Matt Radburn. Daddy, this is Tania's father. He brought me up the river. We had to use the boat to get across—the current was really strong—and he knew how to do it.''

Matt gripped the rough hand hard. Doc had a strong handshake. In fact, he looked pretty fit for an old geezer of seventy.

''Thanks for bringing her back.'' Matt put as much gratitude as he could into the words.

''My pleasure. Understand you've been looking out for Tania, so I guess we're even.''

It wasn't the time or place for Matt to say he wanted to look out for Tania for the rest of his life, that he wanted this tough-looking old man to be his father-in-law.

The fishermen were all crowding around now, shaking his hand, wide grins telling him how glad they were he was back. Benny, filthy apron firmly in place, walked over and nodded as if Matt had just been out on a regular fishing excursion.

"Don't guess you thought to bring me up any fresh eggs or milk or such from town, huh?"

Matt hadn't. The last thing on his mind when he'd finally reached Terrace was buying groceries. He'd bought the parts he figured he needed for the jet boat's engine, but that was only because the jet boat would be essential in the search for his daughter. "Sorry, old-timer. I just wasn't thinking of groceries."

"Humph." Benny gave his typical grunt. "Well, there's no fresh eggs, but there's bacon aplenty and flap-jacks." He waved an imperious hand at Ed, the copter pilot. "You, too. No point flying on an empty stomach—that contraption's dangerous enough as it is. But get a move on, I'm not serving all morning. Come and get it while it's hot or do without." He turned, braid swinging, and stomped back to the cookhouse.

Matt hung back while the others hurried in for break-fast. He'd been watching for Tania, but so far there'd been no sign of her. He was amazed, however, to see Scott and Mario come out of the bunkhouse together, acting as if there'd never been a punch exchanged be-tween them. They came over to him, both looking em-barrassed but determined.

Matt didn't greet them or smile. The memory of his last meeting with these two didn't make him feel exactly friendly toward either of them.

"Glad you made it back okay, sir." Scott was using

his best manners. Looking down at his dirty runners, he added in a fast monotone, "Want to apologize, Mr. Radburn, for what happened down by the creek. It wasn't Gaby's fault, it was mine. Really sorry it caused so much trouble. Won't happen again." The boy's face was scarlet.

Mario took over where Scott had left off, and he, too, was red in the face and perspiring with the effort, hat in hand and long, lank hair falling over his forehead. "Me, either. I mean, me, too." He shuffled and began again. "I mean I'm real sorry for what happened. I won't go around punching Scott anymore. Or anybody else, either," he added hastily. He shot Matt an anxious look. "Hope it won't affect my job. I sure do like workin' for you, Mr. Radburn," he added.

Matt had to smother a grin. Mario had called him Matt since the first day out. As far as Mario's job was concerned, Matt had assured himself a million times on this trip that he'd never hire Mario as swamper again. Now he heard himself say, "Well, I'm not one to hold a grudge. I reckon your job's pretty secure."

From the corner of his eyes, Matt saw Tania come slowly out of her cabin, and his heart began to race.

"Hadn't you two better get in there before that crew eats their way through your breakfast as well as their own?"

"C'mon, Berzatto." Scott thumped Mario's shoulder and they took off at a gallop. The door of the cookshack slammed behind them, and Matt turned and walked over to Tania.

Her fiery hair caught the morning sun, shining like a copper halo around her head. Her skin was tanned a deep golden color, and he remembered vividly the parts of her that weren't tanned at all, the breathtaking ivory whiteness of her thighs and breasts. His body reacted to her just as it always did, and he grinned down at her, loving the way she looked, the clean smell of her.

She was looking up at him, green eyes meeting his, and he recognized both love and anguish in their depths. A warning bell sounded in him, and without a word he gathered her into his arms, holding her close, pressing her beloved body tight against him, not caring for once who might be watching.

"Tania. God, woman, it's so good to see you, to hold you. And Gaby's safe. I was so damned scared. I just met your dad. It's hard to believe we've actually found him at last. Oh, Tania, there's so much I have to say to you...."

She stopped him, shaking her head and pulling away so there was distance between them. She was trembling in his embrace, and she wasn't smiling.

He knew then that there was something very wrong, and he frowned down at her. "What? What's wrong?"

"Matt, I'm going back this morning with the helicopter pilot if he'll take me," she said in a quiet voice. "My stuff's all packed and ready." Under her deep tan she looked drawn but determined.

"You're going... Tania, don't be crazy. There's no reason to do that. I want you to stay here with me till the trip's over. There's so much I have to talk about with you, plans we need to make..."

He stopped because something in her expression told him it was useless. In slow motion, he took his hands away from her shoulders and let them drop to his sides. He felt like shaking her, shaking her till she listened to what he wanted to tell her, until she...

"Why?" He felt the euphoria of the past few minutes

fading and a lump of foreboding taking its place. "Why are you going now?"

"Because I've been doing a lot of thinking, and...and it's just not going to work for us, Matt." Her voice was uneven, and she cleared her throat, not meeting his eyes.

"It's because of Gaby, isn't it?" He was surprised at how quiet and reasonable his voice could sound when inside he was roaring out denial.

She nodded after a long moment. "Yes, it is." She lifted her eyes, her gaze met his, and he could see the effort it took for her to hold the facade of control.

"Tania, I know she's difficult, but she's just going through a stage. Things will get better."

She stepped back again, even farther from him. "No, Matt. She told Benny some things—I won't go into detail, you'll have to talk to him yourself—but she's had a far worse time of it than any of us realized. She needs help, Matt, maybe even some professional help, but most of all, she needs you."

Tania drew in a deep, shuddering breath and released it. "I...I told you a little about my marriage, that there were other women. John was always chasing after young women, and it seemed as if I was always waiting while he did it, waiting for him to grow up, to change, to put me first in his life. To love me." She looked beyond him, to the river, and she tried to laugh, but it sounded more like a sob. "It never happened, of course. I know it's not the same thing with us—Gaby's your daughter—but don't you see? Every time she gets upset and runs away, you'll have to go after her. I know she has to come first in your life—that's what being a parent means. But I...I can't feel the same way about her that you do."

She paused, searching for words. "She...resents me. And I'd always be waiting, waiting for her to change, to grow up, to accept me, to like me." She met his eyes again, and hers were flat and lifeless. "I just can't spend any more of my life that way, Matt, waiting for something to change."

He felt as if he were being torn in two. But there wasn't any choice to be made. In the deepest part of his soul, he knew she was speaking the truth. He knew— he'd always known—that his daughter had to come first this time.

For years he'd avoided being a true parent. Now, there really wasn't a choice. Not if he wanted to live with himself.

Gaby was on one side, and Tania, his beloved Tania, was on the other. She wasn't forcing him to choose. She'd made the decision for both of them. But he couldn't just let her walk out of his life.

"I do love you, Matt. I've known for a while now that I love you. I imagine I'll always love you." The words were only a whisper, but he heard them. They branded themselves on his heart.

"I love you, too. That's what I wanted to tell you as soon as I got here." He reached out and stroked her cheek with the back of his hand, trying to memorize the texture, wanting to pull her into his arms and never let her go.

He was a strong, capable man; there must be something he could do to keep her from leaving him.

"I won't give you up, Tania. I swear I'll find a way through this mess, a way for all of us. I promise you I will. I just need some time, time to think my way through it."

She nodded and made an attempt at a smile, but it failed.

Helplessness and desolation filled his body. He had to

find a way; he couldn't just let her fly out of his life like this.

"Look here, take these." He unhooked a set of keys from the larger ring at his waist. "They're the keys to the trailer. Go out there and wait for me—it'll only be a couple more days and we'll be packing out. I know the trailer's a mess, but—" he tried for a grin "—at least it's got hot running water, and there's not a bear for miles. The sheets on my bed are clean—I changed them before I left. Your suitcase is in my bedroom."

He was begging and he didn't give a damn. "Please, honey. We could talk this through, figure out a plan. Go out and wait for me. The keys to the Jeep are on that ring—use it."

She took the keys, but somehow he knew she wasn't going to do what he asked.

FEELING AS IF A LAYER of ice had her blessedly anesthetized, Tania said goodbye to everyone, shaking hands with the fishermen, planting a kiss on Benny's cheek and even smiling at his pretended outrage. Doc was flying back to Terrace with her. He'd arranged during breakfast to hitch a ride into town with Ed and hired him to fly a load of supplies back up to his cabin.

Everyone had gathered around to see them off. Bob pressed a card into Tania's hand with his phone number and address. "I'd love to show you around Yuma if you ever care to come visit," he said with a wistful look. Then he threw caution to the wind and pulled her into his arms for a hug and a big smacking kiss that missed her mouth and landed on her cheek. "I could get real fond of you, Tania."

Gaby gave Doc a long hug and a kiss. "Thanks for taking care of me," she told him with a captivating grin.

"Maybe Dad will bring me down in the boat to visit your camp."

Tania held out her hand to the girl and said quietly, "Goodbye, Gaby. I hope things go well for you."

Gaby's face froze. She reluctantly touched Tania's fingers and dropped them as if they burned, veiled eyes looking somewhere over Tania's left shoulder. "Yeah, well, same to you."

Tania climbed awkwardly into the helicopter, and Matt stood staring up at her, his tortured eyes never leaving her face until the door closed and the machine lifted from the ground.

In the air, Doc was exuberant, filled with excitement, oblivious to Tania's agony. He pointed out the exact location of his camp. Ed obligingly flew low along the river, and she looked down and saw the tiny roof, the little outhouse, the ridiculous patch of something like order wrested from the surrounding miles of wilderness. Tania wanted nothing more than to handcuff Doc to her side and force him to come home with her. She wanted to scream at him about his lack of consideration for her, his daughter, how she'd worry about him dying in that stupid, isolated camp, with no one to turn to when he needed help.

And what about her? She was so alone. She was miserable. She couldn't stop the images of Matt that kept creeping into her head or control the awful pain that leaving him had caused. And she would be leaving her father here, as well.

She wanted to tell Doc how hurt she felt, how it seemed as if he were deliberately and totally cutting himself off from her, and seemed happy to be doing it. But conversation was impossible in the helicopter, and by the time they'd landed in a small field on the outskirts of

Terrace, she'd convinced herself that not a thing she said was going to make one whit of difference. All she could hope for was that she and her father could at least part on reasonable terms...if she kept her mouth shut.

Ed, good-natured and obliging, gave them a ride into town and dropped them in front of the Terrace Hotel.

Once more Tania felt frozen inside, and she welcomed the feeling. It might get her through the next hours, until she was back in Vancouver, back in her own apartment.

They both thanked Ed, and Doc made arrangements for his return trip the next day.

"I'll phone from the hotel and see if I can get a flight out tonight, Doc," Tania said. "There's really no reason for me to stay." It sounded stilted, formal. But she didn't know how else to handle this parting.

"Well, I'll book a room here—can't get through all I have to do in one afternoon," he replied.

They walked together to the desk, and Tania used the phone. She found there were no available seats on the afternoon flight, so she reserved one for the following morning.

Doc overheard her, and when she got off the phone, he handed her a room key. "Got you one next door to mine," he said gruffly.

She was about to protest that he couldn't afford it, that she could pay for her own room, but she thought better of it. If this was his only way of taking care of her, then she'd accept gratefully. "Thanks," she said. They stood looking at each other awkwardly.

"Well, better get on with my business, I guess," Doc finally said. "Lots to do."

Tania picked up her bags, forcing herself to sound cheerful but feeling relieved that she'd soon be alone. "I think I'll go and have a long soak in a hot tub," she told

him. "See you later." She wanted more than anything to
be able to drop this awful pretense that she was fine and
allow the pain and heartbreak she'd been hiding all day
to erupt.

Doc nodded and started to walk away. Then he turned
and blurted out, "Tania, how about having dinner with
me? There's things we oughta discuss."

Could she make it through dinner without losing the
careful control she'd imposed over her tongue, over her
emotions? She had no desire to eat; she felt as if she'd
never be hungry again as long as she lived. Why was he
doing this? Why was he bothering? It was much too late.

"Sure, Doc. That sounds fine." It sounded like another
woman speaking, some cheerful woman Tania didn't
know.

"About six, then. Here in the dining room? I'll bang
on your door and we can go down together—how's
that?"

SHE WAS AS READY as she could make herself by quarter
to six. She'd had a long bath, and it really had felt mar-
velous to sink into the tub up to her neck and shampoo
and rinse her hair, using as much hot water as she wanted
without fear of Benny's wrath.

She forced herself to concentrate only on what each
separate moment demanded, and somehow she got
through the afternoon.

Feverishly, she dried her hair and braided it. She went
through the crumpled clothing in her bag and found a
pair of clean beige cotton slacks and a turquoise printed
shirt, then phoned down to the desk and asked for an iron
and a board. She washed out underwear in a frenzy and
hung it on the shower rail.

It will get easier, she assured herself. *The pain will*

recede, and when I'm back in Vancouver this will take on some perspective. Time and distance will help. They had to, or she didn't think she was going to survive.

Doc banged on her door, just as he'd promised, at five minutes to six.

Forcing a smile on her face, Tania told herself that somehow she'd get through the next few hours without fighting with her father.

He'd trimmed his beard, bathed and shaved. He must have just bought the new navy cotton T-shirt and stiff jeans he wore; he'd arrived with only his scruffy old backpack, and Tania was sure he hadn't packed what he was wearing. Somewhere, he'd also had his boots polished. He nodded stiffly at her, obviously self-conscious. "Ready?" he asked.

She nodded in a bizarre attempt at jauntiness. "Ready."

They made their way down the stairs and into the dining room.

Through the cloud of misery that seemed to surround her, Tania was vaguely aware that Doc was trying hard to please her. He ordered a bottle of wine to go with dinner, though as far as she knew, Doc had never drunk wine in his life. He even made an effort at conversation, telling her what he'd bought, describing seeds he was taking up to his camp for a garden plot.

He ate with honest hunger, but Tania merely toyed with her food. She simply couldn't pay attention to what Doc was saying, because through the doorway of the dining room, Tania could see a corner of the hotel coffee shop. All she could think of was the morning she'd sat in there with Matt. She remembered every detail of the conversation they'd had; she remembered vividly the way he'd looked, what he'd eaten, the timbre of his voice....

Pain cut into her heart through the insulating gray layer she'd been careful to hold in place all day.

TANIA WAS ACTING mighty strange, had been all day. At first Doc thought it was because she was figuring out how to force him to go back to the coast with her, pressure him into it, but she hadn't even argued once about his decision.

Then it dawned on him that it might just involve Matthew Radburn. Fine-looking man, a real outdoorsman by the cut of him. Gaby had made several pointed comments during their long trek out that indicated Tania and Matt were involved in more than just a business arrangement, and Radburn had been pretty shaken up when Tania climbed into that helicopter this morning.

Doc wished again he'd learned how to communicate with this daughter of his. Women were tough to talk to. You had to be careful how you phrased everything or they got the wrong slant. Now if this were Sam sitting here, Doc would just say… *Damn it all, old man, Sam's gone, and this sad, pretty girl across the table is all you've got left in the world. Do something, you old codger. Time's getting away again.*

"Tania, what the hell's the matter with you, girl? You're not eating enough to keep a fly alive, and you don't fool me with that phony cheery voice you're using on me, either."

Well, he might have blown it good. Probably had. But at least it was out in the open, and she'd stopped messing around with the food on her plate and was really looking at him for the first time all day.

But she still didn't say anything to him. Hell's bells. They'd never learned to tell each other the truth about anything, and maybe now it was too late.

"I...Doc, it's just that...I'm not feeling too well. I think I'll go up to my room, have an early..."

The old sensation came over him, the awareness of the days left in his life flying past while he tried to catch them and failed. But this time, it was his daughter disappearing. He had to catch her, he had to connect before the time was gone forever, but how? His heart was hammering, but his heart was strong again. It was his ways of loving that were weak, that needed strengthening.

She was getting up now, leaving.

He made a lunge for her hand, knocked over a water glass, cursed and ignored the waiter who appeared to mop up the mess.

She pulled away, but he just held on, capturing her long, ringless fingers in his rough grasp, tussling with her for a long, tense moment. Then she gave up and sank back down in her seat.

"I loved your momma, y'know, Tania. You remind me of her, your hair an' all. Eyes, too. You're both such pretty women." Of all the things there were to say, that was the last thing he'd expected might come out of his mouth. But somehow, it seemed the right thing just now.

She still didn't say anything, but those big green eyes slowly filled with tears.

He'd never put these things into words before, and it was rough trying, but not as rough as lying up there in his cabin the rest of the summer and knowing he'd failed once and for all as her father.

"Near broke my heart when your momma left me. Thinkin' back, I shouldn'ta been so stubborn. Had the idea it had to be my way or not at all. Now I reckon I shoulda tried harder." He looked straight into her eyes, willing her to help him a little with this.

"Shoulda tried harder with you, too, Tania. But I never

knew how, see. It was easy with Sam—he was a boy. I knew how to handle boys."

"How I used to wish I were a boy, so I could go with you, too. I hated being a girl." Her voice was tear choked and intense. "For a long time I even hated Sam, because he got to go and I didn't."

Her words hurt, and the enormity of his mistakes filled him with remorse. They were monumental, and for a moment he felt they were also irreparable.

But the past weeks had taught him that he could change things if he tried hard enough. Maybe you didn't get what you deserved in life, but he was beginning to believe you got what you worked for.

He took a deep breath and started trying.

CHAPTER FOURTEEN

TANIA WAVED GOODBYE to Doc as the helicopter took off at dawn the next morning. Both pairs of eyes were wet, and the hug they shared was a symbol to Tania of the new beginning in their relationship.

They'd talked till dawn and then had breakfast as soon as the cafeteria opened and talked some more. Neither had had much sleep, but they didn't feel tired.

"Isn't it crazy? We had years together in Vancouver and never said half this much to each other," Tania said to him at one point.

"Well, take me up on that invite to come and stay at the cabin for a while in the summer, and we'll be able to make up for wasted time."

Her heart clenched, and she shook her head.

"I can't just now, Doc—you know that. You know why. Maybe later, when enough time has gone by."

He understood, because she'd told him about loving Matt. She'd told him in detail about Gaby and why the girl made it impossible for Tania to stay. She found that Doc, just like Benny, had affection and understanding for Gaby. He was even protective of her, and Tania could only wonder why it was these taciturn men were able to understand the girl while she couldn't.

"She's just a kid. She'll change and grow real fast," Doc said. "She's got good stuff in her. She'll come around."

But even he had to admit that Gaby's recovery had to begin with her relationship with Matt and that Tania's presence would make it difficult, or even impossible.

Sharing her pain over leaving Matt didn't diminish it, but being able to confide in Doc, and, for the first time in her life, having him there for her when she needed him seemed to ease an old and aching wound she'd lived with always.

He did his best to explain to her why he'd left Vancouver the way he had, why he hadn't been honest with her about what he was doing. "At first, I didn't have a plan at all," he told her. "I just got so I had to get away from that damned lodge. Spring came, I knew the fish were running up here. And old Emil Sanderson, the only one at the lodge I could talk to, up and died in March, you remember. Emil was a miserable old cuss, much like me."

Doc actually winked at her when he said that.

"He hated the city, hated the lodge, hated gettin' old, just like I did. He used to dream of taking a trip back to Norway, back to where he'd grown up, but his son and daughter figured he wasn't strong enough to make the trip, wasn't able to manage his own affairs, and they got power of attorney. He couldn't touch his own money, and it near drove him nuts. I can tell you, it scared the piss outa me, seeing what happened to Emil."

He didn't seem to understand how his words affected her.

"Doc, did you think I'd do something like that to you?"

He didn't answer for a few minutes, and she had time to remember uncomfortably that when he'd had his heart attack, living out in his little house in the valley, she'd been insistent that he sell his property and move to the lodge.

He had been sick and weak, and she'd taken charge. What else could she have done?

"Hell, gettin' old is tough, and I guess kids don't always know what in blazes to do with ya, so even with the best of intentions, things can go wrong," he mused.

It was true. She realized after she'd gotten him moved to the lodge that she'd made a mistake, that he'd never be happy in the city. By that time though, she and Doc couldn't seem to carry on a civil conversation, so how could she have admitted to him that she'd been wrong, that she felt inadequate, that maybe together they could find a better solution?

"I wasn't thinking none too clear when I first decided to come up here, I just knew I didn't want to die the way Emil had. So I cooked up that phony fishing expedition and I banked on you not checking it out too close. I got my old gear together, bought my ticket and just flew up to Terrace. And it was the damnedest thing. On the plane, I sat beside this guy from Calgary who wanted to take wildlife pictures for some magazine. He could fly a helicopter and he was planning on leasing one and flying into the Spatsizi park area. Well, it just seemed like opportunity bangin' on the door. I told him some cock-and-bull story about my son meetin' me in a few days, and he gave me a lift up to the cabin with a few boxes of supplies. But before we left town I gave a little Indian kid ten bucks to mail those postcards off to you every few days." Doc laughed and shook his head. "Kinda figured he'd toss them in the garbage the minute my back was turned."

"He didn't. I got every one, see?" She opened her purse and took out the cards, held together neatly with a rubber band. "They mean a lot to me, because they're the first letters I've ever had from you."

His eyes were somber. "I got a lot to make up for, Tania."

"I guess we both do."

WHEN THE COPTER DISAPPEARED into the sunlit sky, she hired a taxi to drive her out to Matt's trailer for her suitcase.

The driveway was just as rutted as ever, the setting just as breathtaking.

"You want me to wait, lady? Doesn't look to me like anybody's home around here." The taxi driver idled the engine, squinting back at Tania over the seat.

Matt's homestead looked deserted and forlorn in the early-morning light, and she avoided looking over toward the barn and the corral...and the pile of logs behind it, where he'd kissed her for the first time.

"I won't be long. I just have to pick up a suitcase." She climbed out and walked over to the trailer, inserting Matt's key into the lock with trembling fingers.

Don't crack up now, Tania. Hold on, concentrate on getting the damned suitcase and getting out of here. Just a few more hours and you'll be away from all these places and things that remind you of him. You can start forgetting then.

The door opened and she stepped into Matt's home. The curtains were drawn and the air was musty smelling. The counters were clear this time, but there was still that general air of untidy chaos, of a home uncared for and unkempt. Her shoe stuck to the floor tiles where something had been spilled, and dust balls floated across the rug. Books and articles of clothing lay scattered across the sagging sofa, tumbling off onto the floor.

Matt had said her suitcase was in his bedroom.

She hurried down the narrow hall, passing a bathroom with Gaby's makeup scattered on the counter, a small utility area with a washer and dryer and a bedroom that had to be Gaby's, if the clothing and shoes scattered around were any indication.

Matt's bedroom was at the back, and here Tania was more aware of him than ever. The bed was neatly made, but one of his white T-shirts was tossed on the comforter.

A mystery paperback lay open on the bedside table, a denim jacket hung over a chair, a pair of old and comfortable leather moccasins, worn to the exact shape of his feet, sat on the rug beside the wide bed.

The closet doors were ajar, revealing shirts hung in a row, blue and navy and green. She saw the checked shirt he'd worn the first day they met. Unable to stop herself, she went over and buried her nose in it, drawing in the wonderful scent of his body, remembering the feel of his arms around her.

Wait for me.

She could hear his voice, see the muscles tense along his jaw, the pain in his blue eyes when she'd said she was leaving.

Oh Matt, you were so good to me, caring and thoughtful and kind. Loving, and passionate. Tender. Patient. I found Doc because you took me with you, even though you knew far better than I how difficult it was going to be.

Had she even said thank-you?

She picked up the suitcase and walked back down the hallway. A spider had built a huge web in the doorway to the laundry room, and a dozen bugs were caught in it.

Tania stopped and glared at it. It offended her, that

cobweb. She couldn't just leave it there to catch more
and more bugs, grow larger and larger.

She set her suitcase down and found a dirty towel in
the bathroom and swiped at the cobweb, clearing it away.
This was idiotic, letting one cobweb get to her while the
rest of the place screamed for a good scrubbing.

Perhaps the idea had been half forming since she'd first
walked in. Now it was clear in her mind. It was the last
thing, the only thing, she could do for the man she loved.

She set the suitcase down with a thump and walked
into the kitchen, to the telephone. She canceled her reservation on the morning flight and made one for the following day, instead. Then she hurried out and sent the
mystified cabdriver on his way, asking if he'd come back
and collect her the next morning.

She searched out soap and disinfectant, laundry detergent, bleach, powdered cleansers, ammonia, sponges,
floor wax, a bucket and some clean rags. At least Matt's
intentions were good, she concluded, studying the impressive array of cleaning materials.

She put on her jeans and Matt's white T-shirt, and she
set to work. It felt good to wear something of his. It felt
good to clean his home.

It took her all day, and it was deeply satisfying to work
until her body ached from exhaustion. The hours sped
past, and as she methodically scrubbed and polished and
washed, hanging out lines of laundry and bringing them
in to fold, she experienced moments of intense pain, almost physical pain, knowing she'd never have the opportunity to perform these homely tasks for Matt again.

In the late afternoon, she made herself a meal out of
tinned soup and crackers and cheese she salvaged from
a dry block in the refrigerator. It was the first time she'd
felt hungry since leaving the fishing camp, and she car-

ried her food outside, past the corral, to where Matt's house sat unfinished in the sunshine. She sat down on the lumber where he'd first kissed her and allowed herself to dream.

She saw the house finished, the wide terrace screened, filled with comfortable rockers and longues where they'd sit on long summer evenings, talking nonstop and listening to the nearby song of the Skeena.

There'd be a baby toddling around, a fat, cheeky little girl with his crooked grin. Or maybe a boy with her red hair and his eyes.

In the winter, they'd be snug and warm, the fireplace he'd described crackling, logs piled high to replenish the flames.

Dreams were free, and she spent them with abandon.

When at last, late that night, she showered in the gleaming bathroom and collapsed on Matt's wide bed on the fresh, clean sheets, it gave her a sense of immense comfort to know that when he came back, his home would be in shining order, order she'd created for him. If only she had the power to put the rest of his life in the same order, to wave a magic wand and make things right for him with Gaby.

She tried to write him a note and tell him so, but she couldn't.

SHE WAS BACK at her desk at the newspaper the following Monday. The office seemed smaller and more cramped than ever, and it was raining outside, a dismal, gray downpour that threatened to go on the rest of the summer.

The city felt cramped and chaotic after the time she'd spent in the wilds.

The weekend at her apartment had convinced Tania that she had to keep busy if she were to stay sane. It was far too painful to have enough time to think of what might have been.

She ached inside, but strangely enough, she didn't cry at all. The loss she felt was too deep even for tears.

Jane Kendall greeted her with a hug and a torrent of words when she arrived at work.

"Gads, Tania, it's fabulous to have you back. Look at you, you're as brown as if you'd been in Hawaii. Dennis put that weirdo from the front desk in here while you were gone—y'know the one with the orange hair? Honestly, I think she's committable. She hums under her breath all day long, and I thought I'd end up doing the bridge trip. So quick, tell me, tell me, did'ja find him?"

Tania gave Jane a bare and brief version of what had happened, the trip into the bush, finding Doc at last. She tried to sidestep the rest of it, but Jane had an uncanny ability to go for the jugular.

"So what was that guy like, the fishing guide you kept calling on the phone who never answered? Was he young, old, single, sexy, what? Tell, tell."

Tania swallowed and stared out the window. The daffodils were almost finished blooming by now, and the irises looked drenched and bedraggled in the steady downpour. She remembered the sunshine in the little glade by the Skeena, and suddenly the rain seemed to be inside of her as well as outside the window.

"He was...helpful. He was—" she could feel her throat closing up, and she fought it "—he was a gentleman," she finally managed.

The telephone rang and she blessed the interruption. A society matron wanted coverage of her daughter's wedding on Saturday. By the time Tania had scribbled down all the details, Jane was off on a different conversational tangent.

"While you were away, I met this fabulous guy—
Steve is his name. He's got the greatest set of buns you
ever saw in your life...."

THE DAYS AND WEEKS dragged past. She knew exactly
when Matt was coming out of the bush, and for a while
after that date she found herself tensing each time the
phone rang. But he didn't call.

She packed up the things Doc had asked her to store
for him and cleaned out his place at the lodge so someone
else could move in. She wrote to him several times,
knowing he probably wouldn't get the letters until he
made another trip in for supplies. She used all her writing
skills in those letters, revealing herself and her dreams in
a way she never had to anyone, determined to cement
the tenuous bond she and Doc had established. It was
hard, and she threw away more letters than she sent. Then
she started keeping the rejects instead of throwing them
away, vaguely aware that they were a map of sorts.

They spelled out the gaps there had been between her
and her father, the important things that had been left
out, the places they had missed their way. Perhaps other
fathers and daughters had similar problems understanding
each other.

What would you write about, Matt had asked her, *if
you had the chance?*

What better place to begin than with a father and a
daughter? It was a subject she understood, and she'd always believed writers should begin with subjects they
knew about. A first chapter took form, and then another.

It filled the lonely evenings.

THERE WAS A LETTER from Doc about three weeks after
she'd come home. Tania tore it open, filled with pleasure

because he'd made the effort to write. She read and re-read it. It gave her a new warmth that took away some of the chill that seemed to have settled in her heart.

The spelling and grammar weren't perfect, and he kept apologizing for that, adding that he was new at it—it took an old dog time to learn new tricks.

He wrote of simple things: a chipmunk he'd tamed, a beaver dam on a creek, the huge bald eagle who'd swept down and stolen a fish he'd just caught, the deer that came down to drink each night below his cabin. He'd seen three black bears, a mother and two cubs. He was making repairs to the roof of the cabin. And then one paragraph at the end leaped out at her.

> Matt R. is up at his camp with another fishing party. He came by to see if I'd do a bit of guiding—seems he's shorthanded. He's coming to get me to-morrow. Will spend the next week or so up there working for him. Guess I'm not over the hill yet if I can still get a job, ha ha. Will send this out with him for posting when he goes.

The very next day, there was an envelope with her name in strong, bold lettering. Tania stood inside her apartment door, staring down at the envelope, trembling when she saw Matt's name on the return address.

Heart hammering, she went to sit by the window before she tore it open.

It was obvious that, like Doc, he didn't write many letters. It was barely a page. He didn't waste words, but the few he used made her feel better than she'd felt since leaving him.

Dearest Tania,

Not much time. One party left today and another arriving in the morning, so this will be brief. Wanted to tell you your father's fine. I'm keeping an eye on him for you. He's a tough old bird and seems to thrive on the life he's leading. Before winter comes, I'll find a way to lure him closer to town. Thanks for all you did here at the trailer. The place looks great and I'm doing my damnedest to keep it that way, even though it's missing what I wanted most to find when I came home—you waiting. Darling, I hope you're keeping well. I miss you and I love you. I meant every word I said—I'll find a way through this mess, and then there'll be a time for us, if that's what you want, too. Write me. Reassure me. I need to know you're out there. Excuse the scribble, I'm doing this late at night. Sultan misses you and the rides we took along the river.

All my love, Matt.

Simple, strong and honest. Exactly like the man who'd written it.

She wished with all her heart that she could believe in what he said, believe there would be a time when they could be together. But the fact that he hadn't mentioned Gaby was silent proof that nothing had really changed.

The next day she made an appointment with an expensive hairstylist. He cut off a good eight inches and blew her hair dry in a newer, softer way.

"You've got good cheekbones and eyes. And this hair is a great color. If you've got it, flaunt it."

That hadn't been her purpose at all. She'd come because even though she was in mourning, she didn't want to look as if she were. That and the fact that her thirty-seventh birthday was coming up in November. It loomed

like a signpost, spelling out how few years were left for
having children, for achieving the things she'd always
longed for.

The coastal summer stayed wet and cool, and Tania
marked the passing of the months by the envelopes that
arrived sporadically from Matt and Doc.

At first, writing to Matt was almost impossible. She
finished three long letters and tore them up before she
came up with one that sounded almost right to her. She'd
decided there wasn't any point rehashing their problems,
so instead she wrote to him as a friend, telling him what
she was reading, doing, thinking. Gradually, his letters to
her became longer, and he told her things about himself
that touched her, intrigued her or sometimes made her
giggle.

He had a wicked sense of humor, and his descriptions
of some of his clients were hilarious. He described
Benny's encounter with one of them, a snobbish chef
from an exclusive restaurant who was determined to give
Benny pointers on cooking. He'd driven the old cur-
mudgeon into frenzies of rage with his constant unasked-
for advice and criticism. The chef had boasted that he
was an expert at ethnic cuisine, and he'd condescendingly
asked Benny if there were any Indian recipes he might
be able to adapt to his more sophisticated methods.

Benny had become suspiciously agreeable, preparing
an intricate native dish from wild herbs and roots he had
gathered. He'd served it, with much fanfare, only to the
chef. Somehow, though, the poor man had ended up
spending most of the next two days and nights sitting in
the outhouse. Afterward he'd avoided Benny like the
plague.

As the summer months slipped away, Tania and Matt
relaxed in the pages they exchanged. Slowly, they came

to know each other as friends as well as lovers. There was so much they hadn't talked about during their short weeks together. Tania wrote openly to him about her father, about the bridges they were trying to build between them and how difficult it was not to fall into old patterns.

Matt, in turn, began to mention Gaby, at first only that, of necessity, she was coming along with him on all the fishing trips and was actually starting to be a help with the horses and even the float boats. His writing was endearingly candid.

Although, most of the time I still think there's some damned course on raising daughters that I should have taken and didn't (your father missed it, too, I gather). Still, we are starting to get along a little better.

In his most recent letter, he told Tania he was hoping Gaby would agree to go back to school in September. The letter arrived weeks after he'd written it. It was already October, and the school term would be well under way by now. Tania wondered if he'd been successful. She took the letter to work with her to reread, eating her lunchtime yogurt and sandwich at her desk, hearing the deep intonations of Matt's voice in her head as she read his words.

She folded the letter up slowly and stuffed it back into its envelope, thinking as she so often did of her own failures with Gaby. They haunted her. She was the adult. She ought to have been better able to understand and help the girl. She should have tried harder.

Jane came bustling in, shaking the rain from her fluorescent orange umbrella. "I swear, we had a day and a half of sunshine all summer, and now we're into a rainy fall. I'm going moldy from this weather. Letter from your dad?''

Tania had never confided in Jane, never really talked about Matt or even Gaby, even though Jane was touchingly open about her own love life. Tania suddenly remembered Bob Young, in the middle of the night at the fish camp, needing to talk about his dead wife. What misguided sense of privacy kept her from talking to Jane about her own failed romance?

"No, it's not from Doc." She took a deep breath and said, "It's from the man I met in Terrace, Matt Radburn, the fishing guide. Remember him?"

"Yeah, you never said much about him." Jane polished her glasses on a tissue and plopped them back on her nose, then ran her fingers through her mop of hair until she had it properly on end. "But I figured you must have met somebody up there. You're different than you were before."

"How's that?"

Jane shrugged. "Well, lots easier to be around, I guess. And you were sort of shaken up when you came back. You still don't laugh a lot, but you're more relaxed than you ever were. You look better, too—not that you didn't look good before, but now…well, I like your hair. And the way you dress. It's a lot more fashionable."

Tania had to grin at the younger woman. "Less buttoned-down and frumpy, is that what you're trying to say?"

Jane flushed. "Not at all. Just that you changed after that trip." She added a bit hesitantly, "So what about this Matt guy? Is it serious?"

The old Tania would have denied it, afraid of looking foolish. The new one nodded, instead. "Yes, you could say that." It hurt, Lord it hurt, to talk about him. "But you'd also have to add that it's hopeless."

"C'mon, nothing's hopeless." Jane was an optimist. "Tell me what makes you think that."

In fits and starts, between phone calls and interruptions—work they both ought to be doing and weren't—Tania told Jane about the trip up the Skeena, about Matt and then about the problems she'd had with Gaby.

"Wow, she sounds like bad news, that kid," Jane declared, frowning over her glasses at Tania.

Tania nodded. "She was hard to understand. I made a lot of stupid mistakes with Gaby that I feel bad about. Benny, the camp cook, told me that Gaby might have been sexually assaulted by her mother's boyfriend, which accounts for a lot of her anger, I guess."

Jane whistled. "That's heavy-duty. So, do you think you'll see Matt again?"

Tania shook her head. "I couldn't handle it now—it still hurts too much. But because Doc is living up there, I'll probably visit Terrace sometime. Maybe. But not for a while."

HER BIRTHDAY fell on a Saturday, the first week of November, and Tania told herself over and over that she was just going to ignore it. Jane had given her a small pottery vase with three carnations in it on Friday afternoon, along with a fat muffin holding a single lighted candle. Tania was delighted and touched and said so. There was a new closeness now with Jane that made workdays pleasant.

But there wasn't even a card from Doc. Probably because he couldn't get it mailed in time, Tania assured herself. Still, it hurt a little. He'd always remembered her birthday, even during the difficult years at the lodge.

She woke early that Saturday morning. The sun was shining, which had to be a reason for feeling grateful. It had been the wettest summer and fall in recent history. Her waking thoughts were of Matt, the way they always were, and she wondered where he was, what he was doing at that moment.

Instead of healing, the pain of missing him seemed to grow more intense as the months passed. She went through the motions of her life, but there was always this aching sense of loss. There were so many things they'd never shared, and they came to her most often in this moment between waking and sleep. This morning she dwelt on the fact that they'd never spent a night together, wrapped in each other's arms.

Enough already. It was far too easy to be sorry for herself, and it was nonproductive. She forced herself out of bed, into the shower.

She was having coffee, wrapped in her old blue robe, when the doorbell rang. Her heart leaped. Maybe Doc had sent a card special delivery. She unlocked the door and opened it.

Matt was standing there, a huge grin on his rugged face. He wore gray slacks, a white shirt and a tweed blazer. He looked foreign to her in the city uniform—until she looked into his familiar blue eyes.

He was holding long-stemmed roses wrapped in silver tissue, a huge bundle of them, and he thrust them at her. He'd dropped a duffel bag and a long box at his feet on the hall rug.

"Happy birthday, Tania."

She stood frozen, her mouth open, immobile and speechless.

"Think I could come inside?"

She moved back from the door, still unable to speak,

and he reached down and grabbed his things, dragging them inside and then shoving the door closed behind him.

"Tania. My darling Tania."

His arms went around her, fierce and urgent, and his lips came down on hers.

CHAPTER FIFTEEN

TANIA FELT as if she were dreaming. She held the flowers awkwardly out to one side, her other arm rising tentatively to slide around his neck.

The dear, familiar smell of him enveloped her, the texture of his mustache registered on her senses, and she began to believe he was real. He was here, holding her in his arms, and his lips sent waves of desire coursing through her. She wanted to hold him as close as he was holding her.

"Matt, these roses—"

"To hell with the roses." His voice was a deep, gruff growl.

"But they're beautiful. I should put them in some water...."

He groaned and buried his nose in her neck, planted kisses up the line of her throat, arms locking her to him.

"Tania, I've missed you like the devil. God, it feels good to hold you again." He moved back a little, studying her from top to toe, taking his time, fondling her shoulders, stroking tender fingers along her jaw and down her neck. "You've changed your hair." He reached out and touched it. "It's just as soft as ever, anyway."

She set the flowers carefully on a table and reached up to fluff her still-damp hair, conscious all of a sudden of her old robe and her naked body under it.

"I had it cut. Everybody says it makes me look

younger.'' All this time apart and they were talking about her hair.

''I like you the exact age you are. Thirty-seven today, right?''

She narrowed her eyes at him. ''You've been talking to my father.''

He snapped his fingers and went to the door, retrieving the long, narrow box. ''I damned near forgot,'' he said. ''He sent you this. It's a fresh salmon, frozen. We'd better get it into a freezer, pronto.''

''Doc sent me a fish?''

''Unusual birthday present, but he's making sure you won't go hungry. It's a twenty-pounder.''

She unwrapped the cardboard. The fish was carefully packed in plastic, and it was immense. Together they fitted it into her small apartment-size freezer in the corner of the kitchen.

''Now the roses.'' She found a vase and arranged the lovely, half-open flowers in it, setting them on the low coffee table in the living room. When that was done, she turned back to him.

''Now tell me, what are you doing here in Vancouver? Come and sit down and explain.''

''A week ago, Doc and I were talking and he told me today was your birthday. So I decided to fly down and help you celebrate. I needed to see you, see where you lived.'' He walked to the window, looked out at the quiet street below, then followed her to the kitchen and took a seat at the table where her coffee cup was still sitting, cold now.

''Can I get you some coffee? Have you eaten breakfast?'' She felt nervous, every part of her aware of him. For some reason, she'd never imagined him here, in her apartment. He seemed to belong so completely to his own outdoor world, she'd never in her wildest imaginings dreamed of transposing him here. She kept looking at him, and each time she did his eyes were on her.

"I had one small bun and a cup of instant coffee on the plane, so yeah, breakfast would be nice, thanks."

She poured him a mug of coffee, found a frying pan and eggs and took bread out for toast. He seemed too large for her tiny apartment kitchen, wedged in a corner, shoulders almost touching each wall.

While she cooked, they chatted about Doc.

"He and Benny really hit it off. I think they might rent a cabin together this winter, a small house about a mile down the road from my place. Benny's been living closer to town with a couple of other guys, and he's anxious to move." Matt's eyes twinkled and he grinned the crooked grin Tania remembered so well. "Too many women in town, Benny says. Makes him nervous."

Tania shook her head. "What is it with him and women, anyhow?" She set a heaping plateful of eggs and toast in front of him, along with a bottle of ketchup and a jar of marmalade.

"He was married a long time ago. His wife left him for another man. Benny never got over it, and I guess his resentment toward her gradually spread to the whole female species." Matt spread marmalade on a piece of toast and took a huge bite of egg. "You know, I think you and Gaby are the only exceptions he's ever made. He likes you, although he'd never admit it, and he's good friends with Gaby. He's teaching her to cook—she's getting quite good at it."

Tania toyed with her own eggs. "How is Gaby, Matt?"

His face became sober, and he laid down his fork and

sipped his coffee, worried frown lines falling into a pattern on his forehead.

"She's doing better—at least I hope she is. We talk a lot more instead of fighting. I've learned that a father's sometimes the last one to know how his kid really is. It took you and Benny to get it through my thick skull that there was more wrong with Gaby than just normal teenage rebellion." His face hardened and his blue eyes became cold and remote.

"After I finally found out what happened to her with this Neil character Margaret is hooked up with, I couldn't sleep for days. I wanted to go down there and kill them both, murder them with my bare hands. How could a mother act the way she did? Gaby tried to tell her what was going on, and she refused to believe the girl. Told her to get out of the house. Thank God Gaby had sense enough to phone me when she did, and thank God I happened to be home at the time. As it was, she spent a whole night on the street in Toronto, hanging out with a group of runaways." The pain and frustration he felt showed clearly in his eyes and on his face.

"Oh, Matt." Tania reached across and took his hand in hers.

"The worst part was knowing I didn't give her a chance to really tell me about all of it when she first arrived. I was busy and distracted, and I'd never learned to really talk with her. Hell, she ended up confiding in Benny, of all people."

Tania thought about the taciturn old cook, remembering the night she'd spent with him waiting for news of Matt and Gaby. "I can understand Gaby's being able to talk to Benny," she said reflectively. "There's something comforting about him under all that bluff. He sees things clearly, and he's not at all as tough as he'd like everyone to believe.''

He nodded in agreement. ''Far as I can tell, he's given Gaby fine advice. But I really didn't think I was capable of helping her with the feelings she has, considering how furious I felt with her mother. So I went to a doctor I know in Terrace, a guy I like and trust. He recommended counseling, with some sessions for me, as well. There's a woman up there who's really good, Penelope Reese. Anyway, Gaby's back in school, and she's seeing Penelope twice a week. I've gotten to know her, and I think she's doing Gaby a lot of good.''

Tania noted the affectionate way Matt said the woman's name, and she fought against a sudden rush of awful jealousy.

Matt looked across into her eyes, his expression suddenly bleak. ''I've stopped seeing things through rose-colored glasses, believing it'll all work out. I don't honestly know if Gaby will ever change, Tania. That's really what I came down here to talk over with you, although I didn't plan on getting into it this soon. I thought it was just a stage she was going through, being difficult and resentful of…everyone.''

Not everyone, Tania thought. *Only of me.*

''Now I realize that it's a lot more complicated than that, and I promised you—''

''You don't owe me anything, Matt. I thought that was clear between us.'' And yet she felt bitterly disappointed. From the first moment she'd opened the door, hope had been building in her that maybe, just maybe…

''The thing is, I love you, Tania. I want us to be together, for always, and I know it won't work as long as Gaby's the way she is. This is the hardest damn thing I've ever gone through, and the most frustrating.''

He'd barely touched the food on his plate. She made a monumental effort at a light tone.

"Eat, and let's not worry about all this now. We'll have time to talk later. How long can you stay?"

"Only until tomorrow night. Penelope organized a camping trip for four of the girls she sees. Gaby's gone for the weekend with her."

Tania tried not to resent the fact that even seeing Matt for two days hinged on Gaby's activities. Seeing Matt at all was nothing short of miraculous, however it came about, she reminded herself. "Then how should we spend the day?" she asked him. "What would you like to do, Matt?"

His eyes burned into hers, and he shoved the plate of food away and got to his feet. Tania's heartbeat accelerated.

"It's your birthday—you ought to choose. But I have this really good idea." He took her hands and pulled her gently to her feet. "I've never made love to you in a bed, you know that?"

"But you didn't eat your breakfast."

"I'll have it for lunch. I love cold eggs. Which way's your bedroom?"

She smiled up at him and pointed down the hallway. "That way, but are you sure you can manage this without your rifle, horses looking on and all those mosquitoes?"

His voice was thick. "Well, it's doubtful. I'll just have to give it a damn good try." He scooped her up in his arms and her robe came open, revealing her naked breasts. His eyes caressed her, and a shudder of desire rippled through her, so powerful it took her breath away.

"You know," he murmured in her ear, striding down the hall as if she weighed nothing at all, "I think I can live without those romantic details, after all. If you can."

He put her down on the bed, and she watched, desire building to a crescendo as he stripped off his clothing. In a moment he was beside her, arms and body enfolding her.

There wasn't time for slow exploration...that would come later. Tonight. They'd have hours and hours together.

Now, there was only urgent, demanding heat building inside of her, and she knew by the way his body surged, turgid and burning in her hand when she reached down and curled her fingers around him, that Matt felt exactly the way she did.

"Now, Matt. Love me now—I can't wait."

Her robe was still on her shoulders. He loosened it, freeing her arms. He knelt over her, capturing her mouth with his in a deep, passionate kiss, and then in one long, slow motion he entered her.

She opened herself for him, body, mind and soul, and in the last second before ecstasy claimed them both, he gasped, "Happy birthday, my dearest love."

THE DAY STRETCHED before them like a gift to be unwrapped and savored.

They took a bus down to Vancouver's colorful Chinatown, wandering hand in hand amidst the crowds of Chinese families doing their marketing from open-fronted shops that exuded exotic smells: fresh-caught fish, roasting chicken, Oriental spices, and the pervasive musky, enticing odor of food from the dozens of restaurants scattered through the area. They looked in windows at jade jewelry, silk blouses, rattan furniture and luxurious handmade rugs.

They found their way up two winding flights of stairs to a noisy dim sum restaurant full of entire families out for the chinese equivalent of smorgasbord. Grandmothers tended tiny babies, bashful sloe-eyed toddlers wound among the diners' chairs, young couples exchanged shy and loving glances under aunts' and uncles' critical scrutiny.

Matt and Tania spent two hours choosing tiny round platefuls of delicious tidbits, none of which they could identify, laughing and tasting and pronouncing judgment in a way that would have made Benny crazy. The brisk and beautiful serving women, in red *chong san* with hair that gleamed shoe-shine black, joined in the game, urging them to try this and that, plopping the steaming bowls and plates in front of them and nodding encouragement as they rushed from table to table with mobile steam trays.

Afterward, almost too full to move, they walked in Stanley Park, admiring the graceful swans on Lost Lagoon and laughing at the hordes of tame Canada geese that came racing over as they passed, hoping for handouts of the bread scraps that strollers often brought them.

They talked, free at last to explore any subject they chose without the constant threat of interruption or the difficulty of letter writing. And the more they talked, the closer they drew to each other, even through the inevitable arguments about politics and ideals.

Late in the afternoon, they made their way back to Tania's apartment to change for dinner, since Matt had made reservations at an elegant restaurant. There was a long delay in the dressing ritual—it was probably a mistake to decide to shower together if they really wanted to get to the restaurant on time—but Tania finally slipped into a dress she loved and hardly ever had a chance to wear, an emerald-green tube of the finest silk that fell from her shoulders to her knees in a deceptively simple line. It clung and shimmered and outlined her body with every movement she made.

As it happened, they were outrageously late, but a smiling maître d' assured them he'd held their window table. Tania saw the folded bill Matt slipped him and rolled her eyes, but she agreed that the view of Vancouver harbor was spectacular.

It was after midnight when they arrived home again. They'd toured Gastown after dinner, joining the fashionably dressed crowds who strolled the cobblestone streets, dropping into one of the many noisy clubs to dance to slow, pulsing music.

"You're such a good dancer," Tania said with a sigh as she slid off her high-heeled sandals and sank into a chair.

"I suppose that's why your feet are this sore," Matt teased. "Speaking of feet..." He went into the bedroom, rummaged in his duffel bag and came out holding a large rectangular box wrapped in blue birthday paper. "This is a present from a friend."

Excited as a child, she tore off the wrappings.

Inside was a pair of dark brown, exquisitely tooled Western boots, as soft and smooth to touch as the silk dress she wore. A small card read, "From one liberated female to another. Best regards and happy trails, your equestrian pal, Sultan."

Tania had to fight back the tears. Riding boots. They represented all the tomorrows Matt longed to share with her. She looked up at him, eyes overflowing, unable to speak, and he put a gentle hand on her hair, running his fingers through the soft strands.

"There'll be a time for us, pretty lady. I know there will. Now..." He knelt at her feet, cradling her instep, and slipped one boot on and then the next. "A perfect fit," he pronounced, getting up and pulling her to her feet. The boots felt wonderful.

He put his hands low on her back and pressed her intimately against his body. "A perfect fit," he said again. "Just like us," he added with a catch in his voice. "Let's get your boots off again. Unless you want to wear them to bed?"

SHE WOKE TO THE SMELL of coffee. Her body ached here and there, a pleasurable ache, created by hours of loving. She stretched, and just as she was about to climb out of bed, Matt appeared, tray balanced carefully.

He was dressed in faded jeans and a sweatshirt she remembered him wearing in Terrace. His brown hair and mustache were still damp from the shower, and his wide-set blue eyes were loving when he met her gaze. The smile he gave her was lazy and full of the memory of the night they'd shared.

"'Mornin', sleepyhead. Want some breakfast?"

"In two minutes." She scrambled out of bed, reaching for her robe and deriving voluptuous pleasure from his open admiration of her naked body. In the bathroom, she splashed water on her face, used a brush on her hair and a toothbrush on her teeth, then hurried back to bed.

He was waiting patiently, tray balanced on the dresser. On the tray he'd put one of her roses in a water glass. He'd brought scrambled eggs and toast, juice and coffee and a neatly folded paper napkin.

"How about you?" She felt incredibly pampered as he arranged the tray across her knees.

"Mine's in the kitchen. I'll get it." He was back in a moment with a heaping plateful of food.

"I shouldn't tell you this, but no man ever brought me

breakfast in bed before,'' Tania confessed, sipping her juice and smiling at him.

His eyes flashed at her. "Let's keep it that way. Bob Young would have been delighted, given the chance."

"Still jealous?" She could tease him now and feel secure.

"Damned right." He dug in his pocket and pulled out an envelope addressed to her, care of his business address in Terrace. The return address was Bob's. He flipped it onto the bed beside her. "I debated about even giving you this. It came a few weeks ago."

Tania tore it open. It was a warm and affectionate letter saying how much he'd enjoyed meeting her and reinforcing the invitation he'd made to come to Yuma as his guest.

"You made me realize a person has to go on living, instead of just remembering," he wrote in closing. "I'd very much enjoy the chance to get to know you better."

Without saying a word, Tania handed it to Matt to read.

He skimmed it quickly and then put it on her dresser. His smile had disappeared.

"Tania, I haven't any right to ask you to wait around for me—I know that," he said after a long silence. "You're beautiful, desirable, intelligent...all the things a man looks for in a woman." His voice was strained, and he set his breakfast plate on the bed and cleared his throat before he went on. "But I'm going to ask, anyway. When the time is right, Tania, will you marry me?"

The egg she'd just taken a bite of seemed glued to the roof of her mouth. She swallowed hard and took a gulp of coffee.

"It's a hell of a thing to ask, because I can't set a time limit, but I can't go back to Terrace without knowing, one way or the other.'' He looked at her, and his soul was in his eyes. ''You're the other half of me, the person I should have waited for if I'd had the sense. I love you more than I ever thought it possible to love. I can't bear to lose you now. I'm sure as hell no bargain, but I'll go on loving you until I die. Can you wait for me, Tania?''

It was the hardest question she'd ever been asked. Waiting might mean a large chunk of her life, the years she had left before nature made the decision for her about having children. They both knew waiting meant hoping that Gaby would change, and that might be a futile hope. But it was also an easy question, because she knew she'd never love anyone the way she loved Matt.

''I'll wait. I love you the same way, Matt.''

He knelt beside her on the bed, moved the tray aside and took her in his arms. She felt his wide shoulders tremble beneath her touch.

''I just have one question, Matt.''

He looked at her. ''Anything.''

''Just how old is this Penelope woman, anyway?''

His mouth tilted into a semblance of the grin she loved.

''Penelope? I'd say about sixty, give or take a year.''

HIS PLANE LEFT at six. Tania drove back from the airport, missing him, but also experiencing a feeling of quiet happiness.

She truly belonged to him now, and distance and time were less important.

MONDAY MORNING at coffee she told Jane about the weekend, editing out the more intimate details.

''So that's why you have that glow about you this morning. I should have guessed you spent most of the weekend in bed with him.''

Tania blushed crimson and Jane giggled, but later she became serious. "You know this kid of his you told me about, the one you had all the problems with in the summer?"

"Gaby, yes." Tania told Jane about the counseling and that Gaby was back in school.

"Well, I got thinking about it. My cousin Christine's a youth worker downtown at the Eastside Teen Center. It's a drop-in place for street kids. Anyhow, I saw her on the weekend at one of my grandma's infamous family dinners. Chris was telling me how desperate they are for volunteers. It dawned on me that it might be something you'd want to try. Maybe getting to know other kids with problems might help you with this girl of Matt's. What'ya think?"

Tania shook her head. "I botched the situation with Gaby so badly I'd be nervous about trying with any other teens. And these kids have serious problems I don't know the first thing about."

Jane shrugged. "Well, the best way to learn is to do, right? You're levelheaded. You'd do fine. Anyhow, here's Christine's number if you change your mind."

Tania tucked it in her wallet, privately thinking that it was a waste of time. But during the next week it seemed that everywhere she turned there were stories or broadcasts about street kids and their problems. A major women's magazine had an in-depth article about kids on the street. A television news broadcast interviewed a girl called Fiona, a Vancouver street kid, and Tania found herself unable to change the channel.

Fiona sounded much like Gaby, except her language was more profane. She was the same age, and like Gaby, she gave the impression of being tough and uncaring, but when the interviewer asked about her home life, the young woman broke down and cried. Her story of abuse made Tania physically ill.

"I had to run away, y'know? But it's tough out here. It's awful to wake up in the morning scragged down, filthy from sleeping in stairwells," Fiona admitted. "But the worst part's the loneliness, eh? Just having somebody to talk to down at the center makes a big difference."

Tania couldn't sleep that night. Horrible images of what Fiona described so matter-of-factly kept intruding into her dreams, except that Fiona was Gaby, a Gaby who hadn't had a father like Matt to turn to.

The next day, heart pounding with apprehension, she called Jane's cousin and asked if she could volunteer on weekends.

TANIA WALKED nervously into the center that Friday night and almost walked straight out again. The air was thick with the smell of unwashed bodies, old tennis shoes, tobacco and filthy clothes. There were young people everywhere, lounging on the beat-up old sofas, napping on chairs, sitting on the floor. They all stared at her with a shuttered, suspicious regard that reminded her of Gaby, and with a sinking feeling in her stomach, Tania felt certain she could never be of help to any of them.

Chris, a tall, handsome woman with prematurely white hair, came hurrying over to greet Tania and introduce her to the staff. "You can just hang out with me for tonight, then you'll have more of an idea what's going on," she told her.

What was going on appalled Tania. It was a world foreign to her, one she'd never imagined could exist beneath the surface of the city she loved.

For the first few weekends, she stuck close to Chris, terrified she'd do or say the wrong thing if she tried to help any of the youngsters herself. But one evening Chris was ill, and one of the young boys Chris dealt with, an emaciated thirteen-year-old alcoholic named Sid, asked Tania for her help in finding some clothes from the boxes of castoffs the center provided.

She did her best, and in the process began talking to him, hesitantly at first, then, as he developed an attachment for her, with increasing confidence. She began to make herself available for whatever the young people needed, and she dealt with their problems the best way she could, although often there was little she could do for them except listen. Gradually she began to understand their jargon, and even, to their amusement and delight, to use some of their phrases in her own speech.

She came to realize that just being there was meaningful to these teens, and she remembered Gaby sobbing in the night and herself stroking the girl's back. Maybe she hadn't always done the wrong thing with Gaby, after all. But she hadn't done enough, either.

These young people didn't hold down jobs or go to school. They had no identification, no backup system or money to help them through illness or accident. The majority were runaways, not by choice, but because the situations in their homes were intolerable. Most were victims of sexual or physical abuse.

And in each sad young face, in each tragic story, Tania recognized echoes of Gaby.

As Christmas neared, she had a group of young people who considered her their friend.

DURING THIS TIME, she and Matt wrote letters constantly, and he called at least once every week now that fishing season was over. The bond between them strengthened and deepened. She told him what she was doing at the center, and she knew he understood why. She told him of the difficulties and triumphs she was having writing her book, and he was sympathetic and supportive, even making one or two suggestions that helped.

At times he sounded guardedly optimistic about Gaby. The girl was doing well in school, still seeing the counselor twice weekly. But now and then he had problems, and Matt was honest about them and about the quarrels they resulted in.

Gaby came home drunk after a school party. She stayed out all night on a date. She and one of Mario's friends stole a neighbor's pony and went riding till dawn. She and a group of other youngsters were picked up by the police for speeding down Terrace's main street. Matt fought with her over chores and job lists.

Tania compared these outbursts with Sid's alcoholism, fourteen-year-old Daisy's pregnancy and Madeline's three suicide attempts, and she couldn't help but feel that Gaby was pretty normal, after all.

She wrote Matt and told him so, but she refused his invitation to come and spend Christmas in Terrace.

What if it turned into a disaster with Gaby? Tania didn't feel strong enough to chance it yet.

DOC FLEW DOWN and spent Christmas with her, and it was one of the best Christmases Tania could remember, despite the fact that she missed Matt terribly during the holiday. At times it was like a toothache, a physical pain she could only endure until it eased with the passing of the season. But knowing he felt the same helped in some obscure way.

He phoned, long, intimate calls that must have cost him a small fortune. He sent her a lacy black negligee set for Christmas, with instructions that she was to wait to wear it until he could remove it for her. His Christmas card had Gaby's name on it, but the handwriting was Matt's.

He also sent a picture with Doc, and it was the photo that was her real Christmas present. It was Matt's dream house, and it now had walls, a roof and a half-finished sun deck. Matt and Doc and several of Matt's friends were working on the structure in every spare moment, Doc confided. "Didn't tell you before. Matt wanted it to be a surprise of some sort."

Doc looked fit enough to climb mountains, Tania thought in wonder. He and Benny lived in a warm little cabin, wrangling with each other occasionally but both totally content.

"Benny's no carpenter—couldn't pound a nail straight if his life depended on it—but he can carve like a hot damn. He sent you this." It was a miniature totem, and with amazement, Tania recognized the faces on the tiny figures. Doc was there, Gaby, Matt…and herself, as well.

"Tell Benny I'll treasure this. I sent him a couple of new aprons, but he may not appreciate them."

"Good idea. I'll burn the old ones when I get back. Long as he cooks fine meals, I'll do the carpentry, and I'm not half-bad at it, if I do say so myself," Doc confided. He gave her a huge, theatrical wink. "Modest, too, ain't I?"

Tania laughed with him, delighted at this new, jocular side of her father.

"Benny feeds us while we're hammerin', him and Gaby. She's gettin' to be a fine little cook, too. Real pretty girl now that she's stopped all that foolishness with dyin' her hair yellow."

To Tania's amazement, Doc was inordinately proud of the volunteer work she was doing at the center. "Nothin' better than helpin' those young ones who can't help themselves,'' he stated. Tania had told him in letters about the kids, and he knew most of their names. She invited him to the Christmas celebration the center was having.

"We're cooking that huge fish you sent me, as well as a couple of turkeys and a ham.''

They ate the special dinner Tania and the other volunteers provided, and there were small gifts for everyone. Afterward they gathered around the old, beat-up piano and sang carols, the beautiful young voices so much at odds with their emaciated bodies and old-young faces.

Doc came away from it with tears in his eyes, and that night he told Tania the stories Gaby had related to Benny at the camp the summer before, about street kids she'd known in Toronto.

"Heard her say once she wants to help kids like the ones she met on the street. So I told her about this place and what you do.''

"What did she say, Dad?''

"Never said much at all, but she was interested all the same.''

IN FEBRUARY, on impulse, Tania wrote a letter to Gaby. She kept it chatty and light. She described the center and how much she was enjoying her work there, despite the sadness of not being able to change very much for the kids who came looking for help. She described one of her special charges, a girl who called herself Cat.

"She reminds me of you, Gaby. Her eyes are the same lovely deep brown and her skin would tan like yours did last summer—if we ever got any sunshine here.'' Tania posted it without any expectation of getting an answer.

March came and went. On April 10, there was a letter

in slanted handwriting and vivid purple ink, from Gaby. She wrote about school and her teachers. She said she knew how to make bread just like Benny's now.

"I see him and your dad all the time—it's like having two grandfathers. Doc gives me these lectures, and Benny's such an old phony. Remember how scared we were of him that day I got you some tea?"

She said she'd like to get to meet Cat someday, then she added, "Remember Scott? He writes to me once in a while. He's on his own. He left home last fall and went to San Diego. He's working in a pizza place during the day and playing in a band at night, called the Headhunters. He sent me a tape—they sound exceptional."

Tania thought of Jim, his bullheaded insistence that Scott go to college, and she felt a pang of sympathy for him. Parenting was probably one of life's most difficult jobs, because there didn't seem to be any standard rule book to follow.

On the second page, Gaby abruptly announced, "May 4 is my dad's birthday. He's going to be forty-one. I'm having a surprise party for him, and it would be nice if you could come. I won't tell him if you won't."

She signed it with touching formality: "Best Regards, Gabriella." Underneath was a PS.

"I'm sorry for those things I said to you last summer. I guess I wasn't thinking too straight. Dad said he told you I have a counselor. She's helped me a lot to straighten out my act. Dad's pretty tough to live with, and I'm no prize at housecleaning, but if you'd like to give us a try, I'd do my best to make you tea now and then. He's as grumpy as Benny without you around, and you guys aren't getting any younger. Love, G."

For the first time in many months, Tania cried.

CHAPTER SIXTEEN

DOC MET HER at Terrace airport on the morning of May 4. He was driving Matt's Jeep.

There were still patches of snow here and there, but the morning was bright and almost blindingly sunny.

Doc was in fine form. He seemed to be growing younger each time she saw him, and more loquacious.

"I been helping Matt out at the Fiberglas shop the past few weeks. He's there right now closin' it up for the summer. I told him I had some things to pick up. He don't have a clue you're comin', don't think he even remembers it's his birthday. Matt's gearin' up for fishin' parties—first one comes in next week. I'm goin' up with him as far as my cabin, for the summer again. It's spring—steelhead are spawning. Can't miss that."

Doc had hugged her till she thought her ribs would crack, and his face seemed split by a perpetual grin as he drove along the rough road to Matt's place at a speed that Tania considered downright reckless.

Her emotions were in a turmoil. Ever since the plane had dipped into the green mountain valley where Terrace lay and then dropped to the landing strip carved out of the surrounding forest, she'd been having an attack of nerves about this trip.

She hadn't seen Matt since his trip to Vancouver on her birthday, and she worried that they'd feel like strang-

ers again when they met. What if he'd changed his mind
about marrying her?

Letters were great, but they just didn't fill all the gaps.
Even phone calls were necessarily limited to a time span,
and sometimes there were misunderstandings that took
even more calls and letters to get straight.

What if it wasn't a good time for Matt, her coming
now, just when the fishing season was beginning? This
was only a couple of weeks earlier than she'd arrived in
Terrace last year. The difference this time was knowing
that if things worked out right, she'd stay up here with
him. She'd made arrangements in case that happened. It
depended, as always, on Gaby.

She felt terrible apprehension about meeting Gaby
again. The girl's letter had sounded as if Gaby would
welcome her, but there wasn't any way to be certain.
Gaby had never been predictable. Now, though, Tania
had a lot more experience dealing with difficult youngsters.

All the same, her heartbeat accelerated as Doc swung
off the road and into Matt's driveway, and she clenched
her hands into fists, worried that she'd done the wrong
thing in coming here, yet unable to suppress unbearable
excitement at the thought of seeing the man she loved.

She strained forward in her seat and gasped when the
homestead came into view. "Oh, just look at the house!
You didn't tell me it was finished, Doc."

"Ready to move into anytime. Inside finishin' is all
but complete." He gave her a broad wink, hitting a particularly deep rut in the process. "Don't know what he's
waitin' on, d'you?"

The house was beautiful. It was more impressive than
she'd imagined it would be, even half-hidden as it was
at this angle by the barn and the corral. It was a rambling

natural-log structure whose walls were bisected by huge windows. Matt's stone chimney rose majestically from the roof. She could see the solar collectors he'd told her about, too, and one corner of the wide, encircling veranda.

Tania tore her gaze from the house and looked toward the trailer. The picnic bench stood just outside the door, and the trailer looked the same as it had the year before. She could see the clothesline where she'd pegged wet laundry the day she'd spent here alone. That day had felt like the end of a dream.

Today felt as if it might be the beginning of one.

As the Jeep lurched to a stop, the trailer door opened and Gaby stepped out to greet her, a taller, older Gaby, with long dark hair. She looked every bit as nervous as Tania felt, but she came down the steps toward the Jeep with a welcoming smile on her lovely young face.

MATT FELT GROUCHY and out of sorts, so it was probably a good thing he was alone at the plant. He hated to admit it, but it bothered him a little that not one soul had remembered today was his birthday.

Well, except for his mother, of course. She'd sent him the usual token card, "Happy Birthday, Son," but in her typical cautious fashion, she'd mailed it three weeks early. Even if Gaby had noticed it, she had probably forgotten by now that today was the day.

How the hell did you teach a kid thoughtfulness, anyway?

There wasn't a word from Tania, either. Did she even know when his birthday fell? He tried to remember if they'd ever mentioned it and couldn't.

Sometimes, like now, he grew despondent, missing her, wanting her the way he did. The new house was finished, but he'd be damned if he'd move in until he and Tania were married.

How much longer was it going to take for his daughter to come around? He'd thought there was a definite change in Gaby lately, and with the new ease there was between them, he'd discussed his love for Tania. He'd tried to explain how important it was to him to make Tania a part of their lives.

He'd even told her about proposing last November. He'd gone on to explain why Tania wouldn't go ahead with a marriage unless Gaby was agreeable.

"Yeah, Penelope and me already discussed all that, Dad. It's sort of natural, right? Freudian. Like, girls are jealous of their fathers and try to break up their relationships, right? There's even a name for it—I forget what it is." Gaby had rattled on nonchalantly in that new pseudopsychological way she'd adapted lately.

And then she'd added, "I'm going to the movies with Jemma tonight, okay? And I'll need a ride into town again. You know, really, Dad, it would make a lot more sense to let me get my driver's license—this being driven all the time is just absurd. Jemma's had her license for a whole year already."

And that was the end of that conversation.

He forced thoughts of his daughter and of Tania out of his mind and concentrated on cataloging supplies. There were a million details to attend to this morning. Doc picked a fine time to go off and run errands, he thought irritably.

It was almost lunchtime when the phone rang, and Doc still wasn't back. He answered the phone testily and heard Gaby's urgent voice. "Dad, you'd better come home pronto. The drains are backed up again, and there's sewage all over the bathroom. It's like gross."

Matt put the receiver down with enough force to drive it through the desk and swore with fluent ferocity. It looked as if he'd spend the rest of his birthday cleaning out the damned septic tank.

He felt downright sorry for himself as he clamped his hat on his head and stomped out to his truck. He started it and wheeled around viciously, throwing gravel in every direction as he sped out of the parking area.

THE JEEP WAS in the yard when he pulled in and parked, and he wondered what Doc was doing here at this time of the day. But thoughts of the sewer were uppermost, and he slammed out of the truck and started toward the door.

He was only yards away when it opened.

Tania came slowly down the steps to meet him. Behind her, Gaby stood in the open doorway with Doc's arm around her shoulders. Benny hovered in the background. All of them were grinning at the expression on his face...all except Tania.

She looked at him with her heart in her eyes and a tiny, tremulous smile on her lips.

"See what we got you for your birthday, Dad?" Gaby called with a wicked giggle.

Matt didn't hear her. He wasn't conscious of moving, but suddenly the woman he loved was in his embrace. His arms closed convulsively around her, and she looked up at him with those huge, shining green eyes.

"Time's passing, you're getting older, and I think you'd better marry me, sir, or I'll have to sue for breach of contract," she said with uncertain bravado. "I've got witnesses."

A chorus of catcalls and whistles sounded from the doorway.

"Well," he drawled with a catch in his voice, "then I guess we'd better get on with it, hadn't we?"

He felt a surge of wild joy, and an irrepressible grin spread across his face. He felt like throwing his hat in the air and whooping, but instead he grabbed her under the knees and slid an arm around her narrow back, swinging her into his arms and striding toward the new house.

It had never been an ordinary, logical romance, what with bears and mosquitoes and fishermen and fathers and cooks…to say nothing of daughters.

"I'll carry you across the threshold first, and we'll have the ceremony as soon as possible," he declared.

He stumbled just then and almost dropped her because she moved her head and pressed her lips against his, a promise of fulfillment to come.

The audience clapped and cheered, and behind the new house the Skeena murmured softly in the background.

EPILOGUE

IT WAS EARLY JUNE of yet another spring, and far up the Skeena, the giant chinook salmon were running again.

Doc and Benny were doing their best to guide and feed Matt's fishing party in his absence, but the two old men were distracted this morning. Benny burned a whole batch of bread, and Doc didn't really care whether the fishermen got a good strike out on the river or not. Their thoughts were with the Radburn family and the event they'd all anticipated throughout the long winter months.

With painstaking care, Doc had built a wooden cradle for the grandchild soon to come, and Benny had hand carved intricate Indian symbols into each end to ward off evil spirits and keep the child safe while it slept.

Gaby was back in Terrace with Tania, charged with taking care of her, and just as Matt had carefully arranged, the girl had alerted the helicopter pilot in the small hours of the morning when Tania's first pains began.

He'd arrived to collect Matt at daybreak.

TANIA COULD HEAR her own voice echoing through the delivery room. The guttural sound she made amazed her, but she couldn't seem to stop it.

"Bear down, Tania. One more good push. Wonderful...."

The doctor and nurses were excited as the moment of birth neared. It showed in their voices.

Tania felt beads of sweat break out on her forehead and tried to smile a thank-you when Gaby quickly mopped them away with a cool, damp cloth. She'd been wonderful throughout Tania's pregnancy, caring and considerate, and she was handling this with more aplomb than her father.

Matt had had reservations about Gaby being present at the birth, but the girl was adamant. "Honestly, Dad, I've watched war and sex and everything else in movies and on TV, I'm almost eighteen, getting born's a miracle and Tania wants me there, right, Tania?"

Gaby was still adept at playing one of them off against the other.

Now, Matt was holding one of Tania's hands between both of his. Gaby took the other. They'd attended the childbirth classes with her, and they were here as her coaches, her family, her support team.

She knew she was gripping their hands tight, bruising them with the force of her hold. Both of them were unnaturally pale under the fluorescent lighting, and they looked unfamiliar swathed in their green gowns. Matt's eyes were panic-stricken.

During these last few moments, they both looked scared, and Tania wanted to reassure them, to tell them it probably seemed a lot worse than it really was. But she didn't have breath enough for words. This was hard work, the hardest she'd ever done, and her body had a strength she'd never tapped till now.

The contraction expanded, filling her awareness until there was nothing else, as hot and urgent and all consuming as the act of creation had been.

"Here's the head. Hold it, hold it. Now once more, good and strong. Push...."

The sound she made was more of a victory cry than childbirth agony as Matt's son slid from the security of her womb into the uncertain world. He was a large baby, and he drew in a breath and cried vigorously, the insulted, wavering cry of the newborn.

"Gaby, here you go, take your brother...."

With trembling hands the girl accepted the wet and bloody child from the smiling doctor, laying him on Tania's chest.

His mother, his sister and his father each put a hand on him, fingers interlocking, supporting and protecting him, claiming him as one of them, one of their family.

And they all cried a little with him, but theirs were tears of wonder and gratitude and overwhelming love.

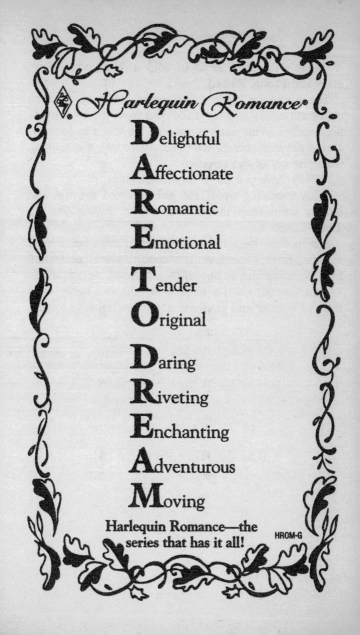

Harlequin Romance®

D elightful
A ffectionate
R omantic
E motional

T ender
O riginal

D aring
R iveting
E nchanting
A dventurous
M oving

**Harlequin Romance—the
series that has it all!**

HROM-G

HARLEQUIN PRESENTS®

HARLEQUIN PRESENTS
men you won't be able to resist
falling in love with...

HARLEQUIN PRESENTS
women who have feelings
just like your own...

HARLEQUIN PRESENTS
powerful passion in
exotic international settings...

HARLEQUIN PRESENTS
intense, dramatic stories that will keep you
turning to the very last page...

HARLEQUIN PRESENTS
The world's bestselling romance series!

Harlequin® Historical

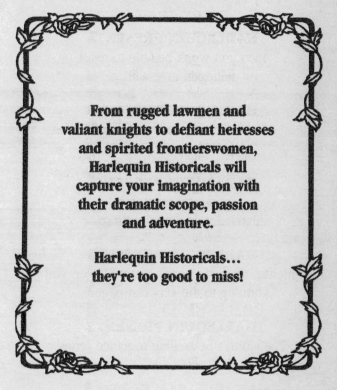

From rugged lawmen and
valiant knights to defiant heiresses
and spirited frontierswomen,
Harlequin Historicals will
capture your imagination with
their dramatic scope, passion
and adventure.

Harlequin Historicals…
they're too good to miss!

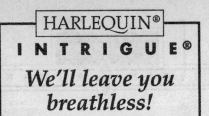

HARLEQUIN®
I N T R I G U E ®
We'll leave you breathless!

If you've been looking for thrilling tales of
contemporary passion and sensuous love stories
with taut, edge-of-the-seat suspense—
then you'll *love* **Harlequin Intrigue!**

Every month, you'll meet four new heroes
who are guaranteed to make your spine tingle
and your pulse pound. With them you'll enter
into the exciting world of Harlequin Intrigue—
where your life is on the line
and so is your heart!

THAT'S INTRIGUE—DYNAMIC ROMANCE AT ITS BEST!

HARLEQUIN®
I N T R I G U E ®

LOOK FOR OUR FOUR FABULOUS MEN!

Each month some of today's bestselling authors bring
four new fabulous men to Harlequin American Romance.
Whether they're rebel ranchers, millionaire power brokers
or sexy single dads, they're all gallant princes—and
they're all ready to sweep you into lighthearted fantasies
and contemporary fairy tales where anything is possible
and where all your dreams come true!

You don't even have to make a wish...
Harlequin American Romance will grant your every desire!

Look for Harlequin American Romance
wherever Harlequin books are sold!